SUZANNAH ROWNTREE

Anarchist on the Orient Express

Miss Sharp's Monsters, Volume II.

First published by Bocfodder Press 2021

First edition

ISBN: 978-0-9942339-7-4

Cover art by Parker Book Design

This book was professionally typeset on Reedsy.
Find out more at reedsy.com

Chapter I.

They call Paris the city of love. The perfect stranger who was, at this very moment, kissing me enthusiastically in an archway of the Gare Saint Lazare had taken this entirely too seriously, in my judgement. But what did I know? As far as I could tell, I had never been to Paris before.

Still, I could not allow this sort of thing to continue unopposed. Not that I had any reputation to think of; the werewolf scars that scored the left side of my face marked me as a fallen woman, the sort of female who would willingly traffic her blood to monsters for easy money.

I did, however, still have my self-respect. I thought that if a young man wished to kiss me, he might at least introduce himself as a basic preliminary, and perhaps consult my own views upon the subject. In his defence, of course, he seemed firmly under the impression that he had at least *met* me before. Upon fastening himself to my elbow and drawing me into this sheltered archway, he had addressed me as "Vera", uttered a few broken words, and then clasped me to his bosom. As a result, I did not respond quite so firmly as I might upon a different occasion. I shifted my hips to one side, broke his embrace with a lift of my elbows, and used the ferrule of my umbrella to administer a gentle, persuasive blow to the knot of nerves below the breastbone. My accoster recoiled with a faint wheeze of pain, and I withdrew the small revolver from the chatelaine purse (in black brocade) that hung at my waist.

"My good man, I think you are mistaken," I said, not unkindly. "I am Miss Elizabeth Sharp."

The young man stood with one hand clutched to his ribs, his eyes wide and staring. He did not look like a respectable gentleman, for he was dressed in a day-labourer's cap and neckerchief, and my face still stung from the rasp of his unshaven chin. Though not a great deal taller than myself, he was broad-shouldered and wiry, like a man who spends much of his time in hard labour.

He said in thickly-accented French: "Why, Vera! Don't you know me?"

He lifted a shaking, stubby-fingered hand to my cheek, and I retreated a step, bringing up my revolver to tickle his ribs. Naturally, the weapon was unloaded. Although I happened to be the bodyguard of a princess, I was not quite so reckless as to carry a loaded gun about with me. All the same, I did not think he could afford to test me.

"Why do you call me Vera?" I countered. "Who is that?"

Taken aback, he looked me up and down, noting every detail of the plain black dress and neat straw boater that marked me as a servant in a respectably wealthy household. Then he looked past me, to the news-stand where my employer, Princess May, and her parents stood exchanging pleasantries with a Russian Grand Duke; and something like despair came over his face.

"They took away your memories."

How shall I describe the way those words went though me?—like a needle, like a knife, like a cutting edge too sharp to be seen! I was without memories. As far as I knew, my life had begun two years ago, when I had awoken in the hospital of Saint Botolph's in London with raw wounds on my face. Before that, every memory was lost, even my true name. The Directors said we were nothing better than used-up "dainties"—unfortunates who had sold their blood to monsters for food. They had taken us in, healed us, and trained us to hold respectable positions in the houses of the rich and noble as servant-bodyguards; but withal they never ceased to remind us that we were wicked, fallen, and monstrous; that we must keep constant guard on ourselves, lest we break out into some grotesque and horrible vice. Lies, I knew. I was no more likely than anyone else to commit dreadful crimes, and I would never believe that *I* was the one most at fault for the brutal attack that had left me half dead on the streets of London.

Now I felt as though I had seen from far away the piercing gleam of truth. I lowered my weapon. "How did you know I have lost my memories?"

He didn't answer, instead pointing to the news-stand with a trembling hand. "Why are you with them? Who are they to you?"

"For heaven's sake, tell me how you know me."

I put a hand on his arm, and he threw it off angrily. "Are you their servant?" he demanded, backing away a step. "Have you gone over to *them,* now?"

Before he could run, I took his elbow in a firmer grip, one he was unable to shake off—for the wolf-bitten, if they survive the attack, are left with an unusual measure of strength. He tried to wrench from my grasp, but I was too strong for him. He looked into my scarred face with a look of sickened disgust. "Look what they've done to you," he whispered.

Even at the time, dear reader, a part of me knew he was not really angry at *me.* But his words cut me to the heart, where all the accusations nested: I had been preyed upon by monsters, and now I was monstrous myself. I released him at once. "Please—if you know who I am, tell me!"

Behind me, a voice rose in imperious demand. "Sharp! Yoo-hoo! Come along, Sharp!"

I turned and stifled a groan. A short way away, the Duchess of Teck waved at me. The Russian Grand Duke and Princess May had both turned to stare at the young man and myself where we had retired within the shadows of the arch.

"It's true, then," the man said in a voice of choking despair.

"No! Wait," I entreated, but he turned his back abruptly, and hurried towards the rear of the station. At the news-stand, the Duchess still waved at me, evidently summoning me to accompany them to their hotel.

Princess May, shrouded in deepest mourning beside her mother, was the closest thing I had to a real friend since Sal Tanner had died in a grimy square in Whitechapel. But even my loyalty to my mistress had little hold on me now. Every spare moment of the two years of my remembered life, I had devoted to wondering exactly whom I had once been; and now—well, it was no good waving at me, and screeching that we must move on to the hotel. Whoever he was, whoever *I* was, this man held the key to my lost past. Sending May a gesture of apology, I dropped my revolver into my reticule and set off on the man's trail.

He glanced over his shoulder as I began to gain on him. "Wait!" I called, but he only broke into an outright run, dashing to and fro among the people thronging the platform. I followed suit, weaving through the crowd, sometimes catching, sometimes losing sight of my quarry, but never quite losing the scent of coal-dust and engine-grease that hung about him. At last I followed through another archway and found myself on a cobbled street, golden with late-afternoon light and slick with a shower of rain that had just passed. The passers-by—mostly comfortable, well-fed Parisians in top hats and respectable gowns—were just putting away their umbrellas; but to my right, some way to the north, I saw the stocky form of the man I was following. He saw me again and put on another turn of speed, disappearing into a small opening on the right, as though doubling back towards the train station. Throwing caution to the wind, although somewhat hampered by the slipperiness of the smoothly-paved footpath, I dashed after him and quickly found myself on a narrow street rising gently to a large and handsome viaduct over the train tracks at the station's rear. I could not at first see the man I hunted, but I supposed that he must have already disappeared over the rise ahead of me. Hastening up the narrow street, I found myself in a large square at the intersection of six streets, complete with gas-lamps and shrubs, all supported on massive stone piers above the steam and racket of the train lines.

There was a dreadful cloying scent over it all, like rotting flesh. To my astonishment, I found that the place was full of the gendarmerie. They were smartly dressed in shining boots and visored caps, but I looked into the eyes of one, and horror struck me to the heart! His skin was grey and waxen; his eyes milky and blind; a deep, livid gash ringed his throat, and the skin was partially eaten away from the awful, groping hand he reached towards me. "Papers! State your business!" he groaned, lurching towards me on ungainly feet.

I recoiled from that blindly reaching hand in horror. I had heard tell of the revenant policemen of Paris, but report could not possibly have prepared me for the grisly reality.—In recent years, anarchist violence had become almost a weekly occurrence in the Republic of France, and the wealthy were in the grip of terror. Their solution was to employ terror of their own. French scientists had discovered the key of restoring animation, if not truly life, to the corpses of dead criminals; and these, raised unnaturally from the scaffold and outfitted as policemen, were sent to haunt the streets of the city.

"Papers! Business!" this nightmarish figure demanded again, and I backed another step. The revenant gendarmes advanced upon me. In another moment I should be surrounded, and I could see no sign of my friend from the train station.

"I have no papers," I said, barely remembering to speak French. "I am an Englishwoman."

"Business!" my undead interlocutor demanded. I had read accounts of innocent people being set upon, beaten, and dragged to prison by these dreadful creatures, and I began to be truly afraid. I had a revolver in my purse, but what good would it do me against these creatures, who already bore the most dreadful wounds, or wore the mottled purple seams at their throats that told of a death by guillotine? It seemed my fate to fall afoul of the police; and this time I had not even an Inspector Short to save me.

In my desperation I said the first thing that came into my head, which happened to be the truth:

"I am looking for a man I know," I said. "You must have seen him—a labourer in a red neckerchief—he must have come along this road a moment ago."

There was a moment's silence, a moment's stillness, as

though they were considering this. Then the nightmare figure groaned again: "Under arrest. Come quietly."

"What!" I cried, as one of those dreadful decaying hands fastened upon my sleeve. "Stand back! What reason can you possibly have to arrest me?"

"Associate with anarchist, section fifty-three of Anti-Sedition Act. Penalty: no less than six months' hard labour."

I gripped my umbrella—it was standard issue at Saint Botolph's, and constructed to double as a stout truncheon. "This is preposterous! I've done nothing wrong—*unhand me,"* I protested as ten more hands laid hold on me. The stench was suffocating; I could feel the wetness as their decaying hands soaked through the black bombazine of my dress. The voice droned on:

"Resisting arrest, section eighty-three. Maximum penalty: death and revivification. Warning given once only."

Revivification? It was too much: a scream broke out of me. I threw myself against the restraining hands. Tearing my left arm free of their steely grip, I raised my umbrella to strike.

A hand caught it. A crisp, sterile scent wafted through the stench—cedar.

A voice, soft and melodious, spoke in my ear.

"Kindly do not harass this lady; she is travelling with me."

I turned to look up at—Grand Duke Vasily. This did not materially restore my composure; if anything, it was a frying-pan and fire sort of situation. I felt the cold perspiration sliding down my back, caught as I was between the monsters I did not understand—and the one I knew entirely too well.

The revenants did not relinquish their hold on me. "Papers!" they groaned again, turning to the Grand Duke. "Business!"

Behind Vasily's dark glasses, I thought one heavy-lidded eye closed in a languid, elegant wink. Reaching into the breast-pocket of his immaculate black-velvet coat, he withdrew an extremely official-looking document, unfolded it, and handed it to the nearest of the undead creatures. "My letter of accreditation from the Tsar of All Russias," he said in an almost bored voice. "I am Grand Duke Vasily Nikolaevitch Romanov. I take it there will be no trouble."

"Monsieur," the revenant groaned, handing the paper back to him. *"Monsieur, desolé."* And they released me, groaning and nodding *"Desolé,"* like a field of black poppies blown by the wind. They were *French* revenants, after all, and must keep up the national reputation for manners, to princes at least. A moment later, and they set upon another foot-passenger with their never-ceasing wail for "Papers!"

"Miss Sharp," Vasily said, pocketing his credentials and addressing me directly for the first time, "what a *delightful* surprise."

To those who have read the first volume of my memoirs, the Grand Duke will need little introduction. Like all the ruling family of Russia, Vasily was a vampire—even now, in the daylight, his teeth looked sharp and extremely white. I had met Vasily in London during the Whitechapel werewolf business, and I realised now with a sinking heart that I must have made an impression upon him, to find my name so ready upon his lips. Frying-pan and fire, indeed: I did not want this fabulous creature, with his madman's smile and his sleek, black clothes cut in the height of fashion, to remember me. I did not want him to ask me, as he had done once, to give him supper. I did not want to stare into his eyes and forget myself before waking just too late, with his teeth in my veins.

It was a little late for such thoughts now, of course. Instinctively, I picked another tactic. "Well, *good* afternoon, mysterious stranger," I said, flattering myself that my voice sounded huskily seductive rather than shakily terrified. "Are you going my way?"

"I came to offer my escort to the Hotel Terminus, since you and I are both staying there," he said, tendering his arm with a bow.

There was a gleam of laughter in his eye, and I could not help seeing it as a good sign. If I could not fade into obscurity, let me act the fool; let me keep him laughing too hard to think of hurting me.

"Thank you; but I know my own way," I said. One last glance told me there was definitely no sign of the man who had accosted me in the train station, so I whisked about without taking Vasily's arm, and went back the way I had come. Vasily fell into step beside me, but for a while he did not speak, allowing me the comfort of a few moments' thought.

They had taken away my memories—but whom? It had not escaped my attention that all the wolf-bitten (and siren-enchanted, and vampire-drained) at Saint Botolph's had come away from their attacks with no memory of the event itself, nor anything from their lives before. We were told that some attacks naturally left the bitten without memory, and that Saint Botolph's had been founded two hundred years ago for the express purpose of caring for such victims. By now, however, I had had the opportunity to meet a number of my fellow bitten, who had never attended Saint Botolph's (nor its sister institution, the *Akbar)* and not a single one of *them* had lost memories.

Yet I *had* witnessed May lose some of her memories, at the hands of one of the siren princesses of Denmark. Was this the method the royalties had chosen of hiding their crimes? With all memory of our attacks erased, all scandal might be repressed. Briefly, I considered the possibility of returning to London to raid the records at Saint Botolph's, but then discarded the idea. During the Whitechapel affair in the winter, I had uncovered very good reasons why the British Crown should be anxious to keep Saint Botolph's records a deadly secret. I very much doubted whether such records even existed, and if they did, they were assuredly not kept on the premises, at Aldgate. I should be much more likely to find them in some heavily-guarded safe-deposit at the Home Office in Whitehall, or perhaps the Tower of London. No—if I wanted to find out where I had come from, I had better look for the man who had kissed me in the Gare Saint-Lazare.

"Those gendarmes were preparing to arrest me for associating with an anarchist," I said as we came to the end of the viaduct and turned down the Rue de Rome. "Can you credit it?"

"Paris has been unsettled of late," my companion said.

"But there are *laws!*"

"And the French laws permit the police to make such arrests at will. Even for expressing sympathy. Even for making foolish jokes." A shrug. "The bombings are a serious matter. The French mean not to tolerate them."

For a moment I could hardly draw breath. "What, arrested simply for being *acquainted* with someone?—which I was not in the least!"

Vasily's sharp, white teeth showed in a sardonic smile. "No? You shock me!"

That was unsettling. Some anarchists had no compunction in attacking men, women, or children whom they saw as members of the exploiting classes. I had myself met anarchists of a different sort, who disowned the bombers in no uncertain terms; but my experiences among the royalties of Europe had taught me that the monsters themselves were outspokenly in favour of shooting or eating any and all anarchists on sight.

It was, therefore, an uncomfortable thing to be suspected of consorting with anarchists by such a creature as the Grand Duke. "What the dickens?" I objected, keeping my tone light.

"Your friend at the station, whom you were greeting with such enthusiasm..."

"I was *not* greeting him, with or without enthusiasm. I had never seen that young man before in my life."

"Indeed! Well, by a remarkable coincidence, I had."

Chapter II.

I choked back the yelp of excitement that rose to my lips—this fish would not rise to too obvious a bait. "Nice friends you have, I must say," I said severely. "Perhaps you might advise them on the proper way to address a lady."

A gleam of tooth; otherwise Vasily's face did not change. "He is no friend of mine. I have an estate in Moldavia, and he was once a peasant there. Now, he is an anarchist."

It seemed to be my fate to be involved with anarchists, and I reflected, with some alarm, that this told me something about my own past. *Have you gone over to* them, *now?*—dash it, had I in fact *been* an anarchist myself once? This was an uncomfortable new reflection, and suggested that if I was fated to be in trouble with my new masters for consorting with anarchists, I was equally likely to be in trouble with the anarchists for consorting with monsters.

I wanted to ask the young anarchist's name, but I did not think Vasily would give it to me—at least, not without exacting some cost.

"You shock me! He *is* an anarchist?"

"He was a good, respectful, hard-working man once. Now he is driven only by rage."

I opened my eyes very wide and innocent. "No! I wonder what could possibly have happened, to embitter him so?"

At that, Vasily really did laugh; but it was a soft sound, ominous simply by virtue of its lazy confidence. It was not followed by any explanation—only by a cold sort of chill that traced its fingers up and down my spine.

"Perhaps someone he cared for was bitten," I ventured, thinking of the way the anarchist had greeted me just now, in the Gare Saint Lazare.

Vasily sent me a swift, piercing glance. "Now, whatever makes you say that?"

I did not like that look. "Feminine intuition," I said airily. I hoped my guess was correct: perhaps it was my loss that had made the man what he was; perhaps when I had known him, neither of us had been anarchists. That would be a great relief. "What brings you to Paris, your grace?"

"I have been invited to the Coburg wedding."

That in itself was ample explanation. Readers of the previous volume of my memoirs will recall that during the Whitechapel business, Princess May's wedding had been called off owing to the sudden and tragic death of the groom—a death, I hasten to remind my readers, with which I had had *practically* nothing to do. At any rate, this had left a gap in the social calendar of the noble and monstrous of the world—a gap which was now to be filled by the marriage, in Coburg, of Princess Victoria Melita of Saxe-Coburg and Gotha to Prince Ernest, Grand Duke of Hesse and by Rhine. Both were grandchildren of Queen Victoria's, and were thus connected with most of the royalties of Europe. Nearly every monster in Europe would be there, no doubt including the creature that had attacked me, leaving me scarred and disgraced for ever. I would have dearly loved to be there, if only for the opportunity to hunt down the creature and exact justice; but May, now that her own wedding was cancelled, had become once more an obscure, landless princess of tainted morganatic blood, to whom no self-respecting German werewolf prince would ally himself. She and her parents had received no invitation; not that they would have accepted one if they had. May had fled England to mourn, not to go into society.

The wedding was still a month away, however, and I did not think the Grand Duke meant to arrive early. "And until then?"

"Oh! it has been some time since I was in Moldavia; I mean to visit my estates there."

"All right; I suppose that must be the official story," I said. I had never known anyone to carry official accreditation from his Emperor in order to visit his own estates.

No sooner were the words out of my mouth than I wished I could have taken them back, for his hand strayed towards the breast pocket where he had replaced his papers, and there was something very shrewd and alert in the glance he sent me. But all he said was, "I see that there is a café here, beneath the Hotel."

By now we had rounded the corner of the Gare Saint-Lazare's imposing façade. Immediately in front of the station stood the Hotel Terminus, a compact building with the steep slate-grey roof I had already come to identify with Paris. Vasily gestured towards it. "Step inside with me. I will buy you a coffee and perhaps a beignet; and I will make you a business proposition."

A business proposition—well, I didn't much like the sound

of *that.* A young woman of my background has only one or two things to sell, and I did not think he was interested in having his hair Marcel-waved.

All the same, I am naturally a curious woman, and although the part of my mind that could not help feeling like prey in his company was shrieking at me to run, another part whispered that it could not possibly hurt to hear what he had to say to me, even if I turned him down afterwards. He wanted my company, and I was not proof against the flattery.

"You hesitate?"

"Oh," I said, to cover my confusion, "it's only that I don't know what a beignet is."

"In that case—" Vasily said firmly, and ushered me into the café, plush and glittering with rich carpets, mirrors, chandeliers, and potted plants.

A beignet, of course, is a fried pastry, crisp and hot with powdered sugar on top. Vasily waited until I had finished eating before he slid his coffee-cup aside, and leaned forward across the table. "And now, Miss Sharp, to business. I would like you to come East with me."

I lifted an eyebrow over my napkin. "As what? As your dainty?"

That razor-edged smile slashed across his face. "Why not? Have you any objection?"

I swallowed, half afraid to look at him. He was no siren, but he did have certain powers of persuasion, and his offer awoke the same strange, seductive impulse that comes when standing on a great height, to throw oneself from the precipice. I ignored the impulse. "That depends. Have you any objection to incineration?"

His smile grew even sharper, and he leaned back in his chair, playing with something in his pocket. "Then perhaps it would be well to remain on a more regular footing. I have no valet at present, and I was unable to visit the *Akbar* before I departed England, to select one that might suit me."

"You want me to *valet* you?"

"It would be helpful. My English valet preferred to leave my service and remain in London." He laughed. "In truth, I find myself in need of a bodyguard. You receive training in these matters at Saint Botolph's, do you not? I cannot always be watching my back, and as you have seen the anarchists are busy on the Continent these days—much more so than they are in London."

"The more reason why I should stay with my present employers, surely." I might have bidden my reputation farewell, but a scarred woman travelling alone with a Grand Duke would be made a hissing and a byword from one end of Europe to another, and I did not much care for that.

"Ah," he said, very softly, "but your present employers are not going east. It is unlikely that they will take you among the people and the scenes of your past life."

My throat went dry. "What do you mean? What do you know about my past life?"

"Only what your accent tells me. It is very faint, but it is recognisable. Saint Botolph's girls are not left with their memories intact; I presume that you wish to go in search of yours."

"You presume a great deal."

"Do I? Do not imagine that you are deceiving me. The young anarchist at the train station—he knew you, did he not? That was why you followed him."

I leaned forward. "Tell me his name," I whispered.

Vasily put his arms on the small table, leaning close—too close; as close as a lover might lean before a kiss. His scent was cold and sharp, like bones picked clean by the vultures. Maybe it was pride that kept me still, refusing to let him see how much he terrified me. Maybe it was that small mad impulse that wanted to throw myself from that precipice; maybe I thought the certainty of death a small price to pay for the risk, the thrill, and the plunge. At any rate I held still, and wondered why terror felt so near akin to desire.

Vasily smiled in a way that told me he knew exactly what I was feeling. Then he said, "I'll tell you his name when you join me on my journey east."

I ordinarily have a high opinion of my own good sense, but I must admit that I still do not know what my next words might have been. As it was, I did not have the opportunity to commit to anything. A shadow fell across us and a woman said in a husky voice, "Why, Vasily Nikolaevitch! I thought I smelled something antiseptic. Eau de Listerine, is it not?"

Vasily smiled mirthlessly, and I made myself sit back, feeling relieved at the interruption and not at all sure I had been in my right mind. The woman who had paused beside us possessed a striking, aristocratic beauty of the sort that increases rather than passing away with age—for she must have been somewhere in her forties, and her raven-black hair was rimed with strands of silver that glittered like frost on a winter's morning. She carried a walking-stick of black lacquer, and wore a sumptuous gown of black velvet, draped and fringed at the front of the skirt. The white lace about her wrists and neck, and a large crimson flower pinned to her bosom, suggested that her preference for black was a matter of style rather than mourning.

Vasily rose and bowed. "My dear Baroness! in Paris! Can the Day of Judgement be far off?" –and he glanced to the heavens, as though waiting for an answer.

The Baroness, if such she was, was not in the least discomfited by his raillery. She waited until he looked at her again, and said in an impressive tone: "Can it, indeed, when the earth cries out for blood, when men are driven to madness merely by contemplating the sufferings of the poor, and when those who would cry out in protest of such suffering are hounded night and day by the ghastly dead!" She lifted a pale hand, winking with jet, and pointed to the door. I followed her gesture, and saw the shapes of two of the revenant gendarmes, waiting on either side of the door.

"No doubt it is very bad, but I daresay it's the price we pay for living in a civilised society," Vasily drawled—a statement which, even at the time, I thought was pretty rich. "What brings you to this Babylon, Countess?"

She ignored the question. "Justice is worth anything, Duke."

"Do you mean to say those revenants are following *you*, ma'am?" I put in, tremendously impressed.

She looked down at me, past that aristocratic nose. "I am Veronika, Baroness Sarkozy."

I had heard of her. Indeed, Saint Botolph's had used her as a cautionary tale. Socialite, writer, and crusader—it was debated whether the Hungarian baroness was in fact an anarchist herself, or merely friendly towards them. What was quite certain, was that she spent a great deal of time meeting with anarchists, and that she had written books about them, and thrown charity balls and petitioned ministers across Europe in support of aims that, if not precisely anarchist, were practically next-door. She was most notorious for having come to Paris around the time of Ravachol's execution for the bombings at the Restaurant Véry, and agitating for a pardon; which, of course, was denied.

As I grappled with the shock of having come face-to-face with the celebrated lady, Vasily took up the reins of the conversation. "Will you be in Paris long, Baroness?" The laziness of his posture was not echoed at all by the alertness of his eyes. "Concerning this Day of Judgement, I am interested in apocalyptic prophecies. Perhaps we might meet, to compare notes."

"Such a meeting would only cause you unnecessary distress," she said scornfully.

"My dear Baroness, I am tougher than I look. Here is my card, if you should change your mind. And do let me know when you finally identify the Antichrist, for my cousin the Tsar will need to know. It has been foretold that the last of his line will perish in battle against that iniquitous gentleman. Good-day."

He extended his hand to me in a proprietary sort of way. I hesitated, but the Baroness seemed eager to be done with the conversation. "If your cousin had a reflection, I should tell him to look in the mirror," she said, and passed on with a nod to myself.

I took Vasily's cold hand, and allowed him to guide me from the café to the hotel's entrance hall. "Well?" he said, releasing me at the foot of the stair.

"The beignet was very good," I said gravely, "but the baroness was spectacular. They warned us about her at Saint Botolph's, you know. I shouldn't mind seeing more of her."

He watched me through narrowed, laughing eyes. "Do you know what I think, Miss Sharp? I think you want things that are not good for you."

"All of humanity suffers from that affliction."

"Shall I tell you a secret?"

"If I refused, would it stop you?"

"Touché.—The secret is that we monsters also want things that are not good for us. Will you come East with me?"

The thought was tempting, but now I had an alternative, I hoped, in Veronika Sarkozy. The baroness might be able to put me in communication with the anarchists of Paris; and then no doubt one of them at least would know the name, if not the whereabouts, of the young Moldavian I sought.

There was something direct and honest in the baroness's manner, which I liked better than Vasily's careful measuring of truth and lies, and his use of information as bait—to what nefarious ends, I still did not know. He was thrilling, and he was dangerous, but I had my self-respect, and it was unworthy of me to let him lead me about like a dog on a leash.

"A woman may want things that are not good for her, without being fool enough to take them, your grace. Thank you, but I am happy in my present employment."

"You desolate me."

"In time, the wound will heal," I said. "Good evening, sir."—With that, I went up the stairs a little faster than absolutely necessary.

Chapter III.

The Tecks' suite was on the second storey, and I entered the large sitting-room in some trepidation. Mine were not exacting employers, but apart from being royalty, they were paying generously for my services and could not be expected to be overjoyed with my wilful absence.

I found myself in a large, handsome corner room looking out upon the Rue Saint Lazare, down which the golden light of evening had begun to fade to purple twilight. Over the scent of decay that still clung to me following my encounter with the revenants, I could tell that the sitting-room could not avoid having the strange, indefinite smell that is a mark of hotels everywhere—but it was papered in Alphonse Mucha and carpeted in Axminster, and even pianoed in Blüthner. It was also, at that particular moment, empty.

"Franz? Is that you?" a voice called from the open doorway to my right. Mary Adelaide, Duchess of Teck, appeared a moment later, having shed her smart travelling dress for a trailing silk dressing-gown in the Aesthetic style, which fell in generous folds from beneath the wearer's equally generous bosom. Although any other woman would have been swamped by the gown's voluminous folds, it says something for the Duchess's strength of personality that she was wearing the dickens out of the gown, instead of the other way around. As she advanced into the sitting-room, it seemed to contract about her until the vast empty space seemed no more than a commensurate setting for a crowd of one.

"Oh, it's you, Smart."

"Sharp, ma'am."

"I beg your pardon?"

"That's my name; Sharp."

"I think I know my own servants' names, my dear," she said severely, and I knew that she *was* put out with me. "What on earth were you thinking, running off from the station like that? This is Paris, where they have a bombing every Saturday! I am relying on *you* to keep my daughter safe!"

"I know, ma'am. I beg your pardon." I briefly considered how much I ought to tell, and decided to risk as much of the truth as I dared—God knew I had had about as much as I could stand of lies. "As it happens, I was accosted by an anarchist at the station. I left in pursuit of him."

"Really?" The Duchess' temper evaporated. She opened her blue eyes very wide, and for a moment looked nearly as china-doll-like as her daughter. "That young man, an *anarchist?* Whatever did he say to you?"

"Very little, I assure you—once he found out whom I worked for."

"You must tell me all about it—no, you must go to May." The Duchess consulted her watch. "Dinner is in half an hour. They will serve her meal up here, if she likes, but *do* try to convince her to come downstairs for it! I have knocked on her door, but she would not answer. Perhaps she was asleep."

My heart twisted within me. "I doubt she will listen to me."

"Don't pull a long face, Sharp! Roust her out, and get

her ready. It isn't as though she was in *love* with Eddy. I understood her hiding while we were still in England, to keep out of the papers; but we are in the Continent now, and it is high time she showed her face. Oh, and when you're done, come in and do my hair for me. I want it in a high chignon."

"Leave her to me, ma'am," I said with a sigh. May's fiancé had died in the winter, and only I and two other persons knew the truth: that it was May herself who had killed him. May herself was not privy to this secret. As far as she knew, she had merely shot and driven off a dangerous stray werewolf on the Balmoral estate; and although Prince Eddy had been discovered dead in his own bed the next morning (whence he had been carefully returned by myself and one other witness), this was to May merely a tragic coincidence. That her own cousin was the werewolf who had terrorised Whitechapel for the previous two months never entered her mind. Eddy had died before May could be initiated into the darkest secret of the British Crown: that despite their boasting, despite their claim to being the one empire in the world not ruled by monsters, the whole clan of them were in fact werewolves.

All this I had hidden from May in an attempt to spare her pain—yet, three months since Eddy's death, she seemed no nearer recovery. If anything, she had only become more lifeless and sorrowful with the passage of time.

I rapped on May's door, and having received a murmured answer, entered the darkened room beyond. The fire had burned down, and May sat over it with her chin propped in her hand. In the other she still held the hat, with its trailing black veil, that she had worn on the train. She must have been sitting there for at least an hour, motionless since she first walked into the room and dragged the hat from her weary head. A pang of guilt struck me: I ought to have been here to make these surroundings more cheerful.

"Wouldn't you like the curtains open, ma'am?"

"Please don't bother, Sharp." May didn't look up from the fire. "It will be dark in an hour, anyway."

"So it will. If you mean to come down to dinner, we had best start dressing you." The princess's valises stood forlornly in the corner, still packed. I threw them open, reached blindly, and pulled out a black silk frock that would do for evening wear. The gown was a little flimsy, but its crepe weave meant it had not picked up any creases in transport. "This would look well with jet beads, I imagine."

May looked at the dress without enthusiasm. "I detest black. It doesn't suit me at all."

"It makes your hair look like gold."

"Put it away, Sharp. I won't go down for dinner tonight. Just have them bring something up on a tray."

I hesitated, but the Duchess's plea returned to mind. "The Duchess was particularly anxious you should join them for dinner tonight, ma'am."

"Tell them I am feeling seedy from the journey. Tell them I have the headache."

"Should I bring you an aspirin?"

"No, don't bother."

"But if you're really in pain—"

"I am perfectly well, thank you, Sharp!" The admission startled out of her, May flushed dully; then turned back to look into the fire.

"Then I will just unpack your things," I said slowly, taking the black crepe to the large-bellied wardrobe in the corner. Perhaps, like her mother, May could be distracted with talk of the outside world. "I had a rather surprising experience at the train station, ma'am."

"Oh?"

"I was accosted by an anarchist."

That got her attention for a moment. "Oh?—You escaped?"

"Not before I was kissed soundly! I think he must have mistaken me for another person."

"Oh."

I had not often been on the receiving end of May's *oh*-ing, but it was never an encouraging experience. May was never good at dissembling: she was only trying to pay attention for my sake. Meanwhile her long pale fingers were playing with the brooch at her throat where she kept a lock of Eddy's honey-coloured hair.

My heart struck me, but I steeled myself to face her, and went to kneel on the hearthrug where I could look up into her face.

She blinked at me. "What is it, Sharp? I'm listening; indeed I am."

"No, I don't think you are," I said gently. "It hurts me to see you like this, ma'am. Especially after so long."

Her eyes were suddenly bright with tears, and she blinked three or four times, very fiercely, before saying, "It is only three months; and he was my cousin."

"But you did not know him well. You neither loved nor respected him."

"How could you throw this in my face?—you of all people, Sharp!"

"I only want to understand."

She looked away, her face red and angry and so very close to tears. "I was wrong to judge him so harshly."

My heart stood still in my breast. In truth, she might have judged Eddy far more harshly than this and been perfectly correct; but how could she have known he was a monster and a killer—not once, but many times?

"What about that poor girl he got into trouble—Olive Bates?"

"He assured me that she was taken care of and neither sought nor wished for his help. I can't imagine what I was thinking, to be so angry with him! He was a good kind boy, and young men must sow their wild oats. I shall never marry, Sharp; but take warning by me, and don't be so choosy when your own chance comes."

My own chance!—and what chance was *that?* My scars marked me in such a way that only a very brave man would ever take the social risk of loving me. Unbidden, a face rose to mind; a quiet, intent, pallid sort of face with a long mobile mouth and drooping eyes. With a wistful sigh, I banished the apparition. I could not expect any man to destroy his career by tying himself to such an unsuitable wife, especially not one I—liked. The only offers I was likely to receive would be from creatures such as Vasily; and I felt a moment's sharp sympathy for any woman who accepted such an arrangement. Degrading as it was, it might represent one's only real hope for security or companionship.

I said nothing of what was passing through my mind. Only:

"Would you have me marry against my own better judgement, then? Against love, against respect, against trust?"

May looked at me with eyes like drowning forget-me-nots. "If I had only given Eddy the trust he deserved, perhaps he would still be alive today."

I stared, aghast.

"Aunt Alexandra was right," she murmured, becoming more agitated. "I killed him. I ought to have forgiven him; but with my cruel words I killed him who was to have been my king. Do not try to comfort me, Sharp: I have betrayed every duty I have—as a woman, as a subject, as a Christian."

I had feared something of the sort. Eddy's siren mother had tinkered with May's mind, forcing her to overlook Eddy's heartless philandering; and ever since, May had blamed herself for his death. Against siren magic, what could I do? My helplessness nearly choked me.

I murmured some empty words and rose from my knees. Outside, the sun must have gone down, for the room seemed nearly as dark as night. I lit the gas, keeping it turned down so as not to disturb May. It occurred to me that the Duchess was likely awaiting me. "What is the time?" I asked.

"I don't know. I stopped my watch, when..."

—When Eddy had died. I knew that, of course, and I could have kicked myself for forgetting it. "I beg your pardon," I said. "Your mother wanted me to do her hair for dinner."

"Then you had better go. Take the evening off, Sharp, and see some of the sights. Here's some money, if you need it. No—don't mind me. I can undress myself, and then I think I will take a drop of laudanum, and go to sleep."

A moment later I found myself in the sitting-room again, heart-stricken and on the verge of tears. I put my hands over my face, trying to compose myself before I had to go in to the Duchess.

I could no longer deceive myself: I had suppressed the truth, and there in the dark it had festered to a poison. But what could I do about it? We had not decided to keep Eddy's death a secret because it was inconvenient. We kept it a secret for the sake of justice, because Eddy had died trying to kill me, and because it made no sense to let either May or myself as a scapegoat hang for what would, in regards to anyone else, be an act of justifiable self-defence.

Taking a deep breath, I wiped my eyes with my cuff. I had lied for a good cause, for the sake of justice. And justice was worth a great deal in this desperately broken world—it was, as the Baroness had said, worth anything.

Even then, a part of me knew that revealing the truth to *May,* at least, could not injure the cause of justice. *She* would not have used the truth against me. No, I hid the truth from May only because I was afraid—afraid that she would refuse to believe me; afraid that she would cast me out; afraid that I would be forced to face the unfriendly world alone. I had lost everyone else who had ever been my friend, and I could not bear the thought of losing May as well.

On that evening, however, I was not able to look this particular truth in the eye—and so after repeating some platitudes about justice, I pointed out to myself that after all, I was not the one most at fault. This done, I marched over to the Duchess's door and entered when bidden.

"I thought you were never coming, Sharp." The Duchess's own waiting-woman had been sick on the crossing to Le Havre, and was still not quite herself again. Now, Mary Adelaide of Teck plumped onto the stool before her dressing-table, beckoning me to begin work on her hair. "Is May ready for dinner?"

"She asked me to say she had the headache, ma'am."

The Duchess' eyes narrowed in worry. "H'm."

I hesitated, wondering if I should betray May's confidences. Instead, I blurted out the question that had tormented me for the last three months: "Why have you never told May that the rest of the family are werewolves, ma'am?"

The Duchess started violently and dropped her perfume-bottle. "I beg your pardon!"

"Didn't you know it?"

She twisted on the stool to look up at me, and I saw that her cheeks had gone perfectly white. "Does—does May know?" she whispered. "Have you told her?"

"I judged that to be your office, ma'am."

"It's not the sort of thing an innocent girl *should* know."

"With respect, she was about to marry one of them. Oughtn't she to have been told—*before* the engagement?"

"There are certain facts," Mary Adelaide said primly, "to which a young lady is not entitled until her wedding."

I frowned. "What, do you mean to say that princesses spend their whole lives turning into werewolves each month, and they aren't told *why?*"

"Dear me, no." The Duchess arched an eyebrow, and turned back to the mirror. "Kindly do my hair, Sharp, and I shall try to explain."

Her explanation was the first chance I had had to learn about the werewolf royalties from one who knew them personally. In summary, therefore, it went as follows:

Werewolves were partly born, and partly made. A child of royal descent, if not morganatic, would grow up with a craving for blood and raw meat, which normally intensified around the time of the full moon; but monstrosity did not develop of itself, and the craving could be satisfied with a bloody steak, or some similar dish. One's first taste of *human* blood, then, was more a rite of passage, than a positive need.

"Wait a moment," I interrupted, when she had gone thus far.

"Do you mean to say that a royalty need *not* to be a monster?"

"Well, in a manner of speaking. I myself never saw any reason to make the change. The culinary world is so varied! and so satisfying! And besides, dear Franz is morganatic, and it would not do for him to have a werewolf as a wife, since it would remind him of everything he has lost.—And then, of course, I was never in line for the throne."

"Do you mean it would have been different, in that case?"

"Why, of course! How could a monarch hold the respect of his family, or the allegiance of his subjects, if he was not the strongest of all of them? Pay attention, Sharp. I don't imagine my dear Cousin Queen has tasted human blood once since the day of her accession, but she must keep the whole family in line, you know—to say nothing of the Parliament, and the public service, and her rival Empires."

"You knew all this," I said with feeling, "and you never told your own daughter?"

"My dear, I was quite shocked when I found out myself. But it's the only way; you must see that."

I didn't see it at all, but I could hardly say so.

The Duchess went on. "A girl ought not to be initiated before she marries. Nine times out of ten, a prince wants his wife to become the same sort of thing as himself, you know; and there are different rites for making vampires, werewolves, sirens, dragons and so on."

"But May is morganatic. I thought she could never become a monster."

"There is a way," the Duchess said darkly. "For a morganatic princess—and only if her intended is actually to be a reigning monarch. I am afraid that it is dreadfully unpleasant."

I wondered if it was more, or less, unpleasant than being left for dead in a gutter. "And you think she would have agreed to this?"

"May has always been ready to do her duty."

"Yes," I said gloomily, "even if it kills her."

"I meant to protect her, Sharp." A steely edge crept into Mary Adelaide's voice. "I meant to keep her innocent, so far as I could."

"I believe that a woman of strong principles will always be innocent, ma'am, no matter what she *knows.*" I deplored the trembling sincerity in my voice, but I felt I had to say *something* for May's sake. "You can do nothing to preserve Princess May's innocence by keeping her in ignorance, and you might do much to injure her."

"Thank you, Sharp, but the decision lies with me, not with you." Hair done, the Duchess rose from her seat, and fixed me with an imperious eye. "You will kindly leave May's education to *me.*"

This said, she swept from the room. A part of me was genuinely sorry that May would continue in ignorance of her family's true nature, but deep down, another part was greatly relieved. The question had been taken out of my hands. So long as May was kept in ignorance, she could never know that she herself had killed Eddy, and I could never be blamed for it.

The Duke and Duchess of Teck went downstairs to dinner, and I was left in the darkness of the empty sitting-room. Mary Adelaide's maid was in bed, and the Duke's valet, having been given the evening off, had gone out on some dissipation of his own. It was the opportunity I had been waiting for. I changed my decay-scented black bombazine dress for a hand-me-down in mustard-coloured brocade; and then, taking hat and coat, I hurried downstairs and asked the concierge if I might have the number of Baroness Sarkozy's room.

Chapter IV.

Veronika Sarkozy emerged from her suite just as I approached it. At first, as she turned to lock the door behind her, I presumed I was looking at a maid; for she was now clad in a very plain cheap-looking walking-suit in dark grey, its only ornament a long shaggy scarf made to suggest fur when seen from a distance. It was not until she turned, and the gaslight blazed lines of fire through the silver in her hair, that I knew her.

"I beg your pardon, Baroness," I greeted her, dropping into a curtsey. "I didn't recognise you at first."

"Then I suppose it's just as well I didn't wear my false whiskers tonight." She smiled, pulling on her gloves, and taking her lacquered walking-stick in hand. "You are the young woman I saw in the café with Vasily earlier?"

"And you're Baroness Sarkozy. I've heard of you, ma'am. I read part of your article on the plight of the wolf-bitten in Berlin."

"What! only part?"

"They wouldn't let us have the whole thing at Saint Botolph's, ma'am. But Sal—my friend and I liked the part of it that we read."

"Ah! You're a Saint Botolph's girl?"

"Yes."

"I thought you might come to me," she said softly. "I was right about you, Miss—"

"Sharp," I said, curtseying again. "Liz Sharp, ma'am."

Her eyes flashed. "None of that, if you please, Liz. Call me Veronika. You and I are equals tonight.—I take it you mean to come with me?"

It barely occurred to me to wonder where she meant to go, and it did not cross my mind at all to wonder if I wanted to go there with her.—After she told me to call her Veronika, I think I might have followed her to the moon. "Of course," I said, and a moment later we had gone down the back stairs, and emerged into the cold wet night of Paris.

Putting our backs to the fading sunset, we set off at once down the Rue Saint Lazare. I glanced over my shoulder and saw two revenant policemen shuffling behind us. Perhaps it was a trick of the sunset, or perhaps their eyes really did glow with a terrible, phosphorescent light.

"Pay them no heed," Veronika said, not looking back herself. "We will deal with them shortly."

We came out into a small square, where a large and handsome church stood, considerably ornamented with round arches, a rose window, and an imposing cupola-shaped belltower. Its façade was dimly lit by the lamps in the square, and by the light glowing from the windows of the tall buildings that surrounded it. We stood in a world of blue clouds, wet pavements, and glowing reflected lights, and the church at the heart of it seemed like a gorgeous treasure-box, a beauty to lift the soul.

"The Church of the Holy Trinity," Veronika murmured. "It was ordered by Baron Haussmann, at a cost of five million francs, each of which might have made the difference between life and death to some poor factory worker. Do you know who Haussmann was, Liz?"

"No," I said, catching myself just in time not to call her *ma'am.*

"He built the beautiful large boulevards you shall see if you stay in this city a little longer. Before the boulevards, when the citizens of Paris had a grievance with their governors, they would barricade the streets and raise the flag of revolution. After—well, there could be no barricades, and the boulevards became rivers of blood down which the armies of the emperors might march and manoeuvre. To build them, the slums were gutted, and a great many poor people were turned out of their homes, and the people's only means of redress against their rulers was done away with. Haussmann himself boasted that the days of riots and barricades were past, and to me, his boulevards and his churches are as horrible as the revenant gendarmes.—But tonight we shall have a little of our own back. Come!"

She set off briskly across the grassy sward before the church. We climbed the broad marble steps past frowning white statues, and passed beneath the arches of the large portico. The door was open and we stepped through into the vast sanctified darkness beyond. At night, the glass windows slept, and the only light was that which flared from the candles upon the altar and the low-hanging lamps in the nave. I stared around me in wonder: it was the largest church I had ever been in, and the most ornate. Except for ourselves, and three or four worshippers with heads bowed, the place was practically empty.

Veronika beckoned me with a jerk of her head, and we

strolled into the shadows of the north aisle, pretending to observe the carvings and paintings that adorned the wall. After a moment I glanced behind to see the shape of the two revenants upon the threshold, at the door.

"They are following us," I murmured.

"Good," Veronika said. There was a smile in her voice.

I was still watching as the reanimated corpses crossed the threshold. What happened then was very silent—at least at first. There was a flash, white-hot, that lit up the whole interior of the church. Intense blue flame burst from the two gendarmes. A wave of heat radiated through the church, carrying with it the ghastly funk of burning decay. One crumpled to the threshold with a groan. The other stepped across the deadly threshold and stalked, flaming, into the sanctuary. Blazing like a fallen star, it made towards us. Every hair on my head stood upright as I saw how calmly, how inexorably the creature moved. The flames scarcely impeded it.

"This way," Veronika said in my ear, pulling me towards the back of the building.

As we hurried down the aisle, the creature behind us burst into motion. "Run!" Veronika cried; but I saw in a flash that the revenant was the quicker, and I could not bear to be seized from behind by the flaming hands of that ghastly corpse! Pulling away from Veronika's grasp, I turned to face the revenant. The skin had melted from its face, the eyeballs had consumed, but a cold spark still burned in the sockets. Had I been Roman Catholic, I might have crossed myself. Instead, I lifted my umbrella and rammed the ferrule straight through the blazing creature's ribs.

"Liz, *no!*" Veronika's scream echoed through the church.

I tore my umbrella out of the revenant's ribs, seized the greasy ferrule in my left hand—it was barely warm—and swung the weighted handle smartly against the creature's jaw. The blow connected with lethal force and I heard the crack as the jaw dislocated. The gendarme staggered sideways. I expected it to collapse in a shower of sparks and bones, like a fire when it is poked. Instead it drew itself up—and went quite berserk.

An iron fence ran along one side of the aisle, blocking access to the apse. The revenant grasped the fence with a now-skeletal hand and ripped away a paling as easily as you might snap a twig, thus providing itself with a stout weapon. The metal rod whistled through the air. I dodged aside, deflecting the blow with my umbrella towards one of the pillars; it struck with a shattering sound, and chips of marble flew through the air, stinging my hands. The creature turned quicker than thought, grinning like a nightmare, winding up for another blow. I retreated a step—and my foot caught in the hem of my skirt. I was thrown off balance. I knew that before I could recover myself I would be dead.

Then Veronika came out of the shadows with a long-handled, razor-sharp knife in each hand. She crossed the blades at the revenant's throat and swept them apart. The creature's head, still flaming, flew from its body and rolled across the floor. Her blades flashed and sliced, dismembering the creature with surgical precision: arms, legs, and torso rained to the floor amidst blackened flakes of fabric. To my inexpressible horror, the creature still writhed and moved, each part still living though severed from the parent body. But it could no longer impede us.

I threw my arms around a pillar and tried to regain my

breath. Veronika turned to me, sliding her knives together; there was a sheath for each blade in the handle of the other, and the two parts fitted together with a *snick,* forming the lacquered walking-stick I had noticed upon our departure. Before she could say anything to me, however, footsteps pattered on the marble floor and we looked about to find a sacristan hurrying towards us with a broom.

"Oh, heavens!" he murmured, "not again, not again! When will they learn not to enter the church?"

"I'm dreadfully sorry," Veronika said. Her accent changed, becoming a little broader. "My friend and I thought we would just step in to light a taper; we didn't know we were being followed."

"Don't apologise," the little priest said gloomily, sweeping the squirming limbs across the floor. "It happens every other week around here. Although I must say that they normally don't fall apart like this, unless they are in a *very* advanced state of decay."

"There were two of them," Veronika said, turning towards the door. "Ah! the pox!"

I followed her glance and saw a charred corpse advancing towards us. The other gendarme had evidently been clever enough to extinguish itself while its flaming companion engaged us.—Now it was on our trail again. My heart leaped into my throat. Veronika turned to the sacristan. "May we take the side door?"

"Of course." He seemed only too glad to be rid of us. Moments later Veronika and I were in the narrow street beyond. At a run, Veronika led me through a network of dark and winding streets until we had thoroughly lost sight of our pursuit. At length, she pulled me to a halt in the shadow of a dark recessed doorway, and we waited with beating hearts for a long time, watching the passers-by. When there was no sign of our charred pursuer, Veronika let out a long breath, and I saw the white flash of her smile in the dark.

"I ought to have warned you, never to attack a revenant unless you are quite sure of killing it, for the rules which prevent the creatures killing every living thing in their path are abrogated once they are attacked. The only thing that can stop them is slow decay or instant vaporisation; try anything else and you might as well sign your own death warrant."

I recalled the revenant's mad attack and shivered. "You *knew* it would respond like that?"

"The anarchists of Paris learned long ago to use bombs on the revenants, or nothing," Veronika said. "It is a lesson they have learned well, for failure means being guillotined and revivified themselves."

"That is the most horrible thing I have ever heard," I said faintly.

"Indeed," said Veronika, "and of course, since the natural decay of the dead body limits the usefulness of revenants to a few short weeks, there is a great incentive to keep up the number of guillotinings in order to replenish the ranks. The terror," she added, "is thought to assist in keeping the peace. ...And now we shall go to Le Chat Noir."

This, it happened, was a small establishment not far away in Montmartre, on the Rue Victor-Massé. Once a large house, it had now been decorated to resemble a whimsical country inn, the sign over the door resembling a large black cat treading daintily upon a crescent moon. Outside the door, stood a fellow in the costume of a Swiss Guard, of all things, laughing and joking with the patrons as they entered.

I followed Veronika through dark passages and at last into a large, smoke-filled room full of the scent of sweat, wine and beer and absinthe, and about half a hundred cheap tobaccos. Heavy antique lamps, statues, and paintings crowded the walls in a haphazard manner; and in place of a chandelier, a large fish was suspended from the ceiling. The room was packed with people crammed in at small tables on small shabby chairs. Every surface was sticky with spilled beer, and from his precarious perch atop one of the tables, a consumptive-looking young man was declaiming in a reedy voice. "Oh, the songs of Bruante in the salons, and dynamite under the coach doors! These two facts are very symptomatic of the end of the bourgeois era!"

"Oh, stow it, Goncourt!" someone shouted. "Nothing but idle word-spilling!"

The young man was half helped, half dragged from the table, and an avant-garde musician quickly got up on the narrow stage at one end of the room, and began to play a dulcimer in the Japanese style, or so he claimed. At the same moment, a chubby little man in a festive waistcoat approached us with a delighted cry of "Veronika! My darling Baroness, what can I do for you tonight?"

"Find me a table, Rodolphe, and something to drink."

"Perhaps, perhaps. And a chair?"

"Two chairs."

"Oh, Veronika, you ask too much!" He turned aside, and leaned over a young couple who were yawning over a shared cigarette. "Don't you two have somewhere better to be? Go away, now. I want this table for my friend."

The pair got up and left, and with a cheerful grin, Rodolphe drew out one of the chairs, and settled me and Veronika in their place. A pair of wineglasses soon appeared, together with a bottle of wine. Veronika poured a generous glassful, and slid it over to me. "Be good and wait here for a little while; I have someone to see about something."

She got up and disappeared into the raucous, foul-smelling shadows, leaving me to watch the show. It was extremely informal. Patrons would leap up to sing, declaim, or read aloud, and the crowd was eager to provide feedback in a free-wheeling form that degenerated often to heckling. My French was not quite good enough to understand everything that was said, but I am pretty sure that at one point, someone read a poem comparing dynamite explosions to flower bouquets. (A critic: "You can write, my dear, but do not forget that action is the highest form of poetry!")

I began to feel a little giddy, and it wasn't because of the wine. I had spent my whole life being warned against anarchists, and now I was actually getting the chance to see them in action, having their forbidden anarchist meetings, and reading their proscribed anarchist poetry!—Evidently these were the sort of anarchists who believed in "propaganda of the deed", but as I listened to the young poet speak of his beautiful blooms of light, I wondered exactly where he meant to throw his bombs. I could understand that if, as the anarchist laundresses I had met in London had claimed to do, one valued human life above property, it made a certain kind of sense to destroy the latter in protest—for instance, if one truly believed it had become an idol to which lives were being daily sacrificed. But of course, many of the French anarchists had become so furious and wild that they went further still, declaring sentence of death against any member of the moneyed or ruling classes, and seeking to carry out that sentence with their infernal devices.

With such thoughts and observations to occupy me, I was by no means bored by the time Veronika returned to me, sat down, and lit a cigarette. "There! My business is out of the way," she said. "What do you think?"

"Of the art, or of the anarchists?"

"In Paris, they are the same thing."

I shrugged. "They are talking about bombs. Very beautifully, it's true. But I'm not sure I can embrace their principles."

"These people have a new conception of virtue and vice, my dear."

"Perhaps, but if it permits the vaporisation of innocent people, it is not mine."

"Then if you were so decided, why did you come?"

"Because you brought me here."

She dragged deeply on her cigarette, and blew meditative smoke at me. "Ah, but first you came to me. You must have had *some* reason."

"I am looking for a man."

Veronika raised a shapely eyebrow. "Any man in particular, or just a man *simpliciter,* in the sense of a featherless biped, in trousers?"

"A particular man," I said, trying not to laugh. "A young anarchist, originally from Moldavia, presently in Paris."

Veronika's eyes narrowed. "H'm." Then she reached over and yanked at the sleeve of the passing Rodolphe. "Be a dear and tell me if you've had any Moldavian *compagnons* in here lately, Rodolphe."

"Perhaps," he said obligingly, topping up my glass with a little more wine. "Describe the specimen?—That," he added, when I had done so, "is Anton Lupei. Normally he would be here, but tonight he must be busy."

"Where can I find him?"

"Oh, he lives somewhere on the Rue Marcadet, but so do all the angry young men in Paris."

He bustled off to introduce another act, and I was left staring, rather apprehensively, into Veronika's white, set face. What had I said to bring about such a reaction?—After a moment she ground out the cigarette in the small ashtray on the table. "And how do you know Anton Lupei, my dear?"

"You know him?"

"I have heard of him."

I waited silently for her tell me more; an invitation of which she made no use, only continuing to watch me through narrowed eyes. "I have lost my past," I told her at length. "From something he said to me today, I think Lupei may hold a piece of it."

"What did you say your name was?"

"Liz Sharp. It's the one they gave me at Saint Botolph's; but Lupei—if that's the man I'm looking for—called me Vera."

Her face turned to a mask. A very lifelike mask, made of wax: motionless, and a little shiny. It stayed that way for a time, during which I do not think that she even drew breath. I did not think much of this until later. By now I had had a large glass full of wine, and my senses were a little drowned by that, and by the smells, and the sounds, and the dimness of the light. I began to wonder whether I was truly there, or whether I had wandered into a dream of the underworld.

Then Veronika took a deep breath and looked away from me, at the two playwrights who were reading from some rowdy play that was half melodrama, half political commentary. "You don't approve of anarchism?" she said abruptly.

"There are anarchists and anarchists," I said, thinking once again of Kendra Larsen and Iaminia Baciu. "I can sympathise with the grievances of the poor, and I have better reason than most people to hold a grudge against the monsters. But I work for the very people your friends here might wish to explode, and I know that it is not a clear-cut matter of guilt and innocence. My princess has never hurt anyone in her life."

"My dear," Veronika said gently, "do you think I don't know this? *I* am one of the very people my *compagnons* here wish to explode."

"Even though you're not a monster?" I took another sip of the wine. "How is it you're still in one piece, then?"—The question had occurred to me more than once this evening.

"Twenty-five years ago," Veronika said very quietly, "when I was very young, I fell in love with a young man who was beneath me. He might have been poor, but he was also brilliant, and kind, and he loved me not for what I could give him, but for who I was. I ran away with him, and for a while—a very short while—we were happy…until my family found me, and took me back. By then there was a child—his child. They took the baby away directly after the birth; I was barely even allowed to see its face. The scandal was hushed up; and since I was my father's only heir, there was no trouble in marrying me to an old baron who valued me for my inheritance. I had lost my lover, my child, and my faith; and I promised myself then, that when my husband died and I was my own mistress, it would be *my* place to do something about the injustices in this world, since there was no one else to do it." She glanced around the crowded room, and a faint, fond smile appeared on her lips. "My friends know what happened to me. They know that in my heart, I am one of them."

For a moment, I was at a loss for words. "They didn't tell us that part of your story, at Saint Botolph's."

"No, I imagine they would not."

"They treated you monstrously," I said. "But how do you imagine it will help matters, to wreak destruction and murder?"

"Oh, these are foolish young hot-heads, who will do more injury to the cause than good, in the long run. I have no time for senseless bloodshed—everyone who knows me will tell you that." She leaned forward a little. "But that is not the real objection, my dear. When the roots of injustice are inextricably entwined with the foundations of society, uprooting the one means doing some violence, at least, to the other. You must understand that. Change is its own price; one the powerful will never be willing to pay, until it is wrested from their hands."

"Is that what you meant, when you warned Vasily about a revolution?"

She nodded solemnly. "The people's vengeance is coming, whether such as I help it along or not. It is not natural that so many people should suffer in silence for so long." She glanced down at her wine with a frown. "That royal leech took a lively interest in my plans. What do you make of Vasily Nikolaevitch, Liz?"

"If you ask me," I said, recalling the conversation to mind, "he was very interested in your talk of revolution, and thought you had some intelligence he might cadge—or buy."

Veronika raised an eyebrow; I thought she was impressed. "Indeed! And are you closely acquainted with Vasily, Liz Sharp?"

"No, indeed, and I don't care to be. Before this afternoon, I had only met him once in my life."

"But he takes an interest in you."

"Yes; he offered me a position this afternoon."

"A compromising one, no doubt!" she said dryly.

I found my face had warmed somewhat. "No, as a bodyguard; but I wasn't fool enough to accept."

"Now, I wonder what makes Vasily Nikolaevitch Romanov so particularly anxious to have a bodyguard," Veronika murmured, watching me shrewdly.

It struck me quite suddenly that perhaps Veronika was trying to cadge information out of *me.* Before I could decide what I thought of this, a distant commotion forestalled us. Somewhere towards the front of the establishment were stamping feet—shouts—a scream. Then a dishevelled young man skidded through the door into the room, flinging his arms wide.

"It's the corpses, my friends! Every man for himself!"

Something struck him from behind and with a groan, he fell to his knees and disappeared from sight. Behind him loomed the shadowy figures of the revenant gendarmes brandishing truncheons.

With this, the room dissolved into chaos. Chairs scraped across the floor, or fell over with a bang, as the patrons of *Le Chat Noir* jumped to their feet. Calmly, Veronika reached out to grasp my arm, holding me in place as a jam of bodies formed at the sole door, trying to escape the room. Meanwhile a gentleman who had been sitting at a table not far from us rose to his feet and stepped onto the small stage. He blew lustily into a whistle, and silence fell over the room.

"I advise you all to sit down," he called. "The police are only here to search for an illegal printing-press. For your own good it is advisable not to resist."

Some of those trapped within the room shrieked invective at him, but no one obeyed. Veronika picked up the wine-bottle on the table, tested its heft, and then handed it to me. "There is a way out beyond the stage. Liz, if you will."

Realising what she wanted me to do, I felt the proper amount of horror—to say nothing of an improper quantity of unholy glee. "I couldn't possibly."

"Then I shall."

Even if no worse fate awaited me, a woman of my precarious standing in the world could scarcely afford to spend the evening locked up in a Paris police-station. I could hear shrieks and groans from the door, and stamping feet and dragging bodies throughout the house as the revenant gendarmes forced their way in upon us like an inexorable flood. It sounded as though they were arresting everyone, resistant or otherwise. I took the wine-bottle. "Allow me."

I threw the bottle with considerable force and accuracy at the policeman's third waistcoat-button. He folded up at once, wheezing with agony; it was nice to see that there were still at least *some* mortal policemen in the Parisian Force. "Nicely done," Veronika told me. Rising from the table, she stepped over the policeman's prone body, sweeping aside the stage-curtain to reveal a small, solid door set in the masonry behind. This she threw open before leading the way down a narrow dark staircase. After a few more twists and turns, during which I banged my toe on what might possibly have been an illegal printing-press, we emerged into a narrow alley at the rear of the establishment—or more accurately, one or two houses over. A small crowd of gendarmes could be glimpsed a little further away, watching *Le Chat Noir* like cats watching a mousehole; and meanwhile Veronika and I stole away into the night, followed by a little stream of artists, musicians, poets, and other assorted mice who had taken similar advantage of our exit.

Our procession quickly disbanded, and Veronika led me back to the hotel by a different route than the one by which we had come. We did not speak, walking briskly and keeping our heads down, but at last we came to the small open *place* on the Rue Saint Lazare, just across from the glass door that led into the café and restaurant on the lowest floor of the Hotel Terminus. When the door opened to let a well-dressed couple leave, it emitted light and the strains of a small orchestra—a comforting, commonplace, civilised sort of sound, bringing us both back to a sense of safety. Veronika stopped walking and turned to me.

"Now you know why I say that justice is worth anything, Liz. Tonight you have seen what we have to put up with. Is it any wonder—"

Her words were cut off by a thunderous sound, and a flash of light redder and angrier than the one we had seen at the church a little earlier. The ground trembled beneath our feet, and I clutched reflexively for Veronika's arm as we reeled in the blast. I smelled something hot and sweet and a moment later was choking in a cloud of acrid smoke.

It took me a moment to realise that the café had blown up.

It took another moment after *that,* for the screams and shouts to begin.

"Murder! Help! Stop him!"

"What the dickens?" I gasped.

Footsteps hurtled towards us on the pavement; and out of that thick cloud of smoke there dashed a young man, hatless, with his coat flying out around him like the wings of a frantic bird. He pulled himself up just short of colliding with us, and I looked into the eyes of the anarchist from the train station.

"Anton Lupei!" I cried.

He started and paled, but then Veronika stepped forward, took his arm, and said very urgently, "Take the rue le Havre, *mon compagnon.*" At once he started forward at a run. In a matter of moments he was gone, and from the other direction I heard the blowing of police whistles, and the shuffle of revenant feet.

I was staring after Lupei in confusion, when Veronika shook me by the shoulder. "Quickly," she said, "there are people hurt."

"Good Lord," I cried, recalling that the Tecks had been going to the café for their dinner. Veronika and I plunged into the billowing smoke together. Shattered glass crunched beneath my feet as I stepped through the broken door into a scene of terrifying destruction.

The bomb must have fallen not far from the orchestra. Some of the gaslights were still flaring, and by that light I could see shards of marble, pieces of shrapnel, and broken glass everywhere. Shadowy figures groaned or sobbed around me. A man brushed past on his way to the door, half supporting, half leaning upon a young woman; his trousers were in ribbons and he left a trail of blood behind.

That blood, thick and coppery and mixed with the cloying scent of dynamite! I can smell it even now!

"Your Graces!" I picked my way between overturned chairs, stopping to help a shaking woman to her feet. Soon, a gaping hole appeared in the wooden floor at my feet. Above, the ceiling was punctured and the large crystal chandelier dangled crazily askew. Flames licked at the edge of the floorboards. I had come to the place where the bomb had gone off.

I stood paralysed by the sight of this wreckage.—So this was the beautiful bloom of light of which the poets of Montmartre had been singing!

A shattered table lay to one side of the crater. It now stirred and was thrust aside; and from the worst of the wreckage a tall, diabolical figure arose. His clothing hung in bloody shreds from an unmarked body, as though he alone of every soul in that place was made of something harder than mere flesh—harder than glass or even marble. His eyes fixed upon me with a mad and rapacious light, and his lips drew back in a snarl to reveal pointed white incisors.

"Vasily Nikolaevitch Romanov," I whispered, lifting a shaking hand, as though I could hold him off merely by the force of my will. "It's me, Sharp. Be calm; you've just been blown up, but you're quite safe now."

There was not a trace of humanity left in those eyes—there was only hunger. With one hand he tore away the shreds of his coat and shirt, as though they hampered him. Now I could see thick black letters scrolling about his collarbone, a tattooed name: *Ioanna.*

His lips drew back further, and his nostrils flared.

"Stop smelling the blood; you can't have it," I said sharply.

Then Veronika appeared beside me, her sword-stick poised in one hand and a long sliver of broken wood in the other. "Stop it," she said to him crisply, "I will stake you if you don't restrain yourself."

She spoke in a language that was neither English, nor French, nor anything I had ever learned at Saint Botolph's, yet I found to my shock that I understood each word as perfectly as though I had grown up with it.

"Help these people get out, Liz," she added, to me. "I will hold the vampire at bay."

I wondered, fleetingly, what would happen if the two of them fought. Vasily was by far the stronger; but something told me that Veronika should not be underestimated. I did not think to disobey her, at any rate. Backing away from the cool-headed baroness and the snarling vampire, I turned around and saw the Duke of Teck looming out of the smoke.

"Sharp!" he cried, "is that you? Help me!"

"Are you hurt, sir?"

"No, but the Duchess has fainted."

Mary Adelaide was already coming around by the time I made my way over to her. She and the Duke, having been tucked away in a corner, had escaped the force of the blast.

"Sharp," she said in a faint, confused voice as we approached. "I feel terribly hungry all of a sudden."

"You've already eaten, my dear," the Duke said repressively.

"Have I?—Oh, so I have. My knee hurts dreadfully."

"Give us a look," I said, crouching beside her.

"But someone might see!"

"Or the half-naked gentleman might drain the blood from all of us! Anything might happen," I said heartlessly. "Is it bleeding?"

"Dreadfully!" But when she allowed me to look at the knee, it turned out to be little more than a scrape, sustained when she fainted.

The Duke lost patience. "From all the carry-on, I thought you must be missing a limb, at least. Come on, my dear, up you get." Between us, we helped the stout Duchess to her feet and supported her out onto the street, where a crowd of dazed patrons, inquisitive passers-by, and gendarmes both living and dead had gathered.

No sooner had we staggered out of the smoke and the scent of blood, than the Duchess turned to me. "What about May, poor dear? Was she much disturbed by the blast?"

"May?" I remembered my princess with a sudden jolt of alarm. "Excuse me, your grace—" and leaving her and the Duke standing on the street, I rushed in at the hotel's entrance-hall. People were out and about, of course, standing on the stairs or in the hallways gossiping excitedly and having smelling-salts or hysterics as mood and opportunity dictated. Brushing past them, I made my way to the Tecks' suite. The sitting-room was suffused with the dreadful smell of dynamite, but May's door was shut, and the whole suite was as silent as the grave. As the grave!—A horrible premonition crawled down my spine, and I flung open the door to May's room where she lay, pale and still, in bed. The bottle of laudanum stood upon the bedside table, and it occurred to me that she had been using it perhaps too freely of late.

All kinds of terrifying possibilities flitted through my mind. "Ma'am," I gasped, swooping down upon her, and putting a hand to her motionless cheek. She did not respond, but living warmth and a steadily throbbing pulse met my touch. She may have drugged herself into a slumber from which not even an explosion could wake her, but she had not taken an overdose, whether by accident or design. I fell back upon my heels, taking long deep breaths to calm my shattered nerves. Then I took the laudanum bottle, and hid it away in the bottom of Mary Adelaide's valise.

Chapter V.

It was hours before any semblance of normality returned to the ravaged Hotel Terminus; and even into the early hours of the morning, a crowd remained outside in the street, gazing upon the scene of the outrage. In the small bed made up in May's dressing-room, I sat sleepless for some hours, thinking of all I had heard and seen that day.

"Anton Lupei," I whispered to the night, testing whether the name felt familiar upon my lips. Had I once loved the man? Had I been his sweetheart—had I been his wife? If not, why did he kiss me like that?

Was I once an anarchist, too? Had he and I sung the song of Dame Dynamite together at *Le Chat Noir* in days long past? Or was it my attack and supposed death that had turned him from a humble peasant to an embittered killer?

My mind shrank from the thought.

If Anton Lupei was not already a killer, tonight had not created one: no person had died in the blast downstairs, although it may yet happen that some of his victims would succumb to their wounds. But he meant to be—oh, yes. A man does not throw bombs in a crowded room unless he means to kill. The testimony of the café patrons left no doubt that a young man of Anton's description, upon leaving the café, had turned back and thrown a package towards the orchestra, which then exploded.

Then there was Veronika. What was I to make of the Baroness Sarkozy? On one hand she had given Lupei directions for his escape; on the other, she had been the first to plunge into the wrecked café to help his victims. Was it not natural that, being in some sort of agreement with Lupei's grievances, she should seek to give him a sporting chance against the undead policemen who had behaved with such savagery at *Le Chat Noir?* Or had she bewitched me into overlooking her implication in a bloody crime?

At length I gave up trying to make sense of it at all. The Baroness was no concern of mine. Anton Lupei alone held the answers I sought. In the morning, if the fugitive had been captured, I would try to see him in gaol before we departed Paris. This decided, I pitched exhausted into my bed, and slept, like the rest of the family, until mid-morning.

May was horrified to learn what had transpired the previous night. "Do you mean to tell me that a bomb went off—beneath me—as I slept?" she asked as I opened her curtains.

There was more life in her voice than I had heard in a number of months, and I seized upon the opportunity to draw her out of her grief. "If you care to step downstairs after breakfast, you will see the scene itself, and I shall tell you everything I witnessed last night."

"Oh," she said, a note of longing in her voice, "but there will be journalists."

"They won't be remotely interested in you, ma'am, and to escape scrutiny, you might wear your veil."

To that she agreed, finishing her breakfast-tray with a greater appearance of appetite than she had shown for some time. I was putting the final touches to her toilette when we heard a loud male voice from the sitting room. "Heard the dreadful news," it boomed, and a moment later, "—look in and see if you were keeping your spirits up, what?"

May went very white, and looked like a hunted thing, sitting perfectly still for fear of the circling hawk. "Sharp! Do you hear that?"

A moment later, a tap on the door. "May," the Duchess called, "who do you think is here? It's *George!*"

"Sharp!" May pled, seizing my hands. "Don't let him see me! I am indisposed! I *won't* be made to see him!"

"But it's *George,*" I protested. "You used to slide downstairs on tea-trays together as children!"

It was a measure of her agitation that she did not reprove me for using his given name, rather than his title. "I won't have it," she hissed. "I won't have mamma or *anyone* throwing me at George, with Eddy hardly cold in his grave."

"It seems to me that his grace is the one throwing himself around, not you," I pointed out. "If he *will* drop out of the sky into your lap, no one can possibly say you have sought him out."

"It doesn't matter what anyone says, I won't have him. After what I did to Eddy, I can't just turn around and marry his brother. Do you think I am perfectly heartless? I know he's here to see me, and I won't be seen. That's all."

In the course of this whispered discussion, Mary Adelaide had continued to knock on the door and rattle the handle. "I'll see what I can do," I promised May, but my heart sank a little as I slid into the sitting room and closed the door firmly behind me. There I found not only the Tecks but also Prince George, the Duke of York and—as of his brother's unexpected death three months ago—the second in line to the English crown. He was holding a small bunch of roses in both hands, and I couldn't resist opening my eyes very wide at him.

"For me? You shouldn't have!"

As ever, George's short beard was neatly groomed, and his morning-suit, while quiet and plain, was cut with eye-watering elegance. If for a moment he could have stopped looking like a rather guilty schoolboy, the effect would have been one of regal dignity. As it was, my words only induced a greater panic: he nearly dropped the flowers, and yelped, "For May!"

As the reader has doubtless divined, I rather liked George. We had got off on the wrong foot during the Whitechapel werewolf affair, but on the whole *he* had come out that sorry business better than most, and what little I had seen of him since had only confirmed my good opinion. I was sorry to disappoint him.

"Well, that is a shame. I am afraid that May is indisposed today."

"What nonsense," the Duchess cried. "It's only her cousin George. Here, Sharp, let me in. I'll talk some sense into her."

Quickly, I placed my back against May's door. I thought she was wrong to hide herself away, but I knew she would deeply resent her mother's interference at this moment, and I did not mean to give up her privacy without a fight. "Please, ma'am. I know she would not care to hear it."

Across the room from us, George cleared his throat. "I say," he said in a stage whisper that sliced effortlessly through Mary Adelaide's protests, "perhaps she'd be more inclined to see me alone, what?"

"What nonsense!" the Duchess cried, "why should *that* make

any difference?"

"It's worth a try, for she certainly won't show herself like this," I put in, shooting George a wink, which did not seem to reassure him in the least.

"I am sure May would prefer to have her mother in the room, if—"

"My dear," said the Duke of Teck, firmly taking Mary Adelaide's arm, "fetch your hat, and let us walk down towards the Tuileries."

So it happened that after a moment I let myself back into May's room to find her standing uneasily before the window, watching through the gauzy curtains the courtyard that separated the hotel from the station.

"Has he gone?"

"Your parents have gone to walk by the river, ma'am, but George has remained in the hope of seeing you, if you will allow it."

"What, alone? What can he want to be alone with me for?"

"Perhaps because he, too, is mourning Eddy, and thinks of you as his companion in grief."

"Oh—poor George!" she said faintly, putting her fingertips to her lips. "Eddy *was* his brother. Oh, how selfish of me! Very well, I will see him. Has mamma gone?"

"Quite gone."

"But you will stay with me?"

"If you wish it."

"Thank you, Sharp." She looked into her mirror—her eyes were dry, and apart from a little paleness, she was quite presentable. I thought it rather interesting that she took a moment to pinch her cheeks, to bring the colour into them. Then she nodded to me, and I opened the door.

It would, of course, have been fatal had George adopted a tender or consoling or in any way loverlike manner. As I followed May into the sitting-room, I wished I had warned him not to try; but as it turned out, he was in no need of *my* help.

"May!" he barked, marching over to hold out the roses stiffly. "Heard about the bombing, what. Wanted to pop over and make sure you were all right."

"Thank you, George," she said, taking the roses and passing them instantly to me. "Do you mean to say you came all the way from London last night?"

"Dear me, no! Happened to be staying in Paris. On my way to Coburg—for the wedding, you know."

"You're travelling terribly early."

I thought he might be perspiring a little. "Well, yes! Always meant to come early, though. Didn't change my plans just because—hem. Lovely weather, isn't it?"

"Weather means little to me at present," said May in a low voice.

After that, there was a rather thorny silence. George was certainly perspiring. May's pinches had faded from her cheeks, and she looked progressively more wan by the moment. I considered setting fire to the curtains, simply to put them out of their misery.—At least it would provide a topic of conversation.

"By Jove, I miss Eddy," George said at last.

"May I ask something?" May said almost at the same moment. There was a frosty edge to her voice that I wasn't quite sure I liked, and I wondered if I ought to intervene somehow.

"Of course! Fire away!"

"Why did you try to convince me not to marry him?"

George shot me a pleading glance; I lifted my shoulders in a shrug. George was one of the two other people who knew the secret not even May knew: that she was the one who had killed his brother. He knew, none better, the sordid circumstances surrounding Eddy's death, and I for one was not going to help him explain them away.

He scowled, looking thunderous—I had come to realise that George's black looks were more often confusion and grief, than anger. "Thought you were too good for him."

"Then you had much too high an opinion of me," May said crushingly.

"And what if I did?"

"You should show greater respect for Eddy's memory!"

"Well, if it's an apology you want, you won't get it, demme!"

May's mouth tightened. "I will not hear such language," she said, retreating towards her room.

"May! May!" George took two steps, and was at her side, pleading. "'Pon my soul I don't know why you treat me like this! Only meant that I think the world—that I think highly of you. We won't speak of Eddy, if it makes you unhappy. Look at the sunshine outside! Doesn't it remind you of old times? Why don't we go down to the river, and I'll buy you a pinwheel, or an ice, or something."

Possibly it was because I had closed her door and was leaning against it much as I had done when her mother had been trying to enter earlier, but May stopped and listened to what he had to say. I think it was one of the longest speeches I had ever heard from George. At any rate, I thought it was rather good, and I hoped May would relent. George might be a monster himself, and his family might be a set of bloodcurdling horrors; but it could only do May good to go outside and enjoy herself.

May said, "I am not a child anymore, George."

All the same, there was a quiver of humour in her voice.

He smiled. "Only as old as you feel, what?"

She glanced through the window at the sunshine pouring past, and the occasional curl of smoke from the remnants of the bombing last night. But she shook her head. "Oh, George, I can't. Someone would be sure to notice, and then there would be more speculation in the papers, about whether we were going to be married."

He reddened a little, but with great courage said, "I can stand that."

"Well, I can't," she retorted. "I don't mean to marry anyone, and I won't have it gossiped about!"

"Don't say that!"

"What, that I hate gossip?"

"No, about marrying someday. Have to marry someday. Not die alone, and all that."

As it happened, May had once confided in me her dread of dying alone in a dingy corner of a palace that didn't belong to her; and I wondered if George knew how unerringly he had put his finger on her fears, or whether it was only that startling gift he had of understanding her.

Whatever it was, it was not an understanding May wanted. "Do you suppose *you* are going to marry me, George?"

He dropped his walking-stick with a clatter. "Good Lord!"

"You will already have Eddy's throne," she went on, quite remorselessly, in that flat emotionless tone that I had come to recognise as a symptom of great feeling. "Do you mean to have his wife too? Have you no sense of what is proper?"

"May! No—yes! Not for the world!"

May, apparently, found this garbled response to be quite comprehensible. "Good." She turned to me, still plastered against the door to her room, blocking it with my body. "What on *earth* are you doing, Sharp?"

I was saved having to answer by a discreet tap on the sitting-room door. "Oh! that will be the tea-tray, ma'am!"

"I didn't order tea."

"Must have been a mistake. Still! Tea!" And before she could object, I sang out: "Do come in!"

The door opened, and I found that I had, in fact, been mistaken. It was not a tea-trayed chambermaid who entered.

It was Inspector Alexander Short, of Special Branch, Scotland Yard.

Chapter VI.

Short was the third and last person who knew May's secret. We had worked together during the Whitechapel werewolf business, and again during the St James siren affair, but I was not entirely pleased to see him now. It occurred to me that with Short in Paris, my attempts to seek out Anton Lupei were likely to come up against his strenuous opposition. As a policeman (if not the undead kind), Short had a dim view of anarchists.

Despite his interfering ways, I couldn't help liking Short—perhaps a little too much for my own peace of mind, given that I was a scarred dainty and he was about fifty per cent. made of starch.

"Short!" I greeted him, "what the dickens are *you* doing here?"

"Ah, Miss Sharp! I ought to have known; where there are explosions, can Miss Sharp be far away?" (The dickens! just what did he mean by *that?*—I had no opportunity to ask, for he bowed to May a little more deeply than necessary, as though to make up for the solecism of greeting me first.) "Good morning, ma'am.—Sir, I've spoken to the gendarme downstairs, and it seems that the perpetrator of last night's outrage is still at large."

Well, dash it! Was Short already on Lupei's trail?

George was evidently grateful for the change in the topic of conversation. "This gentleman has been assigned by Scotland Yard to protect me," he explained to May. Then, turning back to Short: "Any danger of his trying a second time?"

"That depends on his objective, sir. If the fellow merely meant to make a statement, then this ought to satisfy him. If, on the other hand, he was trying to assassinate a particular person…"

His voice trailed away, but both George and Short shot covert glances at May.

Neither she nor I missed the significance of this look, and I felt what seemed to be a cold hand grasping my vitals.—After all, with what a look of hatred had Lupei fixed my princess and her parents! With what disgust had he inquired as to whether I was serving *them* now! Could I have unwittingly brought danger upon my princess? Could that bomb last night have been thrown for *my* sake? Did Lupei think himself in competition with the Tecks for my loyalties?

If so, I must disabuse him at once, before he made a second attempt!

May turned to me, all else forgotten in her alarm. "Are my parents in danger, Sharp?"

I thought about this a moment. "Not at present, I think, ma'am. The dynamiter from last night must be lying very low today, to escape the manhunt."

George and Short had broken off their discussion to hear my opinion. "What about confederates?" George put in. "Might be a gang of the miscreants!"

"Indeed, as a matter of habit, the bombers work alone," I assured him. "Anarchists do not believe in hierarchies, you know."

"And their voluntary associations are more often aimed at mutual aid than bombings," Short put in. As a member of Special Branch, of course he had a fair bit of experience with anarchists. "Miss Sharp is quite correct. Either the police will find the bomber, or he will succeed in fleeing abroad, most likely under an assumed name. Princess May need not worry for her parents. Still, it may be wise to move from the hotel."

"I have already broached the question with the Duke and Duchess," George put in. "They were quite in agreement with me."

"One moment," May said, before Short could reply. "About *what* were my parents in agreement?"

"Oh," George said, in some embarrassment. "Hem! I suggested we all take the Orient Express to Stuttgart together. This very day, in fact."

Beside me, May stilled—a sign of deep shock. Understanding her objections, and having some of my own, I spoke for her: "Today? But their graces had planned to be four days in Paris."

"They can hardly stay *here,*" Short said. "The hotel is about to close for repairs."

"Excuse me," May said in a suffocated voice. Pushing past me, she fled into her room and closed the door behind her. George stepped forward, a look of agony passing over his face, but I held up my hands to bar his way.

"Not now," I murmured. "I will speak to her later."

"Demmit, Sharp, what's the matter with her?"

The three of us conspirators were now alone in the room. Perhaps I ought to have confessed the truth about May's malaise, but it didn't seem right to do so. Short was my friend, but he was none of May's; and George she was quite determined to have as little as possible to do with. "It's not for me to say. You had better go away now. She has already conceded a great deal in seeing you."

"Till this afternoon, then," he said, putting on his hat again.

"I'll count the minutes," I said wickedly. Reddening, George beat a hasty retreat and nearly collided with—at last—the tea-tray. Short shook his head at me and followed, leaving me alone with four macarons and a rapidly-cooling pot of *Thé Mariage Frères*.

It would have been criminal to let such excellent tea go to waste, so I carried the tray in to May and poured a cup for her. She sat on her bed with her head in her hands, only looking up when I put the fragrant infusion under her nose. That brought her to herself again, and she took it from me with a wry smile. "I am afraid you must think I am becoming neurotic, Sharp."

That was a little better, and I wondered whether, after all, George's visit had served to extract her scrutiny from her own navel. Without being invited, I poured another cup of tea for myself. "He's still your cousin, you know," I pointed out. "You'll have to be seen in his company sooner or later."

She shook her head at the macaron I offered her, so I ate it myself. (To my knowledge I had not had a macaron before; it was quite an experience.)

"I suppose I shall," May replied. "I *did* hope it might be put off until after he was safely married—to someone else, I mean. Let them try to gossip then!"

"Would it be so bad?" I coaxed her. "Marrying George, I mean?"

"Oh, Sharp, not you too."

I sighed. For me, George's appearance had whetted all

those appetites that the wealthy satisfy at the theatre. His tongue-tied awkwardness—comedy. May's expressionless rage—drama. That moment when she had seemed to melt before the promise of sunshine and pinwheels—romance. The abrupt denouement—tragedy. Yes, I had enjoyed the play, and I confess I was looking forward with some anticipation to a second act. At what cost, though? Let me not forget that theatre was a rich woman's entertainment. If May married George she must learn the truth about Eddy. She must sacrifice herself to that monstrous family.—To say nothing of the truth that George himself was a werewolf—George, himself, must have tasted human blood!

"Forgive me," I said. "I only meant…"

"Well? What did you mean, then?"

"It breaks my heart to see you like this, ma'am. You hide in your room; you blame yourself for something that was not your fault; you refuse to go and have a little fun with your cousin, when it would do you the world of good." I found myself speaking huskily, as though a crumb of macaron was caught in my throat. "I only want to see you happy again."

"Poor Sharp! I know I must be dreary company! But how *can* I be happy, when I am supposed to be mourning my betrothed?"

A thought struck me. "There is a lovely poem I once heard, about this sort of thing. Let me see, how did it go?

"Remember me when I am gone away,
Gone far away into the silent land;
When you can no more hold me by the hand,
Nor I...Nor I...

"Oh, dash it. Anyway, I *do* remember the last lines: *Better by far you should forget and smile—"*

"Than that you should remember and be sad," May quoted softly.

"Right!" said I. "If Eddy had an ounce of heart in him, surely he wouldn't want to see you moping around like this—no matter *what* you think you might have done."

Which, of course, was highly debatable.—As far as I could tell, Eddy had had no heart at all, and I was pretty sure that wherever he was now, he would be rather pleased than otherwise to think that May should suffer so much guilt and shame on his account. Accordingly, my conscience stung me into adding: "And if he had no heart at all, there's no point in wasting your tears, is there?"

"Sharp!" she protested, but she was already half laughing.

"I can't put it any fairer than that," I said, grinning as impudently as I knew how. "What about it, ma'am? Is it a bargain? Shall you forget, and smile a little, and hang the gossip?"

"Perhaps a little," she conceded. After that she allowed me to pin on her hat and veil, and we went downstairs to look at the wreckage.

Chapter VII.

"You didn't answer my question."

This remark was directed towards Short. It was now about noon, and we were following just behind the Tecks and Prince George as they entered the Gare de l'Est through the pretty round arches beyond which the Orient Express lay ready to convey us to Stuttgart on the next leg of our journey.

Short lifted a satirical eyebrow. "It's good to see you too, Miss Sharp. I apologise for not greeting you more fully earlier."

"That's very handsome of you, Mr Short. This is going to be just like old times, isn't it?"

There was a brief silence.

"Do you know," he said, "just when you said that, I had the queerest sensation, like a shiver, walking all the way up and down my spine."

"Someone walking over your grave, no doubt."

"No doubt," he said, with the barest twinkle of a laugh in his drooping eyes.

I had been feeling distinctly on edge since his unexpected appearance this morning, but his teasing reassured me somehow. I didn't like to think that we might be at odds.

"You still haven't answered me, though."

"I haven't?"

"No. What the dickens *are* you doing here?"

"I have been assigned to protect the Duke of York during his travels."

"What made you want to do a thing like that?"

"The *Akbar* was willing to send someone, but his grace requested a Scotland Yard man. There was a scandal involving the *Akbar* some years back—poor conditions for the boys, I take it, and harsh gaolers. He prefers not to profit from the enterprise."

"That's rather decent of him. Still, last I heard, you requested a transfer to Criminal Investigation. Nurse-maiding royalty sounds like a bit of a come-down."

Short sighed. "My transfer to C.I.D. was denied. It's Special Branch or nothing; and my Chief gave me to understand that after the Whitechapel business—and the siren affair last month—I ought to be happy for whatever he chose to assign me. I had little choice."

"I wish I could say I was sorry," I said frankly. "But I don't think it was my fault. They never meant you to solve either of those cases. Both of them were cover-ups, and they were setting you up to fail from the beginning."

"It seems likely," Short said, more melancholy than ever.

"Why stay in the Force at all? They have evidently marked you as a great trouble-maker. I'm sure you'd make a wonderful private detective; you're the best policeman I know."

"I thought I was the only policeman you knew."

"Not true," I said with feeling. "I've met a surprising number of them since I arrived in Paris."

"Oh, French policemen," he said with distaste. "So that's my competition: reanimated corpses. I'm overwhelmed, truly. …

Did you know there's talk of introducing them in London?"

"Of course there is," I said gloomily.

I might not be entirely comfortable having Short around, but then, I could hardly be rid of him without first ridding us of George. It was only a short trip to Stuttgart, whence I would follow the Tecks south to Switzerland, while Short would accompany George north to Coburg.—Unless George should decide to make a detour to Switzerland as well, which no doubt he would if May gave him the least bit of encouragement! Dash it, it was bad enough having to leave the only clue to my past behind in Paris. With Short breathing down my neck, how was I to hold any sort of communication with the anarchists in Switzerland?

The Duchess of Teck's strident voice cut through my deliberations. "Sharp! Inspector! Were you planning to join us, by any chance?

Fascinating though my conversation with Short had been, it had not distracted either of us from the purpose of our employment, and as we walked, we had both kept a close eye on our surroundings. We now stood upon the platform beneath the great, beautiful arched roof of glass, the scent of coal-smoke and the warm, sticky fog of steam filling our lungs. Our charges had stepped up into the blue Paris coach of the waiting train; the valets and Mary Adelaide's maid had followed, as had the porters with our luggage; and now only Short and I remained on the platform as the Duchess leaned out of the door watching us.

Short glanced at his pocket-watch. There were still ten minutes left before the half-hour. "I should like to inspect the train from outside, ma'am," he informed the Duchess, whose eyes sparkled with interest at this statement.

"Are you going to look for bombs?"

"Yes, ma'am, but it's only a matter of routine. I don't expect to find anything interesting. Will you accompany me, Miss Sharp?"

"Have you any experience in defusing bombs?" I asked Short as we strolled the length of the platform, scrutinising the carriages.

"I am familiar with the theory, but in practice...well. The truth is the anarchists look upon London as a sort of rest cure. A week at the seaside for us, a month lying low in London for them, once the Continent is too hot to hold them. Not a great many bombs, as a rule." He quirked an eyebrow in my direction. "What about you, Miss Sharp? Do you have experience with the infernal devices?"

"At Saint Botolph's, I was top of my class in bomb-defusing. And lock-picking," I added, once again feeling the sting of loss, the certainty that I had forgotten much of what I once knew. I had an unusual mechanical aptitude. Just what *had* I been, before I lost my memories?

Given my affinity for bombs, did I truly want to know?

Short, meanwhile, whistled appreciatively. "You're a woman of rare accomplishments. Do me a favour, and try not to show me up? I've already been told I'm useless in London."

He tipped me a wink and a grin, and for some perfectly illogical reason, my cheeks flushed warm. If Short could joke about his own limitations, especially when compared to a woman, it made him a bolder man than most.

At the locomotive we stopped to exchange a few words with the engineer, who boasted that the train would make it all the way to Constantinople in less than seventy-two hours.

"I hear the new airships might do it in thirty," said I with a smile.

"For twice the price, maybe," the engineer said with a snort. "And a fraction of the safety! Let one spark get into those gas balloons, and bang! Might as well stay in Paris and wait for the anarchists to get you."

"You have no sympathy for the anarchists, then?"

The man snorted. "What good does it do poor people to blow up the rich? It only brings the revenants down on us and makes life harder for everyone."

"Satisfied?" Short asked, as I jumped down from the engine and re-joined him on the platform. He had his hands in his pockets and was looking back towards the sleeping-car. I followed his gaze, and to my no great surprise beheld the upright, slender form and badger-streaked hair of the Baroness Sarkozy, stepping into the Paris coach with a maid behind her. She had told Vasily yesterday that she was on her way east, and with the hotel closing on account of the bombing, it was not surprising to find that she, too, had become our travelling-companion. Just as when I had met her yesterday, she was clad in blackest velvet and carried her walking-stick; little remained to suggest the proletariat woman who had guided me to *Le Chat Noir* yesterday evening.

"No anarchists on the train, then?" Short prompted.

I started at his words. "I beg your pardon?"

"The engineer—I thought you sounded him out very cleverly."

Perhaps I had, or perhaps I had only been indulging my curiosity.—But what need to confess that to Short? "H'm! We're thinking like bourgeois, Short."

"I beg your pardon?"

"If there was anything to see, we would hardly see it from

the platform." Spying the rungs of a small ladder set there for the purpose, I climbed down onto the tracks before the locomotive. Phlegmatic as ever, Short hastened after me.

"Watch the tracks behind you," was all he said.

"You watch them, then; and I'll inspect the train."

We passed the locomotive and went down the side of the restaurant-car, ignoring the engineer's startled cry of, "Here, miss! You shouldn't be down there!" I stooped to inspect the undercarriage—nothing.

"I understand that you were one of the first to appear on the scene of last night's bombing, Miss Sharp," Short said conversationally, as I straightened and continued towards the first sleeping-car.

Drat, thought I. "That's true. I had been doing some sightseeing with an acquaintance, and was in the Place du Havre when the explosion went off."

"You were directly opposite the door of the café, then. Did you happen to see the bomber?"

Stooping to look beneath the Calais coach, I prodded at the shadows with my umbrella—nothing.

"Well?" Short prompted. "You were certainly well placed, and when it comes to curiosity, the proverbial cat is in a paralysis of apathy compared to Miss Sharp."

It was bad enough that Scotland Yard should employ a policeman so distractingly personable; it was positively *indecent* that he should also be perceptive. If I did not answer him, he would conclude at once that I had something to hide, and yet I hesitated to tell him the truth. So far, Anton Lupei was my one link with the past, and I did not like the thought of surrendering him to Short, even now that we were both leaving Paris. Besides—I recalled the look of wounded betrayal in Lupei's eyes when he had realised I was in the pay of the Tecks. Once this man had loved me—trusted me. English law forbade a woman being compelled to testify against her husband in court. Surely if anyone could be excused from betraying Lupei to the horrible French revenants for execution and revivification, it was the woman he had once loved?

But Short was waiting, and there was no time to consider the thing in greater detail. "I was not looking in the direction of the café when the bomb went off," I said, "and afterwards, everything was shrouded in thick smoke." It was a misdirection, not a direct lie, but it was not honesty either. My conscience, to my surprise, was as vigorous in condemning me as though I had looked him directly in the eyes and sworn that I had been struck with a miraculous blindness at the moment of the explosion.

Short frowned slightly, the dour corners of his mouth pulling downward a little. I felt that he was looking straight through me, but fortunately, my face had already turned red from peering beneath the carriage.

"Why does it concern you, anyway?" I added. "I'm sure the French police have the matter in hand, and if they don't, it's not as though either of *us* could help them."

I moved towards the Paris coach. Short plunged his hands into his pockets and followed, frowning slightly. "I did not like to alarm Princess May; but I am far from certain that the bombing was not meant for some particular person. Your mistress was lately the most famous princess in Europe, and it is not inconceivable that some person or conspiracy might have made her their target. It is a rather extraordinary stroke of ill luck that you should have seen nothing of the culprit."

I swallowed, and tried the direct attack. "Anyone would think you suspected *me* of being an anarchist, Inspector."

"Not at all, I assure you."

We had now come to the second sleeping-car, and I stooped to look beneath it—

I might as well tell you at once that I had never dreamed I should actually find something. Consequently, when I realised what I was looking at, in the shape of a shadowy bundle tied to the struts beneath the car, the sensation was like a dash of cold water in the face. At first I did not quite believe it, but then a faint, sickly-sweet whiff came to my nostrils. After a moment of frozen shock, I threw myself on my knees beneath the carriage and inspected the bundle. I could neither see, nor hear, nor smell a fuse burning, but thanks to my education at Saint Botolph's, the scent of dynamite was as familiar to me as your Sunday roast.

Short went pale as I emerged and he saw my face. "Not really?"

"Really and truly." I straightened and looked up at the Paris coach. The window directly above the bomb was empty, but suddenly a window several compartments away slid down, and May looked out.

"Whatever are you doing on the tracks, Sharp?"

"My job," I said briefly, abstractedly. At that, she stared, and I realised I should not alarm her. "Where are their graces, ma'am?"

"Oh, they have gone to the restaurant car. It's nearly lunch time."

"Do me a very great favour, ma'am, and join them."

She flushed slightly red. "You needn't baby me, Sharp; I was on my way." With these words, she closed the window and disappeared.

Short said, "How much time?"

"Don't touch it," I nearly shrieked, as he got down on his knees to peer beneath the coach. He froze, hands hovering either side of the bundle. "If I'm correct," I added, "it's a reversal bomb; the sort that is activated with motion."

He turned several shades paler. "We ought to clear the carriage."

"No time," I said, although I could feel the sweat running down my back beneath my sensible black bombazine. We could not risk the train pulling away before we could persuade them to wait. "It must have been carried here—very carefully—so it can also be carried away. Very carefully. Have you a pocket-knife?"

I put my hands around the package to steady it while Short cut the thing loose with his pocket-knife. Between us, very gingerly, we slid the bomb from its resting-place. A moment later we stood beside the train, supporting between us a heavy brown-paper parcel of irregular shape at exactly the same angle at which we had taken it from the undercarriage.

"Shall we set it down?" Short asked.

"If we do that, it may overturn and explode."

"Good Lord."

"I will hold it steady," I said at last. "You must unwrap it, and I will tell you what to do."

I hope never again to spend such a ticklish five minutes. Short stripped the paper from the item, and I found that I was holding a large pudding-basin at a slight angle. It came with the sort of lid that must be twisted until a pair of notches allows it to be removed. Short was no cook, and unfamiliar with the apparatus. He fumbled with it at one point, and I may possibly have allowed an unwomanly shriek to escape me. In the end, at any rate, he got the thing off. Immediately beneath the lid was a pen-case.

"Lift that," I instructed, "very gently." He did so, and revealed a tea-cup full of some white powder, nestled among a number of dynamite cartridges. The whole mixture was swimming with water, and I must have shuddered then, for the water rippled, and came close to spilling into the tea-cup.

"What now?" Short inquired.

"Have you got that pen-case secure?"

"Yes. What is it?"

"Not a clue; open it up very carefully." He did so, and revealed a dingy grey powder. "Oh, mercury fulminate, I presume, to detonate the dynamite. Put it in your pocket for now; don't on any account jar or shake it. Now, do you see this tea-cup, bobbing around in the water here?"

"Yes?"

"I presume it's potassium chloride and sodium. Go on and lift it out, but be careful. If any water gets into this cup, we shall both lose our faces. I don't care about mine, but yours is too lovely to ruin."

"I'll bear that in mind." He reached in with his long clever fingers, and lifted the tea-cup with infinite care from the water. I could not help admiring how steady his hands were. As soon as he had done this, I put the pudding-basin gently on the ground, for I was feeling a little dizzy with relief. "Well done, Short. Two policemen were exploded right here in Paris, just a few months ago, performing the same operation."

"Very heartening," he said, "but in the meantime, I still have a detonator in my pocket. What ought I to do with it?"

"Oh, we can hand it to a gendarme," I said, glancing at the

clock. "But let's be quick about it; it's two minutes till the whistle blows."

Chapter VIII.

You will laugh, but this in fact is more or less what we did. We could not stay; the train could not be delayed; at least Short was able to show his credentials from Scotland Yard, and prevent us being arrested on sight.—The French gendarmes we spoke to were natural men in their first semblance of life, rather than the dreadful revenants, but they were, if anything, more nervous than the revenants might have been about an agitated pair appearing to ask if they would be so kind as to take possession of a disassembled bomb.

At any rate, when the whistle blew it found Short and myself still at liberty, and racing down the platform in a mad dash to catch our train. We scrambled aboard the baggage van just as it began to stir. In a minute or two the honey-coloured arches of the Gare de L'Est fell away behind us, and we were safely on our way to Stuttgart.

The tension of the last five minutes dissipated suddenly—so suddenly that I fell against the carriage wall and dissolved into laughter. Short must have felt rather the same, for he joined me.

"And to think how dull my life was before you came along!" he said.

"It isn't as though I—*wait.*" I narrowed my eyes at him. "I do believe you're really enjoying yourself!"

"Enjoying myself?—How could I, when my lovely face has been in such mortal peril?"

"Admit it!"

"Well," he said a little more soberly, "this *is* more like it. I didn't become a policeman because I wanted to cover up murders and harass vagrants, you know. I wanted to save lives."

"I'll drink to that," said I with feeling. For a moment we stood in the gently rocking car amidst the dim mounds of luggage thinking again of the narrow escape we—and goodness knew how many others—had had.

"I owe you an apology, Short," I said after a moment. "It does seem rather likely that someone has made up their mind to remove the Tecks from our midst."

"The question is: Who?"

"Perhaps there is a conspiracy, after all." Or had Anton Lupei made a second attempt? But the answer to that must have been left behind in Paris, at the Gare de L'Est. And even if I had been free to remain in Paris, I had had enough of that city to last a lifetime.

Short was thinking aloud: "I don't like to involve the French police; it would only obstruct our travels, and likely trap us in Paris with the assassin. But I do think we should inform our employers, and remain vigilant ourselves."

"Agreed." I was still feeling somewhat shaken. When I scented the bomb beneath the carriage, dreadful images had played through my mind—the smoke and blood and dazed, piteous faces from last night had all risen up before me like a waking nightmare. That same violence had followed us, and now even the luxury of the Orient Express seemed not as safe as it had a moment ago. "Short?"

"Yes?"

"I'm glad to have a second pair of hands. Steady ones, too."

He looked at me in a meditative sort of way, and went on looking a little too long for my peace of mind. I was about to ask if there was something stuck in my teeth when he smiled that swift, sudden smile of his, the one that lights up his whole melancholy face and transforms it to a beacon of warm light. "As glad as I am to have you, Miss Sharp."

With that, he led the way forward towards the sleeping-cars. We made our way through the baggage-car, then across the windy platform into the Paris coach, which had so recently escaped an explosive fate. There was a porter about halfway down the passage-way, facing the door to one of the compartments; and when we entered, he turned towards us.

It was Anton Lupei.

At this particular moment, I was a few steps ahead of Short. Therefore, he did not see the young anarchist start and pale at the sight of me—nor the way my hands tightened reflexively upon my umbrella. Lupei stiffened, his fists clenching into white knots by his side. I scarcely knew what he might do if he felt himself trapped—nor did I wish to find out.

In my bosom, terror warred with renewed hope. Lupei, here! Where had he got that uniform? What had happened to the real conductor? Had he come for me?—I had but a moment in which to determine my next action. Betray Lupei to Short—see him taken into custody—go on to assure May and her parents that the assassin stalking their footsteps would be arrested?

—And then guillotined, and transformed into one of the horrible revenants!

"You must be the conductor," I sang out, before Short's suspicion could attach to the imposter. The plan had come to me in a flash: I must speak to Anton, at least, before I determined what to do next.—I sent him a look of warning. "I am Princess May's maid, in number—" I glanced at my ticket—"eleven. Will you put another blanket in my berth, please? It ought to be empty at present; everyone is at lunch."

For a moment Lupei stood as stiff as a board, like a man reprieved from death even as he stands before the firing-squad. I gave him my most winning smile. Warily, he nodded and stood back to allow us to pass. I felt rather as though I was passing a wild beast, or the Grand Duke himself; I kept an eye on those clenched fists as Short brushed past him. Feeling nearly as shaky as I had in the aftermath of discovering the bomb, I led the way towards the restaurant car and the Tecks, leaving Anton Lupei behind.

Lunch had not yet been served, but the more sociable of the passengers were already gathered in the restaurant car. In addition to these were May and George, and the Duke of Teck, whom we found in a frightful sulk (it seemed, as May whispered to me later, that one of the porters had committed the *faux pas* of addressing him as "my lord" rather than "your highness"). Between his temper, George's awkwardness, and May's shyness, our party might have been on its way to a funeral rather than a holiday—had it had not been for the Duchess, who was in the process of systematically charming the rest of the passengers.

"My poor child has suffered a terrible bereavement," she was at that very moment saying to a retired colonel and a wizened socialite at the table directly behind her chair, in piercing tones that carried the length and breadth of the carriage. "Only imagine—her betrothed, not two days after their engagement had been *Morning-Post*ed, was found cold and stiff in his bed, poor lad!"

"Dear me!" said the socialite.

"Dem' shame!" said the colonel. "Not sure I quite caught your name, ma'am?"

"Lady Killarney," Mary Adelaide said primly.—As though she imagined for one moment that the pseudonym would hold, with her loudly reminding them of Eddy's tragic demise, the superannuated minx! No wonder May—and, come to think of it George too—looked mortified. I swooped down upon them, and adopting some of Mary Adelaide's own portentously secretive manner, desired them all to retire to the Paris coach for a security briefing. The three silent members of the party obeyed with alacrity, and even the Duchess was unable to resist the scent of intrigue.

"Sharp and I have troubling news for you," Short began, when the six of us had squeezed into Short's compartment, Nos. 4 and 5. As a second-class compartment, it was slightly larger than the others, to accommodate two berths; but even with the Duke and Duchess seated on the bench seat, it was rather a tight fit for three gowns, and if the men had not all been so very slender, I don't know that we would have managed it. Short went on to relate the circumstances of our departure. The news fell among our august masters like a cartridge of dynamite in its own right.

"Sharp! I had no idea!" May protested once the sensation had died down. "Why didn't you tell me you had discovered a bomb?"

"I thought you would prefer it to be dealt with quietly and calmly, ma'am."

"I would have been calm and quiet," she said sadly.

"I am afraid this removes all doubt," Short put in. "Someone has chosen to target either the princess, or her parents, or both."

"But why? We're *English,"* said Mary Adelaide. "—Yes, Franz darling, except you; I know."

"Anarchists often choose symbolic, rather than practical targets," Short explained. He might have continued, but George, who had been silent hitherto, grunted explosively.

"Enough talk! Have to decide what to do next, what."

"What to *do?"* Mary Adelaide's eyes opened very wide. "The danger is left behind in Paris, surely? Oh! Just imagine how wild the boys will be, May, when we come home and tell them what they have missed!"

"Not a game!" George boomed. "Demmed serious, what!"

"Please, George," May said faintly.

"Won't have you exploded, demmit! Near connection of the family and all that!"

He stood by her, one arm braced against the wall near her head, very near to actually embracing her. May did not look uncomfortable there. On the contrary, a slight flush crept to her cheeks as she seemed to realise how close they were. "Please, George," she repeated coaxingly. "It isn't as though such an unfortunate could have boarded the train with us."

"Of course not," the Duke and Duchess said together; and Short added, "Naturally we must exercise caution; but Switzerland may be the safest place for everyone at present."

I stood with my back to the window, and now, partly to dispel the perspiration I felt gathering on my forehead, and partly to escape the attention of my friends, I turned to the window and lowered it a few inches to admit the fresh spring air.

Was I putting their lives at risk by not warning them of Lupei's presence on the train? What had become of me? I, Liz Sharp, the seeker of truth, was even now withholding information from my friends and protectors that might save their lives.

Hiding the true cause of Eddy's death—from the Queen and country, at least, if not May—was not something that left my conscience tender. I had not killed Eddy, but I did not for a moment doubt that I would be made the scapegoat should it become common knowledge that he had been shot with wolfsbane. One did not owe the truth to everyone, especially not to those who would use it to do wrong. But if one accepted that, one must also admit that there was a corresponding duty to convey the truth in every particular to an innocent who needed it.

As May and her family might now need the truth of Anton Lupei's name and presence.

As May herself needed the truth of her part in Eddy's death.

At that precise moment, these thoughts did not occur to me very clearly. All I knew was that my conscience was giving me the dickens of a time. I calmed it by observing that it was only for a short time longer—an hour at most. I would find Anton and learn whether he had indeed been responsible for the bomb in the undercarriage; I would ask him who I had once been, and beg him to leave the Tecks alone. And then I would make him get off at the next stop, and it really would be true that everyone was safe.

Truth served justice; and how was I to get justice if I could not speak to the one person who might be able to tell me who gave me my scars?

Besides, look at May! Since our conversation earlier this morning, she seemed better already. She had ceased to shrink from George—why, she had now even permitted him to take her hand and emit some incoherent and fragmentary remarks upon her bravery and his own intention to watch over her safety.

"Then it's decided," said Mary Adelaide, beaming at the young pair. "We shall continue on our travels. I'm sure that Sharp will take excellent care of us!"

They all looked at me expectantly. I swallowed the guilt that threatened to clog up my throat, and said, "I beg you not to let your guard down. Be aware of your surroundings at all time, and it might be best to move around the train in pairs."

George put May's hand into the crook of his elbow. "Sound advice, Sharp!"

May looked mutinous for a moment, but then she gave in: the present situation, it seemed, was too interesting to permit strenuous objection. "Everyone will be in the restaurant-car for lunch. I will be sure to observe all our fellow-passengers, in case it should be of any help later."

I nodded, trying not to feel like more of a hound than absolutely necessary. "Perhaps you should do that now; we must be a little late already."

We filed out of the compartment, and I hesitated in the hallway. Noticing my movement towards my own berth, Short turned back. "What is it, Miss Sharp?"

"Oh, nothing. I am only going to put my umbrella in my berth. Hadn't you better keep watch over our little flock?"

"Take care," he bade me, following the flock into the restaurant-car. Drawing a deep breath, I hurried down the passage to Nos. 10 and 11, the compartment I shared with

Mary Adelaide's lady's maid. As I had hoped, Lupei was waiting at the window. I felt almost faint with mingled relief and triumph to see that he had accepted my assignation.

"Anton Lupei?" I said, closing the door behind me, and shooting the bolt.

He took two steps. A knife flashed in his hand. The next moment he had me pinned against the door with one hand, that razor-sharp blade of his tickling my jaw right beneath the left ear.

"So, you remember my name now, do you?" he hissed.

I held very still. Although I was the stronger of the two of us, the compartment was cramped, and the blade was very close to my skin. "Yes, I know your name, but only because I had it from the impresario at *Le Chat Noir.*"

His teeth showed. He was still wearing the conductor's uniform, which fitted him tolerably neatly; and he had even shaved and washed not long ago. But his hair and eyes were wild, and once again I thought of Vasily as he had been last night at the shattered café, maddened by the scent of blood.

"You have been hunting me. I do not like to be hunted."

"I have followed you," I said, very softly. "And quite natural, too! You are my only link with who I used to be. You know me better than I know myself. I think I have been looking for you ever since I first awoke in that ghastly hospital without my memories."

At that, a little of the wildness went out of his eyes, and the blade dropped from my throat. "Vera," he said gently; but he didn't move otherwise. "I saw what you did to my bomb, so I came aboard—You are protecting them. *Why?*"

It had been his bomb—of course it had been his bomb, yet the admission hit me like a closed fist.

"They're innocent people, Anton. They haven't done anything wrong."

"People of that sort don't have to do anything wrong. Since they were born into the profits of crime, they are guilty by virtue of their existence."

"I don't know about that; but I do know that you haven't managed to kill anyone so far, and I don't think you want to begin with us."

"With us! What *us* do you mean? You and those monsters—you and that policeman?"

"What other *us* can there be, when you won't tell me of any other?" He made no reply to this. "Anton, please—I'm begging you. If you know who I am, *tell* me. If you have a claim on my loyalties, *tell* me. If I once believed as you do, remind me."

He watched me with shadowed eyes. "Vera," he said again. His voice was rough and low, and some instinct deep within me responded to that tone with a mixture of happiness and anticipation: for a moment I thought he was going to kiss me, and for a moment I would have welcomed the caress.—Instead, he turned away with a wild gesture, and put the knife back into a sheath at his waist, beneath his conductor's tunic. I took a long slow breath and put my umbrella in the luggage-rack.

"Anton," I began, but he turned to interrupt me with determination written across his face.

"Leave them, Vera. Come away with me. I'll tell you everything, I swear; but you must trust me first. I dare not risk any less."

What was this witchcraft? A few moments ago my nerves had been jangling with alarm; then with a slight change in his voice I had wanted to throw myself into his arms. Now he offered me everything I had ever wanted, and I did not know how to deny him. Gathering up the shreds of my reason, I said:

"And the Tecks? You will leave them in peace?"

An angry change swept the tenderness from his eyes. "I will never have peace with the monsters!"

"The Tecks are not monsters, and I want them safe."

"And if I don't?" It was my turn not to answer.—"You'll turn me over to your policeman friend, eh?"

Not ten minutes ago I had been promising myself that if Lupei refused to cooperate, I would do just that. Now, I only shook my head. "You asked me to trust you—"

"Only because I must know I can trust *you.* There are things in the past that could be used against me and others—and if I were to tell you..." He shook his head. "I don't ask you to trust me. I ask you to trust yourself. This was your choice once."

"A choice I have only your word for? A self I can know only through you? You've *hurt* people, Anton; that I've seen with my own eyes. How can I trust you won't hurt me, too?"

"Please, Vera."

"I ask only that you promise you won't hurt May or her family. That's *all* I ask. Please."

"I can't," he said thickly. "I'm so close—after all this time—and I wish, I wish..." He stopped himself, before going on. "Do you think I am a greengrocer to be bargained with? I *loved* you, Vera. I still do. It has been more than two years since they told me you were dead and there has not been a single moment of a single day since that I was untrue to you. Not *one* moment." He paused, breathing hard; and then he put up his hand, and touched my face. His fingers, warm and gentle, smoothed the rough stripes of my scars, and a bone-deep warmth unfurled within me. "No bargains, my love, and no threats. If you are not willing to take your place at my side, then you must hand me over to your monstrous friends, or stand out of my way."

He brushed past me, and threw open the door.

"They'll kill you," I said. There was something wrong with my voice. "They'll kill you and turn you into one of those ghoulish creatures. No one deserves that."

He hesitated when I spoke, but made no reply. The door closed, and I was alone.

Perhaps I ought to have seized him then and there, but I could not bring myself to do it. I could still feel his gentle hand upon my scarred cheek.—He had demanded I trust him, and I found that I did. The memories had been stolen from me, but at least some of the emotions remained. For the first time, a new future opened before me: a real choice, not some wistful, foolish daydream about a man who saw me only as a friend. My employment with May had hitherto been the only thing standing between myself and a return to the gutter. With the scars upon my face, if I failed as a bodyguard, there would be no alternative before me but to become a dainty—to sell my blood to some monstrous prince—or to starve. I had been drained by a monster once against my will, and I had sworn I would never endure such a thing again, even willingly. That left starvation; or now, Anton.

No doubt life with a penniless anarchist would be hard, but together we might do it, where alone I would surely starve.—Men's work paid more, and two might live more comfortably on the combined income, than a woman might on her own.

If there was a real choice, would I take it?—Or stay as I was?

—But of course, it was no choice at all. I could not pledge

myself to a man I barely knew, just because he said he had once loved me; and whether he knew me or not, if I could not have his parole, he must be put where he could do no harm.

But how? On one thing I was resolved: I would never hand him over to the French police. Better to shoot him myself, if I must. In the meantime, there must be *some* understanding we could reach. He was not devoid of feeling—not where I was concerned. I was perhaps the only creature in the world who might awaken his pity and draw him out of his anger—and unless I meant to shoot him out of hand, it was my duty to try.

Flinging the door open, I stepped out into the passage again. I had deliberated only moments, and Anton was still visible at the far end of the coach, making towards the rear of the train. "Wait!" I called, hastening towards him.

At that moment, a door opened between us—and Grand Duke Vasily emerged.

He glanced at the retreating conductor, and then at me, with a knowing smile I didn't much like. "Why, Miss Sharp," he said with an amused gleam of teeth, "I hate to say such a thing, but if I didn't know better I should suspect you of entertaining a young man in your compartment just now."

I halted in my rush, and ran quick fingers through my hair as though to smooth it. "Don't tell me! He got his rouge on my collar, didn't he?"

Vasily lounged into the passage-way, seeming to take up all of it with his lazy, catlike grace. "That's not rouge; it's blood. And it's yours. I thought you didn't like to give your blood away."

I put a finger to the corner of my jaw and found a tiny, stinging cut where Anton's blade had rested. "Cut myself shaving," I said automatically. The vampire laughed. "*You* try being bitten by a werewolf and see if it leaves *your* schoolgirl complexion intact. I didn't know you were on the train."

"I have business with the spectacular Baroness, so it behoves me to stay in her vicinity. But you're evading the question, Miss Sharp."

"You didn't ask a question."

"Consider it implied."

"Then no—I don't actually need to shave."

He regarded me with tolerant amusement. "That was your friend from the Gare Saint Lazare, wasn't it?"

Dash it!

"Anton Lupei?" I said. "You refused to tell me his name, yesterday."

"Ah. I must rise earlier in the morning to get the better of you, it seems. Heigh-ho! I'm not sure I mean to bother. If you knew that, you must know that he was the Hotel Terminus bomber."

"If that's so, then why haven't you already turned him over to the police?"

"My dear, I did not know he was on this train until just now." There was a flash of something not quite lazy in his eyes, and I shivered, remembering how I had seen him last night—that barely controlled bloodlust. "Have you considered my offer?"

So much had happened since the last time Vasily and I had spoken, it took me a moment to recall that he had offered to take me as his bodyguard, and help me find my past. After a second useless interview with Anton, the offer seemed more tempting. If Anton would not speak with me, then I might in Moldavia find those who knew him well, and who might know the name of a wife or sweetheart, had there been one.

This consideration was, however, counterweighed by the fact that the last time I saw Vasily, he had come within moments of tearing out my throat.

"Come, Sharp," he purred, moving a little closer. "Your china-doll princess can offer you comfort, and Lupei can offer you truth, but only I can give you both."

My throat went dry, and I fixed my eyes on my feet. Vasily's were planted just before them, far too close. His cold, clear scent was in my nostrils. I put a hand into my pocket and found the long, sturdy wooden hairpin I kept there for the discouragement of vampire interest. "Thank you, but no."

"Look in my eyes and tell me you don't want to say yes."

Look in his eyes—not likely. I had once made the mistake of letting him touch me, and he had used it against me, twisting my mind until I saw only what I wanted to see—gilded lie that it had been.

His breath brushed my ear. "Coward."

I wasn't looking in his eyes, so why did his proximity make my heart beat a little faster, and send flickers of warmth through me? I really did have the *most* ridiculous reactions to mortal danger. "I won't put my head in the tiger's mouth, charm he never so wisely."

"Ah! You think I'm charming."

"I think you're a tiger."

"Mrrowr," he said, laughing.

He was far too close. I could smell nothing, see nothing, but Vasily. In sheer self-defence I lifted my chin and looked him—nearly but not quite—in the eye. "Why are you bothering *me?*"

"I already told you. I want a bodyguard—as a matter of some urgency, since your friend is in our midst."

"We will arrive at Châlons within minutes," I told him. "If the company is dangerous you are always welcome to leave it."

I tried to brush past him, but he put out an arm to bar my way. In the narrow passage, there was no passing him. Vasily smiled, showing a glint of teeth. "I am not free to conduct myself entirely according to my own wishes, Miss Sharp—as no doubt you are aware."

I recalled what I had heard whispered of the Grand Duke in London—that he was an agent of the Russian Emperor's, harvesting state secrets from the Cabinet Secretaries, Lords of the Admiralty, and other great men who frequented the debaucheries over which he presided in Soho.

I recalled the papers of accreditation he had tendered to the revenants in Paris. I recalled—oh, folly!—betraying that I suspected him of being on secret business, his trip to Moldavia only a story put about to smooth his way. I shrank back against the window, and said hastily: "I'm sure I can't imagine what you're talking about!"

"My Tsar's business admits no delay," he said, dashing my hopes of being allowed to escape without knowledge that might be dangerous to me. "Certainly it does not permit me to flee at a sign of danger."

"I'm an Englishwoman," I said desperately. "Why do you ask *me?*"

He grinned—oh, he was enjoying himself! If it hadn't been like poking a snake, I would have slapped him. "Because I've never known a girl like you before, Sharp."

"Whereas I've known plenty of men like you," I spat. My heart was going so loudly, I knew quite certainly that he could hear it; that was what brought such a sparkle of excitement to his eyes. "I was drained and thrown away like garbage once by someone just like you. So tell me the truth: *why me?*"

His grin became a little wooden, and this time it was he who looked down, not I. He had my hand—I didn't recall when he took it, and he smiled down at it, circling his thumb over my palm. "Elizabeth Sharp," he said, "the truth is that if you come away with me, one day you will either kiss me or you will stake me, and I honestly have no idea which."

He looked up again, and now the grin was sharper than ever. "There's something intoxicating in that."

I stared at him, that charming monster, my mind in an uproar. Could it be true? That mixture of terror and longing I felt for him—could he really be feeling the same for me? Was *I* the monster who haunted *his* dreams?

Now that was an intoxicating thought—for all of half-a-dozen heartbeats, until I recalled that I could not be half so threatening to his safety, as he was to mine. I did not hunger to end his life, after all: not the way he did mine.

"Enough of your flim-flam," I said severely, planting a hand against his chest. "The fact remains that I can depend on May not to drain my blood some fine morning when she gets bored of me; which is more than I can say for you."

He stepped back, letting me inch away. "Don't pretend the danger doesn't appeal to you, Sharp."

"I don't," I said crisply. "That's why I'm leaving."

I turned and went up towards the restaurant car. It wasn't until I had made my way to the restaurant and asked an attendant for my lunch, that I remembered Vasily had interrupted me in the midst of chasing Anton.

Chapter IX.

I glanced up and down the restaurant-car, trying to decide what to do next. On one hand, Anton was loose in the train. On the other, I was now desperately hungry, and I did not think Anton would remain aboard for long. Disguised as the conductor he might be, but he could not possibly expect to keep up the masquerade for very long. Besides, I had now given him a few things to think about. I thought I might afford half an hour for lunch.

The restaurant-car was now full of dining passengers. The Tecks and George occupied a whole table, the colonel and the socialite another. The two valets and Mary Adelaide's maid sat together just inside the door. Vasily was absent. Short sat alone watching over our flock from an adjoining table—when I entered, he turned and flashed me a welcoming smile that told me he was pleased to see me, and not because he hungered after my blood. I had been directed to sit at a table at the far end of the car, with the Baroness's lady's maid and a bespectacled young person resembling a secretary; but just this side of them was the black velvet and heavy white lace of Veronika Sarkozy herself. On a whim, I marched up to her table and spoke.

"May I have a word, ma'am?" Since it was a public place, I

dared not draw attention by using the Baroness's Christian name.

"Indeed you may! Sit down, Miss Sharp. Who would have expected us to meet again so soon?"

"It seems that the bombing at the Hotel Terminus has brought us all together," I said, sliding onto the seat facing her.

"Yes. Paris is unhealthy at this time of year—that is, for a certain class."

"I am not sure this train is a great deal healthier." Acutely aware of the lack of privacy in our surroundings, I cast about for a way to discuss Anton with Veronika in secrecy. "You're not the only acquaintance of mine on the Orient Express this week. I didn't know our Moldavian friend worked for Wagons-Lits."

"Does he, indeed!"

"At present, it seems that he does. He had a parcel with him, but I have taken care of it."

Veronika took this news very calmly. All she did was raise an eyebrow.

"I have spoken to him about it, but I don't think he is going to listen to me. Perhaps you might try your influence."

"Perhaps I might. I do not care to receive more such parcels." She smiled at me swiftly, and put her hand over mine. "Let me try. If you see your friend again, send him to me at No. 1."

No. 1—that was the compartment immediately between my second-class compartment and Vasily's. I filed that information away for later. "Thank you, ma'am." Another thought struck me. "Our vampiric acquaintance is also on the train."

Veronika frowned.

I lowered my voice. "He has mentioned to me, at different times, that he has business with you, and that he is in Europe as an agent of the Russian Emperor. I thought that information might be of interest to you. But I see that my meal is being brought, so I had better go and sit where I was told."

She caught my hand. "Why do you tell me this?"

"Because I don't like monsters."

She smiled in thanks, and I went to keep the maid and the secretary company. Curious as to what the maid of an anarchist baroness might be like, I attempted to speak to the girl. She was a young, rather pretty-looking thing with rough, work-worn hands and an accent thick enough to cut with a knife. I complimented her on her mistress's hair and accoutrements, but she only nodded and went on staring out the window. After that, the secretary, ensconced behind a newspaper, made a sound indicative of disgust. Upon questioning, he told me that the German Kaiser was rumoured to be revivifying corpses to serve in his army. Scenting an argument, I asked the secretary what he thought of the ethics of revenant-making, and learned that he was generally favourably inclined to it, so long as it was done by Englishmen; and that in South Africa, where his employer, the colonel, had been stationed until recently, there had been some experiments in undead policing carried out in Matabeleland, with salutary results upon the native population.

I asked him whether he thought an Empire that prided itself on democracy should resort to such measures. After a brief conversation, however, his face went red, and he got up and went away. I was surprised. I had not expected such a self-assured person to be routed by a few friendly questions.

Shortly after, as I was sitting back sipping a cup of tea,

the train drew up in Châlons. To my surprise, a gang of gendarmes, both revenant and living, were gathered on the platform. They seemed to be waiting for us, and within moments of our arrival, I saw the *chef du train* advance to meet them.

Were they upon Anton's trail already? I leaped up and hastened down the step of the restaurant-car, and in doing so nearly collided with Short, who must have alighted a moment before myself.

"Short!" I cried, "what the dickens is happening?"

"Haven't the faintest," he said.

Together we hastened towards the gathering. Already the revenants had swarmed aboard the train, and I heard faint but vigorous protests from the Duchess of Teck. Meanwhile on the platform, the conductor of the second sleeping-car had been summoned to meet with the live policemen and the *chef du train*. By rights there ought to have been a second conductor—the gentleman whom Anton was at present impersonating—but neither he nor Anton were present. I hoped the poor conductor was all right—both for his own sake, and for Anton's.

"Inspector Short, of Special Branch, Scotland Yard," Short introduced himself to the French policeman. "I am the detective at present travelling with the Duke of York."

"And I'm a lady's maid," I said audaciously. I do not think the Frenchman could have comprehended my exact words, for he only glanced at my scars and recoiled a little.

"You are the gentleman who dismantled the bomb in Paris, yes?" he asked Short.

That was a bit rich!

"I merely assisted this lady," Short said, which was jolly

decent of him. The policeman looked at my scars again, then looked away just as quickly.

"The conductor of the Calais coach was found unconscious behind a signal-box at the Gare de L'Est shortly after your departure," he went on. "He was...in a state of undress. That is, his uniform was missing. We have been desired by telegraph to search the train for an anarchist in the guise of a Wagons-Lits conductor."

"I see," Short said, after a momentary pause to digest this startling information. "I'm afraid I can give no information to help you. Miss Sharp?"

My pulses thundered in my ears. The police were swarming the train now. Anton would be dragged off it in another moment—arrested, condemned, guillotined, and revivified! As for me, what if I was implicated in concealing him? Only yesterday I had nearly been arrested for the crime of wishing to speak with an anarchist.

I forced a smile. "Afraid not."

The policeman nodded and for a while we stood waiting on the platform. A few minutes passed, and the revenants disembarked again—alone. Anton was not with them.—But *how?* Had he taken advantage of a previous stop to escape?

The Châlons policeman shrugged when he saw them. "It seems our anarchist is not on the train after all. I am truly sorry to have disturbed you, monsieur, mademoiselle." With a blast of his whistle, he marched the revenants off the platform.

"Very strange," Short said softly in my ear.

"What is?"

He did not answer at once. Already, the remaining conductor was walking down the platform shouting *"En voiture!"* I went to ascend the step to the restaurant-car, but to my surprise, Short took my arm and hurried me towards the rear of the train.

"Here! What the dickens?"

"I want to speak to you. Alone."

This time, when Short flung open the door to the baggage-car, it was dark inside. He hesitated a moment, but the train jolted and began to move. We stumbled forward into the darkness. I tripped and fell gracefully upon a sort of large chest, Short slammed the door shut, and for a moment we sat in the dark, our quick breathing lost amid the clank of the moving train.

"Miss Sharp," he said at last. I didn't like the awful solemnity in his voice, nor the hand that reached out of the shadows and fastened upon mine. "You haven't been completely honest with me."

Grateful for the darkness that hid my face, I adopted a tone of light raillery. "Mr Short, I don't know what to say. It's true; I am a grandmother of ninety, and I owe my schoolgirl complexion to liberal quantities of Pears' Soap, worked to a fine lather twice a day."

There was a silence.

"What?" Short said blankly.

Well, that was hardly encouraging. "Never mind," I told him with a sigh. "Go on."

"There was a second conductor; the one you asked for a blanket." He held my hand in both his. They were warm, gentle, and large.

"Really?" The words came out in a rasp, for my throat had gone unaccountably dry.

"Yes; I remember thinking at the time that he didn't look much like a conductor. He wasn't on the platform just now;

and you didn't mention him to the gendarme." A pregnant silence. "Miss Sharp, is there something you aren't telling me?"

"Well, I like that!" I said. "There are a great many things a lady doesn't tell, Mr Short. Her age—where she buys her stockings—whether she pads her corsets."

I wish I could say that I did not yet know Short well enough to trust him with the secret of Anton's presence, but it went beyond that. Perhaps it was the bone-deep sense of loyalty that had arisen in me at Anton's touch, but I could not face the thought of betraying him to one he surely saw as his enemy. Not when I wished to remain on his good side.

I had singularly failed to shock Short into retreat. "All ladies pad their corsets these days," he responded evenly. "Try again, Miss Sharp. The conductor with the blanket; who was he?"

"How do you know so much about ladies' underthings, Short?"

"I warn you, I am not to be distracted from my questioning."

"But I really want to know! I would never have picked *you* as such a gay dog."

A sigh in the dark. "Corpses," he told me. "We inventory their personal possessions, of course, including all items of clothing. Now, the conductor."

"What makes you think I should know anything about a Wagons-Lits conductor?"

"Only that I have a finger on your pulse, and it's getting quicker."

I might have protested that all *that* meant was—someone I fancied was at present cradling both hand and wrist in a warm, gentle grasp. But this was one of the things a lady never tells. I wrenched my hand from his.

"I thought a *friend* was holding my hand, Inspector, not a policeman!" Still, I was angrier with myself than with him. I ought to have known he had an ulterior motive in touching my hand, but I had been too distracted by the delightful sensation. It was hard that I could not keep my head in the presence of even *one* man of my acquaintance!

A sigh out of the darkness. "I'm trying to be both, Miss Sharp. ...Let's see if I can turn on the gas." Striking a match, he got up and looked about for the light fitting. Almost at once, he tripped. I heard him fall heavily, and the flame went out.

"Short! Are you all right?"

"Ugh! Yes! Something wrapped itself around my ankle, that's all." Another match flared, and Short lifted—the blue uniform jacket of a Wagons-Lits conductor, the light reflecting from its brass buttons.

Speech failed me. Short lurched to his feet, shielding the match with his hand. "It's still warm. *Miss Sharp—the anarchist is here, with us, in this very car.*"

My heart jumped into my mouth. At any cost I must keep Short and Anton from meeting. "That's impossible. The police searched this car moments before we boarded it!"

"I don't like to speak evil of my colleagues, even the undead ones, but that means little to me." Short glanced around the cluttered carriage. "He might have been hiding anywhere—in that chest you're sitting on, for instance."

I got up hurriedly. Short bent over, fiddled with the catch, and threw the lid open.

Within was nothing but a conductor's cap, and the musky scent of a man.

"That's where he hid," Short breathed.

It struck me that I had been smelling Anton without realising it since Short and I first entered the baggage-car. The effort of avoiding Short's questions had pushed everything else to the back of my mind. Now I turned, sniffing the air in an attempt to locate the anarchist.

Something moved among the shadows. I shrieked a warning, but it was already too late. A black figure loomed out of the darkness. There was the sound of a blow. Caught off guard, and unbalanced by the motion of the train, Short fell heavily against me. The light went out as we sprawled upon the floor, and I shrieked as someone trod on my hand. Something long and slithering fell upon us, tangling us in netlike strands. The door to the sleeping-car slammed open and for an instant, Anton was silhouetted against the light. Short made a convulsive effort to get up, kneeing me mercilessly in the thigh and then falling heavily upon me again, tangled in the net. Then the door slammed, and we were alone in the darkness.

"Ow!" I protested. "Stop kicking me for just a moment, will you?"

"Oh, the blazes!" Short growled, but he obeyed. I lay back and groaned; and after a moment, somewhat chastened, he said, "Did I hurt you?"

"At least you didn't tread on my hand," I said.

Short made a penitent noise. "Here," he said, rolling off me. He took most of the net with him, and after a few false starts, hampered by my skirts, I got up, pulled the string that depended from the bulb above us, and flooded the entire baggage car with light.

From an inelegant position on the floor amidst boxes and bags, Short stared breathlessly up at me. "How did you do *that?"*

"It's electricity," I said smugly, holding out a hand to help him up. "It's new."

"H'm." He got to his feet, wiping a trickle of blood from the corner of his mouth, and picked up the net which had brought us to such grief. In fact it was a rope-ladder, of the sort used to climb alps and Himalayas and goodness knows what else. Muttering, he threw it aside, rushed to the door, and burst into the Paris coach beyond. In the baggage-car, I coiled the ladder neatly, threw the conductor's jacket over my arm, and then followed Short at a more demure pace.

He met me in the passage of the forward or Calais coach, chewing his lip in baffled anger and looking more than usually like a Nonconformist elder preaching against gin on a street corner. Glancing up and down the passage-way to ensure that the doors were all closed and there was no possibility of our being overheard, he took hold of my elbow and said,

"Miss Sharp, there is an anarchist on this train. I said nothing to the police at Châlons, because whatever you might be doing, I know you must have a good reason for it. But don't keep me in the dark, I implore you. This is a dangerous man, and you need my help."

The help of a policeman, in defusing an explosive anarchist? "I only wish you *could* help me, Short; but truly, you can't. This is something I can do best alone."

"I find that difficult to believe," he said, giving me that winning smile. "We've worked together so well until now. Can you not bring yourself to trust me, even a little?"

I took a deep sigh. It was true: I shouldn't do this alone. I had been gambling with May's safety, betting that Anton could be convinced to abandon his pursuit before he did any worse damage. Short had shown himself trustworthy at Châlons; the least I could do was trust him in return.

"All right," I said, "I'll make a clean breast of it, officer."

I made my confession quickly and concisely. Short did not interrupt, except once to groan, "Miss Sharp! Oh, Miss Sharp!" when I stopped for breath.

"Are you very angry with me?"

"No," he said, although he looked rather horrified. "Not angry; only a little disappointed."

"I would not have kept it secret, only they would have used him abominably, Short. Whatever else we do, we cannot surrender him to the French police."

"We certainly cannot leave him free to carry out his infernal plans, whatever *they* are! Have you forgotten what he did at the Café Terminus?"

My heart sank. "He may be my only hope of recovering my past, Short. You cannot conceive what that means to me."

"Perhaps I can." There was something in his quiet voice that made me stop and listen. "You are not the only one who has lost a family, Miss Sharp. Mine went down with the *Princess Alice* when I was eighteen. Father, mother, and three sisters. Believe me, if I could bring back so much as one of my sister Emily's hat-ribbons, I would."

I had guessed that Short was more or less alone in the world, but I had not known the reason, and now my heart was wrung for him. It must be far worse to live with such memories, even, than to be haunted by their loss. I wanted to touch him, and my hand stole out to take his—but when the movement caught his attention, I arrested myself. Scarred as I was, I was afraid of my innocent touch being misinterpreted.

"Then perhaps you understand me," I said instead, to cover

my confusion. "Two years ago, my whole life and all my memories were taken from me. The monster that did it will never suffer for what he did, but with Anton's help, at least I might have the opportunity to take back a part of what I have lost. That much justice, at least—"

"Justice?—from an anarchist?" He shook his head. "You misunderstand me, Miss Sharp. I sympathise with your loss, but it is too high a price to pay for justice, to shelter the likes of *them.*"

"Well," I said bitterly, thinking of certain murders that remained unpunished in London, "at least *they* pay more than lip service to the idea."

"What are you saying, Miss Sharp? These are anarchists! Men without laws, without honour—"

"What honour is there in *your* world, Short? What laws? You have seen for yourself how the powerful bend your rules for their own benefit. Give me the anarchists any day over that."

He was pale to the lips with anger, but he spoke very gently. "No. Justice without rules is only vengeance and vendetta and the end of all law. And then what standard do you have by which to measure right and wrong? Without law there is neither wrongdoing nor right-doing. There is only predator and prey, the strong draining the weak."

I wanted to believe him—I wanted it so badly, but I thought I knew the sorts of laws he meant. "So we are to be ruled by laws which were made by the predators to keep the prey docile; is that what you mean?"

He frowned, and backed away a little. "No, I mean a higher law. I mean *love thy neighbour as thyself.*"

"But don't you see," I cried, "that is the very reason I cannot turn him over to be guillotined and revivified?"

Short opened his mouth, but I forestalled him by reaching into the capacious pocket that hung beneath my skirt, and pulling out my revolver. "Look," I said. "I will shoot Anton before I allow him to hurt anyone, but I cannot give him up. Can you accept that much, at least?"

At that moment the door leading to the Calais coach opened, and Prince George burst through looking as black as thunder.

"Where the devil have you two been? All hell breaking loose, and you're gossiping in the passage-way?"

He looked wild with worry, and a stab of renewed guilt went through me. "What is it?"

"It's May's compartment—come."

"Is she hurt?" I cried, but George had already turned to rush back towards the Paris coach. I followed him, my argument with Short already forgotten. The three of us burst into May's compartment to find the princess sitting quite unharmed on the bench seat, staring woodenly as Mary Adelaide rubbed with a wet hanky at scrawled marks on the wall opposite.

"Stop that," I said without ceremony, "I want to see."

The Duchess squeezed back against the window, and I sank onto the seat beside May.

When you enter a first-class compartment on the Orient Express, you find a gorgeously-upholstered bench seat to one side, facing a wall opposite in rich, panelled wood. There are hooks on that wall, and a narrow door which communicates with the next compartment. May's communicating door was bolted, and she was much too tidy a soul to leave her belongings trailing from hooks. Across the panelling, therefore, there was nothing to hide the bold chalk scrawls which the Duchess had been attacking with her hanky. Despite her efforts, a ghost of the words still remained embedded in the grain of the wood.

Death to kings.

Even the Duchess could tell what this meant. "It seems there is an anarchist on this train, Sharp! This is really too much!"

"I'm afraid so," I said with a sigh. Would my deception backfire on me again? "When did you find this? Did you see who did it?"

May spoke in a quiet, controlled voice. "It happened just after the last stop. When lunch was finished, I came back to my compartment to rest, and found it like this already. I rang for the conductor, but no one answered, and I couldn't find you, Sharp."

I glanced up at the door, where beside George, Short watched me with a thin, downturned mouth and a warning in his eyes. "Short and I were discovering for ourselves that the anarchist is still on this train. He was disguised as the conductor: look."

I shook out the discarded jacket, and May took hold of it with a slight frown. "I've seen this coat before. Look: there are dark spots here, on the breast. I remember wondering if he had had a bloody nose." She shivered. "Can you imagine? I asked him to show me to the dining-car just as we were leaving Paris. I thought at the time he was rather rude about it."

At the door, George's moustaches quivered with indignation. "Train ought to be searched at once, by Jove. Knew we couldn't depend on those dead Frenchies to do the job. Come on, Short."

"A moment, sir." Short frowned abstractedly. "Don't forget we have one tool which the revenants haven't."

"And what's that?"

"Brains, sir."

"Oh!" George looked uncertain as to whether he had been insulted or not. "Well, if you put it like that."

Short managed to get himself and George wedged into the compartment, then shut the door. "Keep your voices down," he warned, "these walls are thin. All right: we are looking for a man named Anton Lupei. Miss Sharp is the only one of us who knows him by sight, and evidently he has abandoned his disguise as a conductor. We surprised him in the baggage-car a few minutes ago, at which point he fled forward in the train. I went up as far as the restaurant-car, but the attendants assured me no one had entered since Châlons. I checked the toilets at each end of each coach, but they were empty. That narrows it down to the compartments. I spoke to the conductor of the Paris coach, who informs me that each compartment is occupied." Short stopped, took a deep breath. "You understand the implications, of course."

Mary Adelaide looked confused. "I don't understand anything."

"Oh," I said, aghast. "If he's not in the baggage car or the dining-car, and he's not in the passage-ways or the toilets, why then he must be inside one of the compartments—but that would mean—"

"That someone on the train is hiding him," Short finished. "The only question is: Who?"

There was a silence. I felt my gut churning, churning. But I had promised Short to come clean, and if I was anything less than honest, I'd destroy everyone's trust in me.

"Veronika Sarkozy," I whispered, trying not to think how I might be betraying Anton's trust.

"Eh? Speak up, I didn't hear," said George.

"The Hungarian baroness in black velvet," I said a little louder, "Veronika Sarkozy. She's an anarchist sympathiser, and I—I told her there might be an anarchist on board. If anyone can convince Lupei to make no more trouble, Veron—the Baroness will manage it."

Short sent me a sceptical look. May and George looked aghast.

"She isn't the sort to blow anyone up. She's trying to help."

"Which compartment?" was all Short said.

"No. 1."

"Then we'll start there." He hesitated. "You'll have to come with us, Miss Sharp."

"One moment." May had been sketching something very quickly on a sheet of notepaper. Now, she tore off the page and handed it with a flourish to Short. "This is the man you're looking for."

Short blinked at the page, astonished. I rose, and found that May had sketched Anton in more lifelike detail than even I could have summoned, had I had the skill to do so.

"What do you say, Sharp? Is it a good likeness?"

"Photographic," I said, with a sinking heart. What had I got myself into? It was bad enough having to betray a man for whom I could not help feeling a fierce loyalty—bad enough that Short had not even promised to keep Anton out of the hands of the revenants. It was worse that having got Veronika involved, I was now about to bring princes and policemen about her ears. Baroness though she might be, Veronika was by no means rich enough or powerful enough to escape the consequences should she be found sheltering a man like Anton Lupei, even for the best of reasons.

I didn't like any of it, this having to take one side or another against people I wanted to befriend. But there was no help for it. I heaved a sigh. "Let's get on with it, then."

Chapter X.

The search party consisted of George, Short, and myself. We went directly to Veronika Sarkozy's compartment, the door to which was closed—but muffled sounds penetrated the thin wall. I raised a warning hand.

Even Short could hear the lilting murmur of a hushed conversation between a man and a woman.

"Lupei," George cried, seizing the door-handle. It rattled but did not give way: bolted, no doubt. Within the compartment, the voices fell silent.

"Who is it?" the baroness called.

"Police, ma'am," Short replied, before George could speak. "May we come in?"

"One moment," the baroness said. There was a short silence; then the bolt slid back, and the door opened.

Veronika appeared in the doorway, walking-stick in hand. She looked up at Short with disdain. "You are English. You have no jurisdiction here."

"Stand aside, ma'am!" George burst out. "There is an anarchist in your compartment! Heard you speaking to him, what!"

The baroness shrugged and stood back, allowing the men into her compartment. Hanging behind, I had only the stiffness of their backs to tell me that their search had failed.

"Not that it would be any business of yours what friends I choose to entertain in my compartment," Veronika said icily, "but as you see, I am alone with my maid."

George looked blank. Short checked behind the door; then dropped to his knees and peered beneath the bench-seat. When he did so, I observed Veronika's maid sitting near the window with an odd look on her face, half frightened, half triumphant.

Was it true, then? Had Anton indeed been inside the compartment? And if so, where on earth could he have vanished to?

"This door," Short said suddenly, getting back to his feet, and gesturing towards the door in the panelled partition to his left. "Who is in the next compartment?"

"Grand Duke Vasily," I volunteered, "the Russian vampire."

Short slipped the bolt, tried the door. It must have been bolted on the other side too, for it didn't budge, and he gave a grunt of annoyance.

"Are you gentlemen quite done?" Veronika asked acidly. "We have already been hounded by revenants." She turned to me. "And you, Miss Sharp! I would not have expected this from *you.*"

I flushed to the roots of my hair. "Forgive me, ma'am."

There was no chance to say more, for George and Short beat an apologetic retreat, and the door snicked crisply to behind them. Short looked, if possible, more determined than ever. "What did *that* mean?" he asked, turning to me.

"Don't be so suspicious," I said uncomfortably. "I told you before—I let her know there might be an anarchist on board the train."

"You spoke to her, and not me?"

There was real hurt in his voice. I felt my face reddening, but Short seemed to realise he had exposed more of his feelings than he wished. Instead of pursuing an answer, he reached over my head, and rapped on Vasily's door.

It opened a crack. Through it, unexpectedly, there rolled a powerful reek—cologne, cedar-scented and indeed smelling rather like Listerine, at least in this quantity. It instantly blotted out every other scent in the coach.

"Quiet, please," said a whiskered man I had never seen before. "His Grace is sleeping and does not wish to be disturbed."

"Show me," said Short firmly. The man stood back, and through the open door we all saw that the bed had been made up, and Vasily—pale and angelic in repose—was fast asleep in his berth.

"What's the funk?" George hissed in a piercing whisper.

"I have accidentally spilled some of his Grace's cologne."

"And who are you?" Short added, voicing the question on my own lips.

"I am his Grace's new valet. My name is Schmidt, Igor Schmidt. When his Grace wakes, I will tell him you called."

"No need," George harrumphed. But as the valet went to close the door, I put out a hand to stop him.

"Were you speaking out loud just now? Perhaps you said something to the lady in the next compartment?"

"No," Schmidt said. The next instant he, too, closed the door upon us.

Short and George both looked baffled. To be honest, I wasn't feeling particularly happy either. An anarchist waiting in my berth to be interrogated and coaxed was one thing, but an anarchist on the loose somewhere on the train, breathing out threats and murder, was a different sort of proposition altogether. The longer it went on, the more nervous I became.

"I don't like it." Short echoed my own thoughts. "No matter what she said, that was certainly a man's voice we heard in Baroness Sarkozy's compartment."

"Can't have been," George said, frowning. "Not enough room in that compartment to lose a sock. Unless he threw himself out the window, of course."

"In which case we wouldn't have to worry about him anymore," I said, with more wistfulness than hope.

"No," Short said, "it seems more likely that she *was* speaking to the valet, and chose to lie about it for reasons of their own. Miss Sharp, what do you think of Schmidt's story?"

"Vasily did say he was between manservants, and that he wanted to hire me."

Short reddened slightly. "As his bodyguard, or his dainty?"

"The same question had occurred to me."

"You won't accept, of course?" George put in anxiously.

"You flatter me, sir; but you might as well know that it is all useless. Best to let me go: I could never love a man named George."

Poor George! he backed a step, and seemed to be having some sort of trouble with his larynx. I oughtn't to have said it, but he was *such* an easy mark, and I needed *some* manner of diversion.

Short shook his head at me, but it was rather a laughing than a horrified disapproval, which helped me feel a little less guilty. "Come," he said, "there's no help for it; we must search the rest of the train. Let's split up. I shall work my way forwards; you work back. Will you come with me, sir?" he asked George.

George looked at me as though I might bite him at any moment, but his sense of chivalry got the better of him. "I'll accompany Miss Sharp in case she needs me."

I likely would not require his physical assistance, even if we did unearth Anton from his hiding-place, but his presence would lend me a great deal of the respect that the scars on my face denied me. George always was a decent sort.

"Step this way, *chevalier.*" I beckoned him towards the next compartment, which was Mary Adelaide's.

As might be expected, the other passengers were unhappy to be disturbed a second time in the same afternoon. George and I searched the compartments in the Paris coach, and even gave the baggage-car a second inspection, without turning up any sign of our anarchist. After that, we went forwards and found Short being upbraided by the *chef du train* in the Calais coach, who loudly insisted on being informed why his passengers were being hounded once again, and this time by a policeman who did not even have the good taste to be French.

"I was desired by his grace—" Short began with a look of relief as George and I approached.

The official cut him off with a wave of the hand. "Graces! Bah! I do not care how royal you are, you do not disturb the passengers of the Orient Express! Tell your grace that on this train only the *Compagnie Internationale des Wagons-Lits* is king!"

The irate Frenchman bustled forward into the restaurant-car, leaving a rather chastened-looking Short behind.

"Dem' revolutionary sentiments," George observed as we approached. "Quite sure *he's* not the anarchist, I suppose?"

"I'm afraid he's well within his rights, sir," Short said. "Without the backing of the French police, there's no more we can do."

"You didn't find Lupei?" I asked, feeling a gleam of hope.

Short shook his head. "He could be in one of these compartments, but I've been strictly forbidden to search. I'm sorry, sir. All we can do is keep a weather eye out and hope Lupei shows himself before making his next move."

With the search over, George seemed eager to return to May's side. As he led the way back towards the Paris coach, I lingered with Short in the passage of this one.

"I don't see why Anton would be in any of *these* compartments, Short. As far as I know, Ve—the Baroness Sarkozy is the only anarchist sympathiser on the train. Perhaps he did go to see her, and she convinced him to leave at one of the more recent stops."

Short looked thoughtful. "Perhaps you might go and ask her—privately."

"I will, but I'm not sure she'd listen to me," I said, as gently as I could. "Not now."

That long, mobile mouth was pulling down at the corners again, and the drooping eyes were as sad as I'd ever seen them. Short bit his lip. "Miss Sharp, I consider you a friend."

An ominous beginning! "But?" I prompted.

"But I've seen how proficient you are at keeping secrets," he said at last. "From Princess May; from me; from the Baroness just now. I implore you: if you know where Anton Lupei is hiding, *tell* me. Every life on this train might depend on it."

How dare he allude to May? "That's rich, coming from the one who convinced me to lie to May in the first place!"

"To the rest of the world, certainly. But that's beside the point—"

"To Princess May as well. *You* helped me hide the body." I

turned, but he took my arm gently, and pulled me to face him.

"Only to spare her the double shock. But about Lupei—"

"You have no idea what May has been through these last few months," I said thickly. At the time, I believed I was angry with him; but looking back at thirty years' distance, I see now that I was most angry with myself.

"Miss Sharp, you must face facts," Short said. "Prince George and his entire family are determined to have Princess May. Sooner or later, even if you conceal it, she *will* learn what they truly are—and then she will piece together the terrible truth of that night."

My throat dried at that thought. "She will never forgive me," I whispered.

"Who knows? Your only hope is telling her the truth—now—before she learns for herself." Short stopped—took a deep breath. "That's why I'm begging you now, Miss Sharp. If you know where Anton Lupei is, tell me. I won't hold it against you. Nor will I hand him over to the police, at least until we're safely in Germany. Word of honour."

It was like a nightmare I couldn't escape, and I had only myself to blame. I released a long slow breath, and taking his hand in mine, I pressed it against the pulse on my wrist. "I don't know where Anton Lupei is. I want him off this train as much as you do."

"Your heart is racing," he observed, his fingers warm and steady on my pulse.

"Yes," I snapped, "contemplating the fact that apparently the only way I can convince you I don't have Anton Lupei hidden inside my hatbox is to present him to you—but that's just what I can't do!"

He watched me for a moment longer. How shall I describe

the look on his face? It was not distrust, exactly. I could see that he wished to believe me, but could not quite bring himself to do so. At last, with a sigh, he released my hand. "I'm sorry," he told me. He did not say for what, but I read it all too clearly in his eyes before he followed George into the hindermost sleeping-car.

For a moment longer I stood in the passage-way. I was terribly angry, but not with Short. How had I allowed myself to be trapped in such a web of half-truths and lies, that I seemed likely to alienate the two friends that remained to me?

I had injured even Veronika by trying to play this game. Recalling my promise to Short, I sighed and went in search of her.

Chapter XI.

This time I found the baroness alone in her compartment. A lap-desk was set over her knees, and she appeared to be working on a stack of correspondence. She looked up at my entrance with a carefully neutral expression that struck me instantly with guilt.

"Please, I wanted to explain," I said.

"For what?" Veronika said coldly, looking back down to her papers.

"About the search. I tried to give Anton the chance to speak to you and leave of his own accord, but things moved too quickly."

Veronika looked at me with an odd expression. "Oh! Is *that* what bothers you?"

"But—I thought I had offended you."

"Sit down, Liz."

Closing the door, I obeyed her. She turned her papers face-down for the sake of privacy, and sat for a moment rapping her long, tapered fingers on the surface of the lap-desk before turning to me again. "Naturally, with a bomber on the train, your colleague searched for him. He is a policeman. You could not have prevented him."

"But I helped him search."

"And no harm done."

"Did you manage to speak to Anton, then?"

"This isn't *about* Lupei," she said crisply. More gently: "The thing is, my dear, I have been rather selfish. I may not agree with Anton Lupei's methods, but I don't want to live in a world like this any more than he does. My title—my wealth—my privilege—all these things, I use only to undermine the whole rotten structure. It is not right that the weak should be oppressed by the monstrous. I thought that you, of all people, would understand that. It hurts me, Liz, to see you living in their pockets like this."

Could she not see how my heart was torn by what she said? "I only mean to protect my friends from a violent and horrible death. *They* have done nothing wrong."

"Yet still they benefit, every day, from the greed and rapacity of others."

"Unknowingly," I insisted. "If they knew—"

"If they knew, they would only harden their hearts." With that, I remembered how often I had told myself that once May knew the truth about her extended family, she would forget every disdainful thing she had ever said about monsters.

"What other choice do I have?" I asked. "I have lost my memories, and with them everyone I ever knew or loved. I lost my reputation when I gained these scars. The Tecks are my only family now."

"You deceive yourself, Liz. They know very well who their family is, and it is not you. It is the monsters."

I could not deny that, either. "Perhaps I ought to leave them, but I was not born to be a heroine. I cannot quite bring myself to starve."

"Can you bring yourself to hang, then?" An edge of steel

crept into her voice. "I am no great seer, but neither am I blind. Can you not see that the whole world stands upon the brink of a cataclysm—the *Götterdämmerung,* as the Germans call it? And they think it is a fairy-tale!—when their doom is spelled in the tears of each unfortunate soul who suffers to appease their appetite for gold, for blood, for flesh. No, Liz, if this goes on, sooner or later we shall have a revolution to end all revolutions. On that day, perhaps it would be better to have starved in the streets, than to fall in the company of your fine friends."

My hair stood on end—I saw the blood flowing in the London streets, and felt the noose tighten about my neck as I was rushed to the nearest lamp-post. Oppressed by this thought, I laughed. "A revolution worse than starving in the streets! What an extremely tempting prospect!"

Her black brows drew together. "You laugh?"

"What else am I to do? It's that or go mad in white satin, I suppose."

"You could leave them. Most anarchists, rather than fling bombs, choose to open mutual aid societies, and do a great deal of practical good. You would not be left to starve."

She looked expectant. Ordinarily I would have laughed off such a suggestion: what, exchange a comfortable, well-paid position as a lady's maid for a life of hardship and poverty, reliant on the whims of charity?—And yet, such a life would be easier in one way at least. I should not be forced constantly to choose sides, to spin lies. I should be able to live an honest, open, and simple life.

Still, a part of me was dissatisfied with the prospect. If I truly believed what Veronika said of the coming revolution, ought I to retire into obscurity? Ought I to abandon May to her fate? I recalled how she had stood up to Eddy during the Whitechapel business, and my heart warmed. There was hope for May, and if for May, then for all of them—even the monsters.

"There doesn't need to be a revolution," I said at last. "Not if they *choose* to change."

"And why would they do a thing like that?" she said contemptuously. "It's hardly in their interests."

"Because they have consciences," I said. "Don't you believe in redemption?"

"When it comes to these people, I believe in justice."

"As do I. But not like this." I got up, and she reached out as though to stop me.

"Where are you going?"

"Back to Princess May. I have a job, you know; and—I think I know my purpose at last."

Alarm rose in her eyes. "No. You don't understand, Liz. Stay with me. I'll help you. You won't starve—*please!*"

I hesitated, disturbed by her sudden desperation. "Why? What do you fear?"

She stared up at me, lips parted. Then, abruptly, she shook her head.

"Nothing," she whispered, "it's nothing."

"Then I'll say goodbye." I retreated to the door, feeling unaccountably lighter. "I'm grateful to you, Veronika, for talking with me."

She didn't look at me, and there was something terribly dejected in the line of her neck, as she turned from me to look out the window. "Well: I am sorry."

"For what?"

"For failing you. Go away, child. I can't bear to see you just now."

There was something muffled about her voice. Was she weeping? I didn't understand it, but instinct told me now was hardly the time to ask.

All the same, I went back to May's compartment feeling better, and sharper, and more purposeful for the conversation. Was this what it might have been like to have a mother? The thought came wistfully, but I had spoken the truth when I thanked Veronika. Our conversation had cleared my mind wonderfully.

It wasn't until I stood outside May's door that I realised Veronika had never answered my question about Anton Lupei.

Well, I could hardly barge back into her compartment now. Instead, I scratched on May's door and entered when bidden.

May was not alone. George sat beside her. From the silence that had reigned in the passage before my entrance, I divined that the conversation between them had not been particularly animated. All the same, surely May would not wish me to intrude. "I beg your pardon, ma'am. I only wanted to make sure you were safe."

She smiled up at me wanly. "Thank you, Sharp. George has been taking care of me.—Don't feel you have to go," she added, suddenly, as I made to withdraw. "You might as well sit with us."

There was a mute appeal in her look. George reddened a little and half rose. "Should I go?"

"No, please—it's all right—I should like the company."

She shifted a little closer to George, making room for me near the window. Hesitantly, I took a seat. May's sketch of Anton Lupei was lying there, discarded. I picked it up, sat down, and looked into the pencilled eyes.

Where was Anton? What dreadful things might he not be planning at this very moment?

A stiff silence reigned over the compartment until May said, "The sun is getting low."

"Yes," George said obligingly, "it is."

"It is so nice to have longer days."

"Much pleasanter than short days."

Thus far, the second act I had been so eagerly awaiting since the morning's performance in Paris seemed to be getting off to a rather lacklustre start. But then May said:

"I'm told we get to Strasbourg at ten. I am sorry to be passing through at night; they say the Rhine is very pretty just there."

"You may yet see it by moonlight. Full moon tonight. Ought to be up by eight."

"Oh," May said admiringly, "what a lot you do know about it, to be sure!"

At that, George fell into a yet deeper silence. Of course, he would know the precise details of the moon's cycle, but May was unaware of his semi-lupine nature.

"It reminds me of poor Eddy," she said, after a long silence.

"Eh?!"

"The moon. It is exactly three months now since he died. I don't suppose I shall ever see a full moon again without thinking of him."

"Ah," said George. There was another long, awkward silence. Then, with a somewhat reckless air, he said, "Sorry to be such d—dreadfully bad company."

"Oh, no."

"Don't suppose I'm much of a substitute for Eddy."

"I don't think of you as a substitute, dear."

"I mean—that is to say—hang it! Does Sharp have to be

here?"

"Oh, go on, and don't mind me," I said, in reply to this outburst. "If the show doesn't improve presently, I shall be flinging myself headlong from the window, anyway."

"On no account, Sharp," May said severely. "George can have nothing to say to me that you cannot hear."

Ah! so I was present in a prophylactic capacity: I was meant to prevent George proposing to her. Short's warning resounded in my ears: if George persuaded May to marry him, it was all over with me. Well, no doubt that was true, but Short didn't know May. She was quite determined not to be persuaded, and I'd back my mistress against the entire royal family of England, as humans *or* as wolves, any night of the month.

Still, George seemed to have the bit between his teeth now. "Then Sharp will just have to hear it, that's all. You said something this morning about my taking Eddy's bride as well as his throne, what?"

May blushed a little. "It was a horrible thing to say, George. I didn't mean it, truly."

"Yes, you did," he retorted. "What's more, I agree with you. Feel like a hound. Especially so soon. But I might as well come clean about it: the family wants it. Grandmamma sat me down and lectured me about it before sending me off after you."

May shot him a diamond-hard glare, as if to say, "*Sent* you off? After *me?* I ought to have guessed—and moreover, how dare she?"—but of course, one could not say such things of Queen Victoria.

So she confined herself to saying "Oh?"

George reddened, but persisted. "Don't mean to persecute

you, what? Don't expect you to give me an answer right away. Thought we might get to know each other first. As friends. Or as…as Eddy's friends. And perhaps one day, when you're finished mourning…"

It was a good speech, somewhat weighed down by the fact that George was not being entirely honest with her. No doubt he had also been lectured about keeping his lupine condition a secret until he should have convinced May to cast in her lot with him. Of course, I was in no position to condemn him for it myself, so I kept my mouth shut and waited to hear what she would say.

"That is very fair of you," May said coolly, at last. "I will be equally plain in return. It ought not to disappoint you too greatly to hear that I have no intention of changing my mind, even after the mourning period is over."

"Oughtn't it?" he asked, and I thought I detected a note of anxiety in his voice.

"I beg your pardon, I presumed your feelings were not engaged. Was I incorrect?"

"Oh, entirely disengaged," he said, altogether too quickly.

"As are mine."

"Excellent. Frightfully glad to hear it."

"As is only natural, Eddy hardly being cold in his grave."

"Oh! I don't doubt it. No skin off my nose! Ha, ha!" George laughed, in a heart-broken sort of way.

Well, I had only been waiting for them to warm up. They were now in fine form, and the second act was shaping up to be just as entertaining as the last.

There was a companionable silence, before George added, with a scowl: "Only wondered, that's all. Suppose I'm not to everyone's taste. Not much art or music or poetry in me, and there you are, simply bursting with the stuff."

"Oh, no."

"But it's true."

"Don't be silly. It's not as though Eddy—I mean, you said yourself he was—"

"Oh, yes. Brains of a canary. I stand by that. But I'm no better myself."

"As I was going to say, I hope I am better than to object to marriage on *that* score. I did not object to Eddy for that, and I do not object to you for that either. Only, you are the last man in the world I could possibly marry, because you have succeeded to Eddy's place. It would be disrespectful to his memory. I injured him badly enough during his life; I cannot injure him like this now that he is dead. I will not benefit from—from my own misdeeds."

"Misdeeds?" he cried. "What misdeeds? Sharp, what have you—"

I stiffened, rigid with horror, sure that he was about to reveal the secret I had kept for so long. But it was May who saved me:

"Oh, Sharp will tell you that it is all in my imagination! Still, truly, George: But for me, would Eddy have died?"

There was a long, cautious silence, during which I began to scent nervous perspiration. "Suppose not," he said.

May was silent a moment. "I knew you would understand," she said at last. I wondered if George could detect in her habitually level, quiet voice the signs of strong emotion.—Even after all these years, it takes a great deal to elicit obvious feeling from May; but it would be a mistake to assume it was not there, and at that moment, my heart was wrung with pity for her. "I said some very hard words to Eddy on his last day, and I wish you knew how much I would give to take them back."

"Oh, *that?*" George said blankly.

"So you see that I cannot marry you, George, even if I liked you well enough to do so, which I do not. Pardon me for saying so, but it is *so* nice to feel that I can be perfectly honest with you."

Well, of all the crashingly stupid things I had ever heard May say, that was the frozen limit! If I were George, I might have been tempted to thump her over the chignon with a cushion in hopes of knocking some sense into her head. Instead, he looked ferociously miserable. I half expected him to burst into tears.

He swallowed convulsively. "Er—likewise! But, hang it, May! You can't mean to die a spinster, just because Eddy took ill after a lovers' spat."

"Well, perhaps not. Perhaps I shall marry some nice commoner, like dear Louise. What is quite certain is that I cannot marry *you.* I do not wish to be disloyal or undutiful, but I am quite firmly decided. I cannot with a clear conscience do otherwise."

Defeated, George rose from his seat and shot me a look of mute dismay before speaking to May again. "Can't put it any more fairly than that, I suppose. Cheer up, May. Have to see if I can scare up a nice commoner for you at the Coburg wedding, what?"

And so, putting a brave face on it, he went away.

I had been working for royalties for three months now, and they still occasionally came out with the most startling things. "Dear Louise" was the eldest of George's sisters, and the "nice commoner" to whom she was betrothed was no less a personage than the Duke of Fife, who must have bled bluer than just about anyone else in the kingdom. Still, I gathered that this was rather a come-down in the world for a princess of the blood. I understood, moreover, why May considered this rather a distant possibility as regarded herself. A princess's duties consisted of various public appearances and court events, all of which cost a great deal of money. There were relatively few commoners in the kingdom wealthy enough to support such duties, so that those performed by the Teck family had to be sponsored by a not-always-grateful nation.

"I think that went rather well," May remarked brightly in the silence that followed George's departure.

"Do you, ma'am?"

"Now that I have told him the truth, very honestly and firmly, I think we shall be able to go on without any awkwardness, just as we did before. Why, didn't you think it went well?"

In all honesty, I felt that the match would be a bad thing for May—not because of George personally, but because of her ignorance of his condition, and his mother's terrible siren powers. Still, I could not help seeing how naturally they turned to each other, nor how attached they evidently were, despite their protestations.

"You will say I am too bold, but I have sometimes thought you not indifferent to George."

May blushed—that is, a very faint colour rose in her cheeks. "Really, Sharp, that is going too far! How would you like it if I asked to know whom *you* fancied?"

I thought of Short. And (with some mortification) of Anton—and Vasily. "Oh, but that can hardly interest *you,* ma'am."

"Can it not?" She looked gleeful. "You are blushing! Come, confess. There is someone, isn't there?"

"There isn't!" I protested.

"On my life, there is! Out with it!"

"Well, there *is* Short, but then I'm a simple woman, and he is awfully good-looking!"

May's eyes became as round as coins. Whatever she had been expecting to hear, it was not this. *"Short?—Good-looking!* Why, Sharp, whatever is the matter with you?"

I opened my mouth and then closed it again, quite at a loss for words. This was not a sensation I had felt above once or twice in my life; nor have I felt it often since. "Nothing's the matter with me!"

"But he's *old,"* May protested, still very gleeful. "He has *wrinkles."*

"Nice ones," I protested. "Smiles and—and sorrow. And what do you mean, old? He can't be above thirty-five at most!"

"But that's precisely what I mean! He must be ten years your senior!"

"Well, it's not as though anything will ever come of it," I said, trying to sound cheerful. "A fellow like him would never look at a girl like me."

"Oh." Her gleefulness dissipated. "Do you really think so?"

"He's a policeman, ma'am. He has his career to think of."

"Oh," she repeated softly. There was a moment's silence. She didn't try to give false reassurances, as comforting as they might have been; but then, May was never capable of an untruth, even for the sake of politeness. In the end, she gave me an apologetic smile. "Well, I suppose he isn't the sort of man for me, but now that you mention it, he *is* good-looking in an ugly sort of way. *Une jolie laide,* or whatever the male equivalent is. Besides, there are much worse men to like! Will you read to me now?"

Too late, it occurred to me that May had used my own tactics against me, and had escaped my question with an argument! There was nothing for it: I dug *The Small House at Allington* out of our baggage, and we settled in to read. Outside the train, by degrees, the sun fell away into the west, and purple shadows gathered on the rolling green hills and serried vineyards of Moselle. At about half-past six, the train stopped for eight minutes at Nancy, and then continued towards the Rhine valley, and Strasbourg. I put the book down and helped May dress for dinner. The train moved remarkably smoothly, making my task little more difficult than it would have been at home in Richmond. At seven o'clock, I sent the princess off to the dining-car, meaning to follow as soon as I had tidied my own hair and dress.

I was arrested, however, by the sight of a scrap of paper on the floor of May's apartment. I picked it up, and once again the sketch of Anton Lupei looked me in the eye—compelling, almost mocking—as though to say, "Ha! ha! did you think you would catch me when I did not wish to be found?"

The sketch was so lifelike, I could almost smell him. Bother this train, where we were all so trammelled up together that it was almost impossible to follow a scent!

Then, much too late, a blinding revelation struck me.

I snatched May's pencil from the small table beneath her window, and with a few strokes of the lead I added a pair of whiskers and a bushy beard to the sketch. The dickens!—it was Vasily's new valet.

Chapter XII.

Spilled cologne! Oh, how foolish we had been!

That at one stroke solved two mysteries: Anton's whereabouts, and the meaning of the voice in Veronika's compartment. But the solution only raised more questions. If Veronika had spoken to Anton, had she failed to convince him to leave the train?—And if so, why had she not told me, at least, of his whereabouts?—And *what had happened to Vasily?* Since our conversation shortly before arriving in Châlons—hours ago now—I had not seen him awake.

What if Anton had killed him?

Impelled by my fears, I stepped out into the passage. Veronika's maid was there, making towards the dining-car. "Where is your mistress?"

"In her compartment."

Surely I ought to tell Short that I had discovered our fugitive? But after our last conversation, I shrank from confiding in him. Let me try what I could discover alone, and I would speak to him, if I must, once I had my bearings.

I stepped towards Vasily's compartment and at once detected the sound of a woman's voice. Veronika must be in there, with Anton! I advanced to Veronika's door and pressed my ear against it—silence. I pushed the door open and found it quite empty, noiseless except for the mutter of the train across the tracks, and the murmur of the man's and woman's voice from the next compartment.

If I was going to eavesdrop, better to do it in here than in the passage. I closed the door with shaking hands—omitting to shoot the bolt for fear of the noise—and seized the glass tumbler beside the bottle of mineral water upon Veronika's table. This I pressed to the wood panelling, laying my ear against the base. At once the voices within became clear.

"—see the creature is awake," Veronika was saying, her voice hard as ice. "Well, my friend? What a headache you must have, after all that laudanum. It's made from the juice of poppies, you know. I'm not a vampire myself, but I hear it can be rather...draining."

There was a confused sound: a snarl, a rattle—a blow, a groan.

"Keep him in the restraints," Veronika said a moment later. From the cadence of her voice, she seemed to be breathing rather quickly. "If you value your reason, don't look him in the eyes."

What had they done to Vasily?—Poppy-juice? Memory came back to me: the forbidden knowledge we had traded late at night in the dormitories of Saint Botolph's. Sal believed that a drop of poppy-juice could put a vampire to sleep for hours. That was how they must have dealt with Vasily, drugging and then restraining him.

They—and there was the rub! It was clear they were in the thing together. I repressed a groan as I recalled Veronika's joke about false whiskers when I had mistaken her for a maid in Paris. Was *that* where Anton had found his disguise?—Where else could he have discovered whiskers at the very moment he needed them most?

I felt almost sick with disappointment. How could Veronika join forces with a bomber?

"Wait." Anton spoke for the first time in a *basso* growl. "When do I get to kill him?"

"Not until he has served his purpose."

"And that is?"

"As I told you."

"You said something wild about starting a revolution." Anton spat. "If I had a sou for each time I've heard an anarchist say *that*—! No. If I'm going to nursemaid this creature all the way to Budapest, I need more than that."

"Our plans are too sensitive to be distributed to just anyone. The Vengeance means nothing less than to liberate first Europe, and then the world. All flags, all crowns, all empires must fall. If any of the monsters were to discover what we planned, all of them would band together against us."

I pressed a hand to my mouth to stifle my gasp. Revolution ?—Veronika was about to start a revolution? In my agitation the glass slid against the thin partition that divided me from the conspirators, making a faint sound.

The pair on the other side of the wall seemed not to hear the scuffle I had made. Anton said stoutly, "Well, if you need my help, then I'm not just anyone, am I?"

There was a brief silence. "I am taking the vampire to Doctor Livius. There are—experiments he wishes to perform."

This time, the silence was longer. Anton spoke again, his voice quite changed: "Why did you not tell me at once the doctor was involved? He is making weapons?"

"Of a sort."

"But you will give the creature to me afterwards. For justice. What he did to Ioanna..."

Ioanna—surely that was the name I had seen tattooed about Vasily's chest, over his heart. I frowned, trying to imagine under what circumstances a monster might enshrine on his skin the name of a woman whom he had destroyed.—Well, I had heard of the prosthete troopers in the American West carving a notch into their bio-steel arms for each native they killed. If the self-made men of the west did this, perhaps the vampire princes of the east had a similar tradition.

What had happened to this Ioanna, anyway? Anton did not explain, and Veronika went on: "Join us in our work. So long as you are there to claim him, you may have the vampire when we are finished with him."

"How many others are with you?"

"Nearly three hundred."

"Quite the *organisation.*" Anton sneered, as though it was a dirty word.

"Yes, but ours is strictly voluntary," Veronika said smoothly, "like the Red Cross."

Oh yes, thought I: *exactly* like the Red Cross. I thought my hands might be shaking. It was bad—it was so much worse than I thought. I did not pay much heed to Veronika's talk of world revolution, but who knew how much havoc might not be wreaked by three hundred determined men, armed with the weapons of the mysterious Doctor Livius, and dedicated wholeheartedly to a common cause?

"If Livius is with you, I am with you," Anton said at last. "But I tell you it is too dangerous to stay on the train. The Sharp woman and her tame policeman know I am still here. We should leave the train when we are in Germany, at Strasbourg."

"Do not worry yourself about Liz Sharp, my friend. So long as you lie low, she cannot know for certain that you are still aboard; and she and her monstrous friends will be leaving the train at Stuttgart in the morning. And after that—why, this train is nearly the fastest, easiest way to get a wanted anarchist and a missing vampire across Europe. Until Stuttgart, you may leave Miss Sharp to me."

It sounded as though the conversation had reached its end, but before I could pull away from my listening-post, Anton spoke again.

"You *do* know who she is, don't you?"

There was a moment's silence. "She's *his* daughter," Veronika said after a moment. "The one who was lost."

"Vera." There was a world of pain, a world of longing in Anton's voice.

"It makes no difference," Veronika said after a moment, her voice ominously hard and cold. "She is not—"

I did not hear the rest of the sentence, for a rap sounded on the door behind me. I turned as it opened, and looked into the wide eyes of Veronika's maid.

It must have been instantly obvious to her what I was doing, for her eyes widened, and she drew breath to cry out.

There was no time to waste. I leaped upon her, tiger-fierce. The unnatural strength that had been mine since I was wolf-bitten aided me now. It seemed to me at that moment that if Veronika knew I was acquainted with her plans, I could expect no mercy. I grasped the other girl in a stranglehold, one elbow around her neck and the other around her waist, pinning her hands. She lashed out with a foot, but I pulled her away from the opposite partition, and we collapsed upon the seat.

The door to the passage swung quietly shut, concealing us from passers-by.

It was, perhaps, a cowardly thing to do, but I could only keep her quiet if I used threats. "We know your mistress is an anarchist," I hissed in the other girl's ear. "If you value your life, you will make no sound except as instructed."

She went limp in my arms. I could feel her heart racing, the heaving of a sob in her ribs.

"Romona? What is it?" The communicating door between compartments rattled as Veronika tapped it with her walking-stick. I had taken the precaution of bolting it before I sprang.

"Say, *Nothing, ma'am,*" I instructed, very softly. Well I recalled the twin blades concealed beneath the shining black lacquer of that walking-stick, and I did not wish for a closer acquaintance with the weapon.

"Nothing, ma'am!" the girl called. Her voice was a little shaky as she followed my whispered instructions. "Just wondering where you were!"

"Bring my shawl when you come to the restaurant-car," Veronika ordered from the other compartment. With that, she went out into the passage, and her footsteps faded away in the direction of the restaurant.

Finding herself alone and abandoned, as she thought, to me, the maid let out another sob. My own heart was going like a steam-piston. What to do—what to do? Anton was still next door, at any rate. I must keep silent—I must somehow deal with the maid.

I did not much like the thought of what I would have to do next. The girl had never injured *me.* Still, justice was worth anything, or so Veronika had said to me only last night. If that was what she believed, then let her drink her own medicine.

"All right, my dear," I whispered, "I must put you out of the way for a moment, but I don't wish to hurt you," and adjusting my chokehold, I squeezed.

That put her into a panic, despite my reassurances, and she began to fight me with desperate strength. I tightened my grip, and within a few heartbeats she slumped against me in a dead faint.

I rolled her onto the seat beside me and set to work. My handkerchief and a strip torn from my petticoats became a gag. I then reached under my skirts for the fine, strong cord which I had dug out of my valise a few hours earlier, upon realising that Anton was on the train. I used it to bind her hands, knees, and feet—the girl was already waking from her faint—then threw her over my shoulder, cracked open the door leading to the passage, and peered through.

Having satisfied myself that the way was clear, I hurried Romona into the compartment I shared with Mary Adelaide's maid, who was thankfully gone to dinner. The berth was not made up, so I lowered the dazed girl onto the bench-seat and used the cord to tether her feet to the small table near the window. After that, I stripped off my skirt and petticoats, replacing them with my trusty bloomers, and substituting my boots for thin, flexible slippers.

This done, I closed the door on Romona and stood in the passage with my heart thumping. Already, time was running like sand through an hour-glass. I could not keep the poor girl confined forever. Sooner or later she would get free and tell her mistress that I had been discovered eavesdropping. I must move quickly—I must deal with Anton at once and free Vasily of whatever durance they had him in.

Mustn't I?

I recalled Anton's words—*what he did to Ioanna...*

What had Vasily done to the girl? Why did Anton want to kill him?—All now became clear: the Tecks had never been Anton's target at all. The bomb at the Hotel Terminus, the reversal bomb tethered beneath Vasily's compartment, the continual haunting of the train—all of it was to kill the Grand Duke, not Princess May. Vexation reddened my cheeks. How farcical!—to waste all this time and energy trying to save the life of a creature such as *that!*

But it was not merely about trying to save the life of a ruthless monster, I reminded myself. It was about spoiling whatever game Veronika was playing with the lives of her three hundred followers and all the people of Europe...

I closed my eyes, finding here the explanation for why I stood idle when I ought to be in purposeful motion.—Veronika Sarkozy.

Veronika, too, had lied to me.

She knew exactly who I was. When Anton had spoken those words—*she is his daughter*—Veronika had not been surprised. I could now guess why she had begged me so desperately to leave my employment and join the anarchists.—And perhaps I should! Break the monsters, break the empires, just as they had broken me and countless others—throw in my lot with Anton and Veronika—prove myself worthy of their confidence, learn the truth of my past and get justice for my scars!

A prospect so tempting that for a moment I could almost forgive Veronika's lies. Did she not have ample reason to distrust me? Had I not proven myself willing to ally myself with the police?—Yet surely Short was right: what was justice without rules, but vengeance and vendetta?

God knew I had tried my best for them, but Anton and Veronika were hand-in-glove, plotting to ignite rebellion across Europe. Saint Botolph's had painted a grim picture of revolution for us: bodies swinging from the lamp-posts, heads rolling from the guillotine, the reign of unchecked terror! I had learned now what they omitted from our syllabus: the ruthlessness with which the monsters ruled, the grinding helplessness that drove sane men to despair and madness. Yet in this thing at least, they had been right: revolution was a horrible thing. When used to shred flesh and break bones, dynamite was not a poetic bloom of light but a dreadful weapon.

I believed, with Short, that one must love one's neighbour. I believed, with my anarchist friends in London, that if human life was truly more precious than property it ought not to be wantonly destroyed. I could never join with Anton or Veronika; I must do all I could to stop them.

I went swiftly through the Calais coach where the sole conductor was hurriedly making up beds and entered the restaurant-car. As before, Short sat near the door with his back to me—at the same table, George's valet seemed to be trying to get him to join the Temperance League. At the table beyond, May swivelled in her chair and glanced in my direction. I smiled at her—*nothing wrong, turn around, go on eating,* my expression told her—laid a hand on Short's shoulder, and bent down to murmur in his ear:

"Come, I have found Lupei."

He did not question me. He got up at once and followed me.

"He is still aboard?" Short murmured as we stepped into the Calais coach.

"Speak quietly; we must not disturb him," I said. "He has the Grand Duke as a hostage."

We entered the Paris coach with caution. All seemed calm. I led the way past Vasily's compartment and into my own, where Short uttered a stifled sound of surprise as he saw Veronika's maid bound in the corner where I had left her: her gag was a little disarranged, but otherwise, she was secure. I pulled the door shut behind us.

"He's in league with the baroness," I said without preface, and then filled him in on everything I had overheard in Veronika's compartment.

"This is a ticklish affair," Short said when I had finished. "I suppose we will need to tackle the man first. Then, once the Grand Duke is free, he must lay a complaint against the baroness before we can afford to touch her. And as to that—Miss Sharp, I fear the police cannot now be avoided."

"Not with a revolution actually planned." I took a deep breath. "You were right, Short. I should never have trusted her. I'm sorry."

"No," he said quickly. "It is I who should apologise. I ought to have trusted you better."

There was an awkward silence. It struck me once again that few men would have admitted to fault like that—certainly not to a woman, let alone to one of my sort.

In the cramped compartment, there seemed nowhere to look that was not Short.

"Right," I said, after a moment. "Apology accepted, then."

"Right," Short said briskly, unholstering his revolver, and beginning to load it. "How shall we spring our trap?"

"I have a plan." Reaching into the luggage-racks, I produced the rope ladder with which we had become entangled in the baggage-car. Short's eyes widened, but before he could say anything, there came a tap at the door. Then it opened.

"Sharp?" May's voice was rather scandalised, no doubt at the sight of Short and myself ensconced together in seeming privacy. As we turned to face her, however, she got an eyeful of revolver, rope ladder, and the trussed, indignant maid.

Her eyes lit up. "Sharp!" she repeated, squeezing through the door. "The moment I saw your bloomers, I knew the game was afoot! Why didn't you *tell* me?"

Short nearly choked in surprise, and no wonder. This was a side of May few had ever seen. I said severely, "Because last time I did such a thing, ma'am, I nearly got you killed."

"Oh, come! Don't you need someone to—to mount guard over the prisoner, or anything?"

"Out of the question!" Short spluttered.

I wasn't entirely sure. I had no idea what Veronika might be capable of, once warned that we had learned her secrets, and I had not liked leaving Romona to her own devices. I knew from personal experience that any determined person with small and dextrous fingers could loosen any knot, in time. Really, we did need a sentry.

Still—"It's tempting, ma'am, but what will you do if she makes a determined effort to escape? You may have an excellent memory and a talent for drawing, but those will not help you if—"

I was interrupted by another rap on the door. "I say! Miss Sharp, are you there?"

"George!" I cried, "just the man! come in!"

Short's protests were overwhelmed as May opened the door and welcomed the Duke of York to our increasingly crowded midst. He was looking, as I recall, rather pale and agitated.

"Something dreadful has happened," George gasped. Then stopped, as he made out the gathering, and the tell-tale signs of impending action. "Short! Demmit, man, what is going on here?"

"Short and Sharp have found the anarchist," said May. Apart from two bright spots of colour burning on her cheeks, she might have been commenting upon the clemency of the weather. "They need us to watch the prisoner while they apprehend Lupei."

"But—I say—Sharp!" George barked, apparently in an agony. "I must speak to you alone!"

"It's no use, sir. I'm sensible of the compliment, but my mind is quite made up."

May sent me a startled look. George nearly choked. "What? No! I don't know what you're talking about! Something *important!*"

"Is it more pressing than an anarchist on the loose?"

"Yes—no—demmit! Something has been taken from my compartment."

"There's no help for it, sir." That was Short. "Even now, the anarchist is holding Grand Duke Vasily hostage in his compartment. We must go to his assistance at once."

That seemed to cut through his pother. George gulped. "In that case I can certainly guard the prisoner. Only, I need—"

The door banged open, striking George forcibly between the shoulders and sending him staggering into May's startled arms. The Duchess of Teck flooded in with a rustle of silk, sweeping all before her and jamming me into the extreme end of the compartment. Rather than fling myself against Short's manly bosom, I collapsed upon the small seat beneath the window, where Romona took advantage of our proximity to give me a nasty little kick.

"I say," Mary Adelaide said reproachfully, "what fun you are all having without me! I insist on being included! What is it, anyway? Have you found that dreadful little man with the bombs?"

Chapter XIV.

Really, that was the frozen limit! In that moment it was May who took charge—just as well, too, for I was close to suffocation, mostly from the laughter.

"This is not a game, mamma! The best way to help us now is to return to the dining-car at once, before anyone else finds out what is going on here."

"Why, May! is that any way to speak to your mother? I only want to help!"

May had given me an idea. "Indeed, ma'am, you *can* help." I climbed up Short's proffered arm and stepped onto the seat, where I could make my presence known. "If you could possibly make sure that everyone in the dining-car *stays* there for the next quarter-hour?"

"Of course!" The Duchess looked eager. "Should I sprain my ankle? Or—I know—a sudden attack of chest pain?"

"Whatever you can keep going convincingly for fifteen minutes. I leave it to your sense of artistry."

"Chest pains, then." Mary Adelaide's eyes sparkled. Then she reeled into the passage, already clutching theatrically at her breast.

"All right," I said, jumping down from the seat. "No time to lose. One can only hope Lupei hasn't noticed the public meeting going on in this compartment. Short, you take the door from the passage. I shall go in by the window."

"The window?"

"Short—," George put in.

"The window, yes—he'll never expect me to come from that direction."

"It sounds frightfully dangerous."

"Not for me. Come on, let's go."

"Short," George repeated, as the inspector made his way to the door, "please tell me you have such a thing as a pair of handcuffs about you."

"Of course, but this young person is quite secure, and I shall want them for Lupei."

"Oh, give him the cuffs, Short! We can sort it out later." Short did as I said. A moment later we were in the passage.

Vasily's compartment was silent, a thin sliver of electric light showing beneath the door.

"Keep an eye out," I whispered, pulling on a pair of kid leather gloves, "and listen for breaking glass."

Silent and dextrous in my slippered feet, I ran down the passage and knelt at the coach door. Happily, I kept four curiously-shaped hairpins in my chignon for just such an emergency. I had the lock picked in a moment and opened the door, latching it back.

Night had fallen across the hills of Alsace. A dim landscape of hills rushed by before me, the distant eastern horizon silvered by the rising moon. Taking a deep breath, I turned until the fleeting landscape was at my back, raised my arms, grasped the curved edge of the roof—and leaped.

I was stronger than any unbitten woman and most men, but it was an anxious moment; and when my fingers slipped just as I had pulled myself half-onto the train roof, I was sure I had made a terrible mistake. Another instant and I would fall from the train, ruining our one chance of catching Anton if I was lucky, and catching in the wheels if I was not. Horrible images rushed through my mind—and then I reached out and caught hold of one of the air-vent protrusions on the carriage roof. The wind plucked at my body, seeking to tear me from the coach, but the air-vent held.

Shaking a little, I drew myself up and began to creep as silently as possible from vent to vent along the carriage. Despite our speed, I found the journey was not extraordinarily difficult, for my bloomers prevented the wind from catching hold of me and there were plenty of handholds along the roof. In time I arrived silently at the coach's middle, unhooked the rope ladder from its coil at my waist, and fixed it to the nearest vent. This done, I leaned over the side of the coach to count the compartment windows until I was quite sure that Vasily's was the one directly below.

I hesitated only to check that my revolver was secure in its holster at my hip. Then I wrapped my hands tightly in the rope ladder, rose to my feet—swaying slightly on the broad roof of the train—and leaped.

I went through the window feet first in a shatter of glass. Jagged edges clutched at my bloomers and scraped the whalebone of my corset, but the heavy layers of my clothing protected me. Only one arm, taking an instant too long to release the rope ladder, scraped against one of those edges. At once, I smelled my own blood.

The wound could wait. I landed in a crouch within the brightly-lit compartment. At the other end of the space, I had a swift impression of a man poised in decisive motion, throwing up a hand with a revolver in it. I wrenched my weapon free a second later—then arrested my finger on the trigger as I met the man's eyes.

Breathing hard, Short and I looked down the barrels of each other's gun.

Between us—between the smashed window at which I had entered, and the broken door that Short had kicked in at the same moment—was an empty compartment. Empty, but for the vampire lying prone in his berth. Anton was gone.

Lowering his revolver with a growl of annoyance, Short motioned to me. "Stand back." He put his foot through the flimsy door in the partition separating this compartment from Veronika's. Beyond, that compartment was empty too.

"Gone!" Short cried, returning from his reconnaissance. "Is the man a figment?"

"Wait," I said breathlessly.

While Short searched this compartment and the one beyond it, I had turned to Vasily. He was awake, in a manner of speaking, but he looked very bad—white as paper and feverish. The stench of blood—no, of raw flesh—was now strong enough to overwhelm the lingering scent of the spilled cologne. As I twitched aside the bedcovers, my stomach turned.

A strip of skin across Vasily's chest had been peeled off, leaving raw flesh behind. The tattoo, I realised: the name *Ioanna* was gone. I let out a gasp of horror. Anton had exacted one piece of his revenge at least—but Vasily was a vampire; why did the wound remain unhealed?

The vampire lay breathing hard, his eyes wide and red and full of horrors. Suddenly he threw himself against the restraints that tethered wrists and ankles, his teeth bared and snapping.

I recoiled just in time to save my fingers, and it was at this moment that Short re-entered the compartment, and demanded to know if we were chasing a figment.

"Wait," I gasped. "Something is wrong with Vasily. He's not in his right mind."

The vampire lunged against his restraints once again, his lips drawn back in a snarl, his elongated canines bright in the lamplight. For an instant we could only watch as he thrashed in his berth. Then he lay still, shivering. Some of the madness seemed to pass from him.

"Blood," he whispered. "I smell blood."

A shudder ran through me: for the first time I saw the bandage on his wrist. Suddenly I understood: Veronika's mockery, the unhealed wound, the fact that something as strong as a vampire could be restrained by the mere leathern straps around Vasily's wrists and ankles.

"They've drained him of blood," I murmured, trying to staunch the flow of blood from my own wound. "Just enough to leave him weak—and maddened."

"Oh, he knows us well enough, I'd wager," Short said, displaying a tough-mindedness I would not have suspected in such a sad, sensitive-looking man. Leaning over the creature, he grabbed him deftly by the chin. "Sir, we're going to find the man who did this to you. Do you know where he went?"

For a moment I thought Vasily didn't hear, but then his red eyes focused on Short's face. "Anton Lupei," he whispered.

"Yes. Where did he go?"

"I don't know. Give me blood—I smell blood."

It took me a moment to realise that he wished to drink from one of us, and I could not help recoiling a step.

Short glanced up at me. His voice was utterly without inflection: "I don't think so.—Here, give me your arm, Miss Sharp," he added, taking out his hanky.

"Please!" Vasily groaned.

"There'll be a hospital in Strasbourg where you can get what you need," I said, answering Vasily's plea with some difficulty as Short wrapped his hanky around my cut and tied off the makeshift bandage. Right now, I had no time to be distracted by his deft, gentle touch. I should be considering Anton instead: "The dickens! I was afraid of this."

Short frowned as though he, too, had been lost in thought. "Afraid of what?"

"Anton must have guessed that we were onto him—oh, drat! What if he's already spoken to Romona? I thought her gag was askew when we returned from the dining-car."

"All right." As he released my hand, Short's eyes narrowed in concentration. "Let's presume he knows. What's his logical next step?"

I closed my eyes. "He's one step ahead of us. He knows we'll try to rescue Vasily. But Vasily is his hostage, and must be taken to Budapest, so why abandon him?"

"Perhaps for the very reason that he *does* need Vasily alive."

"You think he's after an expendable hostage, then.—*May!*"

I threw open the door and dashed into the passage, where the sight that awaited me blotted out all my fear for my mistress.

The moon had just now peered above the horizon, its silvery rays flowing through the windows lining the passage. A full moon—oh, dash it. I *knew* that. But I had forgotten it.

A black shadow crouched before the door of the compartment where I had left May and Romona. It was a man, breathing heavily, as though experiencing some deadly pain: I heard the bellows-like wheeze of the breath in his lungs.

When I stepped into the hallway, he turned on me with glowing, phosphorescent eyes. A nearly-human face peered up at me—George.

"Told her," he panted, "no account—open door—what?"

He doubled in pain, and it seemed that the passage-way shrank about him as he grew—sprouted grey hair—whipped a doglike head to and fro in dreadful agony.

It was a werewolf who had marked my face with three livid, slashing scars. I did not recall the attack, except in my nightmares. Now, it was as though those nightmares had all come to life to swallow me. I whimpered in fright and recoiled into Vasily's compartment, colliding with Short.

I knotted my hands into his shirt, clinging to him like a drowning woman. "Short," I gasped. "There's a werewolf in the passage."

His hands closed reflexively over my wrists.

"What," he said, flatly.

"Those restraints—"

Both of us looked down at Vasily—at the leathern straps holding him in his berth. I let out a high-pitched laugh. "So that's what George was trying to tell us. Someone took his straps."

"Why didn't he *tell* us?"

"Because May was in the room—and because Vasily needed immediate rescue."

I closed my eyes, drawing in a deep breath to calm my terror. Short said resignedly, "I knew this would happen the moment I saw you board this train."

"What, you knew an anarchist would try to kidnap the

Grand Duke, and that George was going to turn into a werewolf while the Duchess feigned a heart attack in the dining car?"

"We-ell, not as such; but my guess wouldn't have been terribly far off."

"I suppose with a werewolf outside May's door, we needn't worry about Anton getting—"

Through the unglazed window of Vasily's compartment came the sound of breaking glass as another window smashed. In the same moment I heard May's voice uplifted in startled protest.

"The dickens," I gasped. A moment later Short and I were in the passage again. The transformation was now nearly complete. A wolf-man crouched before May's door, but now I saw that one hind paw was tethered to a bit of radiator by a glinting steel chain. Short's handcuffs. I imagined George sticking it out as long as he could, hoping Short and I would finish our business before the change gripped him; then finally beating his retreat—so far, but no further. Anyone who wanted to get to May must now pass him.

Those sulphurous yellow eyes watched me distrustfully.

"George," I whispered, putting out a trembling hand. He'd told me himself that some wolves could control themselves—could hold back the madness and behave like the men they were beneath—even speak. "Good boy—good dog. Let me pass."

His nose wrinkled. He backed a step. A whine rose in his throat. "May!"

"I know, I'm trying to get to her."

"Miss Sharp." Short's hand dropped on my shoulder, holding me back. He'd taken a flat case from his breast-pocket, and now he drew out a shining syringe filled with some pale liquid. "Allow me.—It's a sedative; that's all I know," he added, in reply to my questioning look.

A sedative for use on werewolves! Now *that* would have been helpful at Balmoral a few months ago—but evidently our royal masters were loath to permit us the smallest means of protecting ourselves.

I stood aside as he passed me, syringe poised. "It's me, sir," he told the wolf, soothingly. "It's me, Short."

He reached for the wolf's head with those long, gentle fingers. I held my breath. George whined a little as Short stroked his fur, bringing the syringe nearer the beast's neck—

From within the compartment came a piercing scream.

May.

"George, no!" I cried, but it was too late.

The George-wolf surged to its feet with a snarl. The shreds of clothing still clinging to his limbs burst and fell away as he completed his transformation, becoming larger—stronger—full of madness. With a sweep of one powerful arm, he sent Short flying towards me. We fell in a tangle of arms and legs.

The sound of breaking glass told me the syringe was gone. I fought my way from beneath Short's slack weight and found his breast torn and bleeding from George's claws. I could spare no time to examine his injuries. The door to my compartment twitched open. May stood there, silhouetted against the light that filtered in through the broken window, struggling in Anton's grasp.

As her captor threw the door open, her eyes widened and her mouth opened. For only the second time in her life May faced a werewolf, and this one was furious. She screamed. Anton's eyes widened—he must not have expected to find the creature on his very doorstep—and he recoiled, flinging the door shut.

"May!" I screamed.

The George-wolf lunged, ripping the door and part of the wall to splinters—then fell back with a snarl of pain as the handcuffs bit into his hind paw. Instantly, his rage building, he threw himself forward again.

The radiator groaned. Somewhere in its depths a rivet popped, and it leaned away from the wall by two inches.

There were wood-splinters in my hair. Through the gash in the wall I watched as Anton and May backed towards the window. Romona was there too, freed of her bonds. At the sight of the maddened werewolf lunging against his chains, snarling and scrabbling, she put a hand to her mouth and fainted dead away on the bench seat. May looked as though she might like to follow suit. "Sharp!" she screamed.

"I'm here!" Desperately I patted my bloomer pockets—nothing. My revolver was loaded strictly for anarchist. My silver bullets were in my luggage in the compartment I could not reach. Otherwise I had nothing: no wolfsbane, no silver but the moon-shaped pendant at my throat, which Sal Tanner had given me before dying in a werewolf's jaws. It would burn George—madden, but not kill him, still less remove him from this narrow space.

With a groan of metal the radiator came half away from the wall and George lurched one step forward, snapping and growling, half inside the compartment now.

"Don't move!" I shrieked to May. "I'll come through the window and get you!"

As George lunged forward again, I saw my chance. I leaped over the radiator and past him, raced down the passage-way, and turned for the fresh air and the lock I had picked.

This time, I barely noticed the dangerous climb to the roof. This time I scrambled madly across the roof for the rope-ladder, heedless both of the wind and of the speed with which the train hurtled through the night. We were now in a sort of outpost of the Black Forest, and the full moon silvered the pine-trees overhead. The rope ladder now flew from a different vent than the one I had tethered it to: evidently, this was how Anton managed to get in at May's window. Catching hold of those frail twisted strands, I let myself down the ladder and peered in at the smashed window where May and the two anarchists were crammed against the window in terror, and George still battled the radiator beyond.

Anton turned to me. I pointed my revolver squarely at his head. "May first. Then, if you've an ounce of real manhood, you'll help Romona."

The maid gave my rope ladder a look of terror. "I'll take my chances with the wolf!"

I didn't try to argue. May shuddered at the sight of the flimsy rope-ladder, the jagged glass. "I can't," she said faintly.

"You must."

Anton looked me in the eye, but it was May he spoke to: "Do it or I'll throw you to the wolf."

Behind them, the radiator groaned again, and the ravening George-wolf lurched forward another step.

That seemed to decide her. Whimpering, she stepped up onto the seat. I put away my revolver and helped her through the broken glass, onto the rope ladder. A dizzy, terrifying moment passed as the ladder tilted and swung; and then I got onto the roof again and reached down to draw her up behind me.

May slithered onto the roof with her eyes shut, and I guided her hands to the nearest ventilator, where she lay soundlessly, clinging for dear life. Beneath us, the rope ladder pulled taut as Anton emerged from the window.

Below came a snap as the radiator broke at last.

The whole coach rocked on its wheels as a large body hit the outer wall of my compartment. Romona screamed, and the freed George-wolf howled in triumph. Still dangling from the ladder, Anton jerked aside with a cry of terror as a powerful, hairy arm reached for him. My heart leaped in a thrill of fear for him. I lunged forward, seizing him by the wrist and hauling him bodily atop the train.

Now there were three of us crammed on that windy roof. It struck me that I had thought of no way to get us inside again. No sooner had this occurred to me, than a sinewy paw reached up from below, clamping into the coach roof with five iron-sharp claws.

Anton glanced from me to the pursuing monster and back again. His words were lost in the wind, but I saw his lips form my name: *Vera—it's me he wants.*

"No!" I cried, reaching for him with that blind, reflexive loyalty that still bound my heart to his.

Before I could intervene, Anton grabbed one flapping end of the ladder and threw himself bodily from the roof on the opposite side. Glass smashed below as he hurtled through the window into the passage.

At the same moment the wolf swung up and clawed himself onto the roof.

May raised her head just in time to see it. She screamed.

I levelled my revolver at the monster and emptied three bullets into its chest. Being cast from lead, they made little impression on the creature. But as it happened, the George-wolf was not remotely interested in May or myself. His ears must have caught the sound of Anton's re-entry into the train. Snarling, he threw himself after the anarchist.

Without warning, the train swerved around a corner. The wolf's claws slipped upon the smooth roof. It seemed that for an instant he hung in the air, poised between balance and disaster.

One claw reached out and closed upon the ladder.

Then he was gone—and so were we.

There was a sickening yank and a snap. It wasn't until afterward that I realised the ventilator must have come away. The slack at the anchor-end of the rope-ladder suddenly tightened. Each of us had a limb twisted into the rope for safety. It jerked cruelly and swept us away. Off the train—after George—and into a sudden blinding darkness.

Chapter XV.

No doubt the reader will be surprised to learn that werewolves can suffer concussion. I did not know this, but I was glad to discover it, for that night it quite possibly saved our lives.

May, who conceals a surprising streak of sentimentality beneath her common-sense exterior, will no doubt argue that the creature was only trying to harm Anton, and would scarcely have bothered us. For myself, I will continue to return fervent thanks to my Maker that the fall brought George's head into a brief, sharp argument with a rock—and that the rock prevailed.

As for myself, the first thing I knew was the fact that every inch of my body hurt dreadfully. I groaned and found that my head, at least, was cushioned upon something soft.

"Oh, Sharp!" May whispered from the darkness above me. I realised my head was resting in her lap. "You are alive!"

"Yes," I said, wincing, "but are you?"

She tried to stop me, but I sat up and twisted to look at her. It was dark, for the moon was gone from the starlit sky; but my eyes are very sharp in the darkness, and I saw that she looked frightfully pale and disarranged. I could smell a little blood on her, no more than a couple of scratches, but otherwise her composure was complete. It was only her second encounter with a werewolf, but she seemed to have accustomed herself to the experience with great fortitude.

Nor was I greatly injured, I found upon a cursory examination of my body. Some scrapes and cuts had already begun to heal, for I mend faster than most. My left arm pained me like the dickens. I hoped it would not have to be broken and re-set.

"Broken bones?" I asked May.

She shook her head. "I'm afraid you broke my fall, Sharp. I've been sitting here for hours, praying that you'd wake. Oh, dear! Do you suppose that George is all right? He left the compartment only a minute or so before that creature broke in."

I remained speechless, my brain running in a thousand different directions at once. Had she really not guessed the werewolf's identity?

(And—what had happened while we lay in the shadow of these hillside pines? Surely a search party ought to have been sent out hours ago? Had Short survived his altercation with George? What about Romona? And the other passengers—Mary Adelaide—the Duke—were any of them still alive to miss us? What might Anton and Veronika have done to them all?)

They were beyond my reach now. The rope ladder lay unspooled across the ground, trailing west in the direction from which we had come. It struck me that May's question was more pressing than she knew. George—where was George?

With any luck the moon had already set, but all the same I thought I detected the fading scent of wolf in the air. George could not be far off. I dug into my pocket for a paper of matches, and set light to a fallen pine-bough.

"Stay here," I told May. Lifting the makeshift torch with my good arm, I made my way between the pines, following the fallen rope-ladder slantwise across the slope. Underfoot were only soundless needles. At last, I topped a little rise in the ground, and a small hollow opened before me.

The George-wolf lay motionless where he had fallen at the foot of a rock-face, and the torchlight played over a dark smear upon the stone that smelled like blood. A terrifying thought struck me. Perhaps George was dead! Perhaps a second prince was dead because of me!

Then—a footfall on the pine needles beside me, a faint whiff of orange-blossom, and I knew I was not alone. May was beside me, a soft gasp escaping her lips. "Is it—dead?"

"No," I said. Reason had once more returned to her throne. "They turn into men when they die."

And also when the moon set—which it would do at any moment. Throwing my torch down, where it smouldered among the damp needles that littered the ground, I turned to grasp May by the shoulders. "You ought not to be here. Go back!"

"Back where? Aren't you supposed to protect me?"

I could say nothing to that. "Please, if it wakes…"

She smiled bravely. "As long as you're with me, Sharp, I think I can face anything."

"All right," I said. "We go back together." I tried to steer her away from the wolf, with a vague idea of climbing up onto the train-tracks, and walking east until we found a station, or a search party, or wreckage…

May, however, resisted my guidance. Her eyes widened as she looked past me, to the George-wolf. *"What's happening?"*

I turned. My makeshift torch still burned, just bright enough to shed a little red light upon the monster. It stirred, groaned, and stretched out its limbs. And then the moon must have gone down, for the figure shrank, and the shaggy grey hair melted like summer snow.

May stared at the man lying among the pine-needles, mother-naked save for the steel cuff on his ankle, and the tattered rags about his hips and wrists.

"George?" Her voice shook.

I could not bear to look at her. Instead, I fell to my knees beside George and felt his pulse. Strong and steady, and he had not a scratch upon him. At my touch he stirred and opened his eyes.

"George?" May gasped, stumbling forward to look more closely into his face.

Groaning, he turned to look up at her. "May," he began, uncertainly. "Please—I can explain."

As he moved, she flinched and paled. "Explain what?"

"May—"

"It can't be," she said, shaking her head. "It's impossible. We're English. We aren't like that.—*Explain what?"*

He got to his knees. "May—"

She recoiled another step. "Stay away from me!"

A moment's silence passed. George remained on his knees, shivering. May stood at the lip of the dell with her hands clenched. Her eyes were like two enormous dark stains in her face, and I stood between them, unable to do anything but watch.

"You're a monster," she whispered. Her gaze flickered to me. "Sharp."

"Ma'am."

"Did you know?"

I closed my eyes. "Yes."

She made a sound of distress and stumbled away into the dark. George leaped to his feet, but I put a restraining hand on his shoulder.

"Not now," I murmured. "Here, wrap yourself in this." I had been fumbling with the buttons of my jacket, and now I stripped it off and handed it to him. After that, I followed May.

She had not gone far, and my nose led me directly to her. I found her standing on the raised train-tracks, looking east but not moving.

What could I say? What excuse could I make? I thought of a dozen—I thought of how I feared to break her heart after Eddy's loss; I thought of my own fears of the hangman; I thought of just tonight, barely an hour ago, when I had determined to stop deceiving myself and others because my name was supposed to be Truth. But in the end, there were no excuses that would do.

"Ma'am," I said, "I have nothing to say. I ought to have told you."

She didn't answer. She was not crying, I determined after a moment—only standing there, cold and silent.

"There will be a search party eventually," I went on at last. "We should wait by the tracks. It won't be long."

I was, thank goodness, correct. Before we had waited much longer a light pierced the forest, and a small locomotive came within view, moving at a walking-pace. Lanterns flitted around it, and—oh, joy!—I heard Short's welcome voice, calling steadily: "Miss Sharp! Your Highness!"

"Here!" I shouted, and a moment later, relieved-looking

men in railway uniforms were enveloping the two of us in blankets, and asking if we were hurt.

Hearing that May and I were both unhurt, Short pulled me aside. "I'm well," he said in reply to my question, "only scratched—what about Prince George?"

"She has seen him—she knows."

He lifted his lantern, shining the light into my face. What he saw there pulled his mouth very tight and rueful, but he did not remind me of his own former warnings.

"Short?" a voice hissed. A pale, dejected shape loomed out of the dark, my jacket tied around its waist like an apron. "About time you got here, hang it! Lend me your coat, will you?"

"And the others?" I inquired anxiously, as Short handed his greatcoat to the shivering prince, before bending down to unlock the handcuff that still trailed from his ankle. On George's slight frame, the coat practically dragged along the ground, concealing all inadequacies of his wardrobe. "Vasily? Anton? Veronika?"

Short glanced towards the waiting locomotive, where strident cries of joy told us that the Duchess of Teck was welcoming her lost daughter. His voice dipped. "It isn't good, Miss Sharp. Your friend Anton Lupei and the maid Romona got the jump on me while I was still wool-gathering. By the time I got free, we were in Strasbourg, on German soil—and Lupei and the baroness had taken the Grand Duke and disappeared."

Chapter XVI.

The journey to Strasbourg was not above two hours, but the trip seemed interminable, crammed as we were within the rescue locomotive. By the time we had reached our destination and been delivered to our hotel—a large white edifice in the city's New Town, full of smooth dark wood, green-shaded lamps, and russet carpets—it was dawn, and the city had begun to stir.

A doctor was already waiting to tend May's scratches, and she was bundled into her room to be examined for more serious injuries. George, upon learning that his valet and luggage awaited him in an adjoining suite, disappeared in search of them. Mary Adelaide, who had insisted on accompanying the search party, would not be parted from her daughter; and the Duke of Teck, upon welcoming them home, slipped a ten-pound note into my hand by way of thanks and took himself off to bed.

Left in the sitting-room, I sank into the cushions of the armchair nearest the fire. The ten-pound note was heavy in my hand, as heavy as though I had been holding its worth in gold. It felt such a burden that I briefly considered consigning it to the flames. Instead, I smoothed it and put it into my pocket, for I thought I might very soon have reason to need it.

Then I slipped like a ghost into May's dressing-room, stripped off my filthy clothes, washed in the jug of cold water that waited there, pitched into the narrow bed, and slept.

I was awakened around noon by a clipped voice from the next room.

"No, mamma, I do *not* wish to rest."

I must have forgotten to close the door that communicated between May's bedroom and the dressing-room in which I slept. It sat half open, and though each bone protested as I moved, I found that by rising up on my elbow I could see into the room beyond. There, clad in her silk dressing-gown, May sat ramrod straight in bed with a cup of what smelled like hot broth clasped between her hands. "I do not wish to rest; I wish to see George," she declared.

A breathless silence echoed in the room before Mary Adelaide replied.

"Oh, May! You are going to make your old mother very happy!"

I blinked hazily, wondering what I had missed. But it seemed the Duchess had only been leaping to conclusions, for May said frostily, "I have no intention of making anyone happy. You, or—or anyone else."

"But, darling!"

"George can plead his suit, if that is what he means to do, far more effectively than you can."

Well, that was cold as a December wind. There was little inflection in her voice, but I could tell she was bitterly angry. Mary Adelaide withdrew, and at length the door closed.

George did not speak at once, and I knew he had entered the room only because I caught a whiff of his cologne. May did not speak, either, but she pinned him with a forthright gaze that spoke volumes.

"Hem!" he burst out at length, loud enough to make me jump. "Awake and well, I take it?"

"Quite," May said crisply. She eyed him up and down. "No scratches, bruises, or abrasions for *you,* I see. I take it that is a result of your...condition."

Ineffable distaste in the word. The silence lengthened.

"Came to apologise," George gasped.

"Oh?"

"Been concealing it from you. Not cricket. Ought to have told you. Part of the family and all that. Ought to expect a fellow to tell you things like this."

The sharp, jagged sentence fragments sounded as though they were being dragged out of him by May's merciless gaze.

"I'm not quite sure I understand, George. Why the apology? Do you think I will marry you, now that I know?"

"No, but..."

"Good. I find I am tired, after all. If you are finished, you might as well leave. You have a train to Coburg to catch, I take it."

"Not finished," he said thickly.

"Oh?"

I heard his advancing footsteps. May's composure cracked as though she had found a snake in the bed beside her. Suddenly she was on her feet by the window, clutching her dressing-gown close to her body and breathing rather hard. "Sharp!" she cried, and then, "Stay back! Stay away from me!"

Aches or not, I was already moving. My mistress called me—it was George she blamed, not myself—I half wished George *would* leap at her, so that I might have the honour of saving her once again. I flung my own dressing-gown around my shoulders—my arm twinged—and rushed through the door. May stood by the window on the opposite side of the bed, which she had put between herself and George. He must have heard me enter, but he did not turn.

Nor did he allow himself to be distracted from what he had to say. His shoulders lifted with a deep ragged breath: "Not asking you to marry me—no. Could never marry someone who didn't care for me. But there was one other lie I told you."

"Oh?" she said, rather shakily.

George's neck flushed red. "Told you my—feelings were disengaged."

There was a long silence. Two bright hectic spots of colour kindled in May's cheeks. Her mouth opened, but no sound emerged.

"Sensible girl, I thought. Do Eddy a good turn if I could get him to propose to you, I thought. By the time he did, I…oh, hang it!" he finished explosively.

"Why, you *were,*" May whispered, shrinking back against the curtains. "You *were* jealous of him."

Well. *I* could have told her that. In fact, that is just what I *had* done. Not that she believed me.

"The truth is…the devil, I can't seem to say it," he said grimly. "Truth is, I—love you, May. Felt this way for months. Never really supposed you'd care for me, so I didn't bother you about it. Not sure why I'm saying it now. Dem' foolery. Good morning."

He turned away from her, stalking towards the door. May arrested him with a low, trembling question.

"How did Eddy die?"

George stopped in his tracks—as still, and as silent as my own heart.

"Did you kill him?" May asked.

"No," he burst out, turning again.

Silence.

May clung to the curtains as if in need of their support. "Was he a w—a werewolf too?"

George looked at me. Despite his worried scowl, I knew he meant to give me room to spin whatever truth or lie I chose, conscious even now that whatever lies we had told, they had been for one person's sake:

Mine.

And so I must tell the truth.

"Yes," I whispered. "Yes, Eddy was a werewolf."

Now there was a look of sickened betrayal in her eyes—that look I had been awaiting, and dreading. "Sharp! How long have you known?"

I stared at the carpet. "Exactly three months."

"I ask again," she said in that same low, haunted voice. *"Who killed Eddy?"*

George's head was bent; he would give me no help. I wanted to burst into tears and beg her to spare me this horrible truth, but it was far too late for that. Instead, I gathered about myself some remaining odds and patches of bravado, and said: "You, ma'am. You killed Eddy, with an arrow dipped in wolfsbane."

"Oh," she said, very faintly.

There was, it seemed, an age of silence.

May let go of the curtain. "I knew. Deep down I always knew it was me. I knew I had killed him."

I closed my eyes.

"I knew when I loosed the arrow that it might kill a man—a prince—and I was too frightened to care. Then, when Eddy died... Each time I thought of him I felt the twang of the bowstring in my hand. I knew I had killed him; only I didn't know how. It *couldn't* be, because he wasn't..."

"I'm sorry," I whispered. "I ought to have told you. I'm sorry."

May was deathly white. "Told me? You ought never to have meddled with the werewolves at all. Eddy would still be alive if not for you."

"No." George's voice cut through my apology, startling both of us. "If not for Sharp, Eddy would have escaped the just rewards for his crimes."

May bridled. "His *crimes?*"

"The two dead women in Whitechapel," he said doggedly. "And two more by Deeside if you hadn't shot him."

"Why, George! your own brother! how could you say such things? It was that horrible Ernst Gunther who killed the women in Whitechapel!"

"Have you forgotten that Eddy was in the very act of springing on you when he died?" I put in.

"He would never have harmed me—I was his promised wife."

"God knows it ain't the kind of thing to say of one's brother, but he was the murderer, May. Told me so himself."

Her eyes flashed. "And am I to believe *you,* you—monster!"

"Got to face facts, May," George said, more shrewdly than I expected from him. "Eddy and I are both monsters, or neither of us are. Can't have it both ways, what?"

"Usurper," she said in a deadly calm, terribly frightening voice. "Beast. Liar. Go. Go away. Never let me see your face again. Nor you, Sharp."

Everything seemed so far away. I felt like a puppet-master working at an endless remove from my own body; my face was numb and stiff. "Ma'am—" I began, at the same moment that George began, "There's something else—"

"Not another word, or I will have Short in to remove you. You have deceived me into regicide, and I will have no one about me whom I cannot trust."

She was deadly serious, and I was all adrift. George beckoned me. Still feeling numb, I went into the dressing-room, took up my umbrella, bundled my few belongings into my carpet-bag, and followed George from the room.

Chapter XVII.

There are some passages in these memoirs of mine which are too painful to dwell on too deeply. How the Duke and Duchess of Teck reacted to their daughter's surprising intransigence; how May was begged to take back not only George but also myself; how slowly the truth dawned on everyone, save myself who knew her best, that May was indeed quite determined never to see either of us again, I can hardly bear to remember, much less relate. Through it all, George wholeheartedly took my part—leaving me too abashed even to flirt with him. As for Short, bless him! once or twice I thought he was taking the whole thing harder than I did myself.

And as for myself? Well, I had known for some time now that any effort to tell May the truth would be disastrous. It was only now, in the calm eye of the storm, that I realised how unquestioning my hopes had been of her never finding out—and how utterly hopeless. Worst of all was the conviction that now came upon me, of having wounded and driven from me my dearest friend. For it struck me—alas, too late—that May *had* been my friend. The sense of justice that had brought her to my assistance during the Whitechapel affair—the generosity with which she had attempted to protect me at Balmoral—the courage with which she had faced a maddened werewolf on that fateful night by the River Dee—at that moment I could not help feeling that she had been truer than I.

In the end George promised to find me a new situation, and not to abandon me until I was honourably settled in employment. That was how I discovered what a cold comfort monetary security can be. It was perverse ingratitude, but I could not help feeling it.

The Tecks meant not to resume their journey for two or three days. George, who had nursed such recent hopes of being asked to accompany them, sighed and sent Short out to book his tickets to Coburg. Thereupon Short came to find me, and insisted on my putting on my hat and sallying out with him: the fresh air, he said, would do me good.

Strasbourg, as the whole world knows, is a charming town. A massive medieval wall and moat still girdles the old city, where there is a very fine Gothic cathedral and a great number of very tall and charming old houses. The Tecks' hotel was in the New Town, which boasts a profusion of fine buildings in the prettiest modern style, and from there Short and I walked side-by-side along the moat on our way to the station. It was a fine, sunny spring day, and there were small boys fishing in the canal. Short remained silent for most of our walk, although I made a half-hearted effort to argue Temperance with him. Perhaps he had had enough of that with George's valet, or perhaps I was not feeling particularly inspired that day. At any rate, after some non-committal answers, Short changed the subject.

"Prince George desired me to buy you a ticket to London," he said.

Back to England! That was a blow, and when he said it, I knew it was the last thing I wished for.

"Must I go home?" I said, drearily.

"I'm afraid the Duke of York has little use for a lady's maid."

"Nor a bodyguard, I suppose. Not when he has you."

Short smiled—that swift, curiously sweet smile that transforms his long face. (With a twinge of sorrow I remembered that May had thought him ugly. If he was, *I* did not see it.) "If you wished to accompany us to Coburg, I might remind him how very well we seem to work together."

"Coburg," I said with a sigh—"no. Somehow Coburg doesn't seem to be where the action is." As I said the words, I knew exactly what I wanted to do next.

Short must have sensed what I was going to say, for he stopped in his tracks. "Miss Sharp, I don't like that smile on your face."

"And I don't like the frown on yours. It makes you look like a Nonconformist."

"I *am* a Nonconformist."

"Then oughtn't you to be banging a tambourine for Temperance, too? I imagine that if there was a Spirit of Temperance—"

"Spirits? Couldn't possibly be. The Temperance League wouldn't allow it."

"A patron saint, then."

"We don't have those either, as well you know.—And don't think you can distract me with an argument, Miss Sharp. I'm the one holding the purse-strings. I've half a mind to buy you a ticket to London, and pack you off care of a nursemaid."

But only half a mind! I grinned, adopting a coaxing tone. "Come now! I know that you've cabled Scotland Yard, and Paris, and spoken to the German police, and set all Europe searching for Baroness Sarkozy and her three hundred bomb-throwing maniacs! But don't forget, I have something none of them have."

"And what's that?"

"Anything like the appearance and antecedents necessary to pass as an anarchist myself."

"You terrify me, Miss Sharp."

"I'm not asking *you* to come to Budapest. Just to buy me a ticket there."

"Hang it, dear girl, I can't let you go haring off into a nest of anarchists on your own. I don't object to your making *my* life interesting, but I wish you would occasionally consider your own neck."

"But I shan't be alone. Half the policemen in Europe will be there, thanks to you. I'm sure you can give me some sort of introduction to one of them."

"Is that a wile, to induce me to say yes? Or if I do give you an introduction, will you make use of it?"

"Of course," I said, unblinking. I did not say to which of his questions this was an answer.

Short sighed. We walked on without speaking for a time until he said, "I am not authorised to pay for a jaunt around Europe. If you truly wish to go to Budapest, I am sure Prince George will oblige you, but you will be striking out alone. You would be without all the assistance he wishes to give you, and if things should go badly for you in Hungary, you would be unable to call on us—on him, I mean—for help."

"I suppose that's fair."

"Then why take the gamble?" Short asked, a flicker of unaccustomed passion in his voice. "How will you make a decent living, without a patron, and with those marks on your face?"

I flinched.

"Forgive me," he said at once. "That was brutal of me. I only worry for you; that is all."

"I know." I let the raillery drop away from voice and face, let him see a fraction of the weary sadness beneath. "I know, and I am grateful to count you as my friend. Of course it is a gamble. Of course I don't know to what kind of fate I might be consigning myself. But for some months now I have known that my past lay in the East, and since the hour I learned it, I have only ever been trying to make my way East. And now—now that the worst has happened, with May, what is there to keep me? In the East may be nothing but danger, but there may also be a home, and family—a *real* family, that would never cast me out. Anton knows who they are; Veronika knows who they are." I took a deep breath as tears threatened to cloud my eyes. "I overheard it on the train, you know. Anton said *she is* his *daughter.* Somewhere, I have a father."

Short did not speak until I felt I had myself well enough in hand that I could look him in the eye again. His eyes and mouth drooped sadly. "And the only way you can find this family of yours, is to chase the anarchists?"

"Had I any other lead, I would follow it."

He didn't like it. I saw all sorts of premonitions of doom in his face, but he said nothing of his fears. He smiled mournfully at me, the kind of smile that barely touches the corners of the eyes. "Then come along, and we'll get you a ticket. And—promise me one thing, Miss Sharp."

He reached out. When I took his hand, the fingers contracted involuntarily at my touch, as though shocked. Abashed, I tried to withdraw, but he clasped my hand gently between his own and said, "If you find you can't make it on your own, send me a telegram. If there's anything at all I can do, I'm at your service."

Beneath his earnest gaze, I found myself in greater confusion than ever. I had already betrayed too much by taking his hand when he only meant a comradely gesture, and in another moment he would feel my pulse beating entirely too quickly for blameless friendship. What madness, to risk my one remaining friend in this way! Extricating myself from his grasp, I stammered some sort of assent.—Not that I meant to call upon him, of course. He would have far too much to occupy him in Coburg.

In this way, the following Saturday evening found me boarding the Orient Express once more for the journey to Budapest. I stepped into my second-class compartment with a sharp sense of *déjà vu:* from the smooth wood panelling to the lush brocaded upholstery, everything was exactly as it had been three days ago before George turned into a wolf. For a moment, I felt as though I had woken from a bad dream. Then the thought pierced me like a blade: it was no dream; this was not the same coach; I was not with my mistress.

My journey, which lasted twenty-five hours, was uneventful. Certainly, my actions on my last train journey did not result in any unpleasantness this time. It seemed that the Orient Express, catering as it did to the upper crust, was not unaccustomed to occasional outbursts from those monsters among its passengers. George, rather shame-facedly, had confessed that his family meant to blame the destruction upon the missing Vasily rather than himself—had in fact already been in communication with St Petersburg about it. In this way the events of the previous Wednesday evening had been hushed up or smoothed over, to no lasting ill effect.

All the same, I boarded under an assumed name and a heavy black veil, and kept to my compartment until the following evening, when the train crossed the Danube. I had been asleep in my berth until the conductor called me just in time to watch the lights glimmering on the broad expanse of the river as we crossed. At a quarter past eleven we pulled in at the station in Pest, on the river's east bank. I disembarked to find myself alone and shivering on the platform, as streamers of cold wind rushed to and fro beneath the pitched-glass roof.

Yawning a little, I unwound the thick black veil from my face, picked up my valise and trudged towards the entrance. The station was nearly empty. Quite a different arrival, this, from the comfortable hustle and bustle, the deferential bows accorded a princely family and their entourage! I tried to scold myself out of my melancholy, but it was no use. It was not the comforts of wealth that I missed.

I stopped to ask a porter about a respectable hotel, not too expensive, and he gave directions to a humble establishment not far away, where I could get a bed for—a quantity of money in a denomination I felt I ought to recognise, but did not. Thanking him, I moved on. Passing between tall slender columns, I emerged onto the pavement before the station. The street was nearly empty, save for a hansom cab which slowed as I approached it, then—as Fate would have it—continued on its way when I did not hail it. No sooner had it sped away than I realised it had been empty, waiting to receive me.

"Now, then, Liz Sharp! This will never do!" I muttered to myself, as I shifted my valise from one hand to another. "If you'd been keeping your eyes open, you might have saved yourself a great deal of trouble! Now who knows how far you must walk!"

"That's all very well," I retorted, "but I'd like to see anyone keep their eyes open after the sort of nights I've been having."

From which the reader will perceive that after twenty-four hours alone in a sleeping-car compartment, I had been reduced to arguing with myself. For some years my husband has assured me most solemnly that this is not a thing done by rational people, but I beg to differ. My predilection for debate comes not from a lack of rationality, but if anything, an excess of that faculty.

Not, I grant, that this was functioning at its greatest strength at this moment. I crossed the broad pavement before the station and began to inspect the streets, lined with neoclassical tenement buildings, which radiated from the square. It was dark, and the street signs were in a language that seemed somehow familiar. I had just made up my mind that the street I was standing in, which was the only one not signposted, must be the one I wanted, when a door slammed to my left, and I looked up to see a burly figure standing in the doorway to one of the shabbier tenements. The distant figure's silence and stillness filled me with a sensation of dread, until a breath of cold air gusted between us, and I scented—Anton Lupei!

He had seen me—he was waiting for me. Glad to have my stout umbrella with me, I picked up my valise and trudged over to the door, where I found him waiting with folded arms and an impassive face.

"How did you know I would come?" I inquired.

"The Vera I once knew would come," he told me, standing back, and opening the door. Beyond was a dark entrance-hall lit by a flickering gas-lamp. I stood my ground.

"What is this place?"

"The threshold to something greater."

I remembered I had a part to play. Our positions had reversed somewhat since our last meeting aboard the Orient Express, and now I was in the position of weakness. Perhaps that would put Anton at ease, and help me to find what I sought.

"You were right," I told him, putting a quiver in my voice. "Veronika was right. Those people were not my family. When it came to a choice between me and the monsters, they cast me out."

Anton's face darkened. "What's this you say?"

"They threw me out." I found that the tears sprang naturally to my eyes. "I had nowhere to turn—so I came looking for you."

"They will curse the day they turned their backs on you, Vera. I swear it."

The words ought to have alarmed me, but they did not. It was something in the way he said my name—some long-forgotten part of me could not help but respond with trust and affection.

I stepped across the threshold. "I want to know who I once was. I am ready to put myself in your hands now. Tell me, Anton, is it too late for that?"

Having closed the door, he stood with both hands on the latch, unwilling—or unable—to meet my eyes. "Veronika thinks it is."

"And you?"

He turned to look at me. "You came, didn't you?"

It was a dangerous game I played, for I played it against my own heart. I could not give in to the temptation to trust him. Vasily must be recovered, Veronika's apocalypse averted. I told myself the deception was unlike what I had practiced on May. If Veronika and Anton meant to illuminate Europe in a deadly spring of dynamite-blooms like the one I had witnessed in Paris, then there were one or two things I owed them—but not the truth. Once I knew the anarchists' plans, I must foil them.

And yet—the thought of warm fingers brushing my scars, tenderly, with neither fascination nor disgust. For a moment I sensed old memories stirring like sleek, dangerous monsters in the depths of my mind.

"I loved you once," I murmured, and knew it for truth. "I can feel it, somehow. But that's all I know."

"It is enough for me," Anton said, and then he led me upstairs to a large room in the tenement's garret, where we found five other anarchists sleeping on mattresses, or conversing in hushed voices over glasses of cheap wine. Neither Veronika nor Vasily were present. "Sleep," Anton told me, gesturing towards a broken-down old sofa. "We set out first thing in the morning."

Chapter XVIII.

So began the second stage of my journey. That morning Anton and I, together with the five other anarchists, boarded a train to a bustling provincial town named Eger, which lay in the shadow of the mountains about seventy miles east of Budapest as the crow flies. At Eger station a driver in a dilapidated shooting-brake awaited us. There followed a very long and bumpy four-hour journey up into the mountains, on a windy evening, with flakes of snow blowing against our faces, as the vehicle rocked precariously upon the massive, frowning black crags up which the narrow road climbed. None of us spoke a great deal; I gathered from the few words exchanged, mostly in German or Russian, that the members of the group were strangers. It made me uneasy that no one did anything to conceal the location of my destination. Anton might wish to trust me, but Veronika did not, and she was not a careless woman. Once I had ascended this road, would I ever return?

I thought wistfully of my promise to telegraph Short should I need assistance, and wondered if I was really doing such a clever thing as I had thought.

These gloomy meditations were interrupted at last when we reached our journey's end. After fording a stream in a craggy valley, the road lifted us steeply to the peak of a lofty crag upon which stood what appeared, to my delight, to be a genuine castle. Not the mannered whimsy of Balmoral, but a real fortress: a sturdy wall of grey stone surrounding a broad lower courtyard in which were a great number of outbuildings full of the sound of hammers, voices, and industry. Upon a higher level of the crag was perched the hall: a handsome Renaissance house flanked to one side by a lofty grey tower of much more ancient provenance.

At first glance, in the gathering darkness, I thought there was something wrong with the roof of the house. A small forest of weathervanes had been erected there on the attic roof, and I thought there was a blue flicker within the windows, rather like lightning.

I shivered, and not only because the spring evening was biting cold.

The brake drew up at the foot of the steps leading to the house. Anton leaped to the pavement and turned to offer his hand as I stepped down.

"Welcome to Castle Sarkozy," he announced.

So this was Veronika's home! Others had flocked from the castle's outbuildings to welcome my fellow-travellers, but Anton led me up the steps into the house. Once, perhaps, the place had been very finely decorated, light and airy with its high ceilings and whitewashed walls. Now the carpets had been taken up and the curtains torn down, and furniture and paintings had been removed. Only the ceiling of the entrance hall, with its vividly painted coffering in red and blue and gold, remained to suggest the house's former glory. I supposed Veronika must have sold off as much of her late husband's property as she could, in order to fund her revolution.

Taking a candelabra from its place on a sideboard, Anton

started up the broad dark staircase, and I followed him. There was no gaslight in the house. "Are you taking me to see Veronika?" I asked in some trepidation.

"Perhaps later. First, there is a promise I must keep."

"A promise—to whom?"

"To you, Vera." He threw a glance over his shoulder, then shook his head with a wry smile. "You really don't remember."

At the top of the stairs he turned left and led me into a part of the house even plainer and barer, and darker, than that we had left. I perceived we were in the servant's quarters. Presently we came to the end of a long dark passage, at the termination of which was a sturdy-looking door in a grey stone wall, but Anton stopped short of this. Instead, he pushed open a door on our left to reveal a small room furnished with a narrow white bed. On the chair before the dressing-table was a pool of what seemed at first to be blood, dripping red and liquid to the floor.

It was not blood. It was a gown of red satin. Wasp-waisted, low-necked. In this place, in this bare and ugly room, it glowed like a lamp to attract light and warmth and all rich fluttering things.

"For me?" I murmured, trailing my fingers through that slippery red silk.

"Your dress for dinner," Anton said behind me. "Wear it."

With that, he set my valise on the floor and the candelabra on the small wooden dressing-table before closing the door, leaving me alone. I looked at the dress again, and again it shimmered like a pool of blood. I didn't like it, this sense that I had been expected—that Veronika had prepared for me, despite not trusting me—but there was nothing else to do. I had put myself into the power of the anarchists, and must play the game to the bitter end.

"Dinner," I murmured to myself. She would hardly provide me with a gown like this if I was meant to dine alone in a cell. That was heartening. I had fresh linen in my valise, and Veronika's people had thought to provide a jug of water and a bit of flannel. Shivering—for the place was as cold as the grave—I performed my ablutions and then stepped into the dress. It fit far better than I could have imagined, although it would not fasten around my waist, which was unfashionably thick.

I put my head into the hallway, where Anton was waiting for me.

"Might you happen to have such a thing as a lady's maid about you? If I'm to fit in this dress, I'll need to be laced a little tighter."

He hesitated—ran a nervous hand through his hair. "We don't have maids around here. Will I do?"

"Thanks." I turned, offering him my back. He did not touch me, and after a moment, I turned to look at him. "What? Have you never done this before, then?"

He was actually blushing. "I told you." His accent became a little thicker, a little more difficult to interpret. "There has never been anyone but you."

"Not even Ioanna?"

"Don't," he said, almost before the words had left my lips, and I knew they had been a mistake. There was a silence. His voice, which had been so warm a moment before, turned bleak. "You don't even remember Ioanna."

There was such pain in his words. "I'm sorry," I whispered. "Will you tell me about her, then?"

Anton began tugging briskly at the lacing of my corset. For

a while I thought he would not answer, but at last he muttered, "Veronika says you are not the Vera I loved."

"If you believed that, you would not have brought me here," I ventured. I tried the waistband of the skirt, and found that it would now close about my corset. "That's enough; thank you."

"Don't worry, I won't give you up so easily." He finished the job with a jerk—I imagined him tying off the cord with a workmanlike reef knot—and sat on the bed. "On the train, I wanted to tell you everything. But there was too much at risk. If I promised not to touch your aristos, you would know I was hunting your friend, the vampire."

I buttoned the skirt. The bodice of the dress was made of gleaming folds that crossed over the bosom and fastened at each side; a scrap of white chiffon covered the décolletage. In any other situation I would have been enchanted with the gown, and when I looked up, I found Anton gazing at me with wistful but unconcealed admiration.

"And now?" I asked, turning away to hide the colour in my cheeks.

"You must join the Vengeance."

I opened my valise to find a comb, the business giving me time to think. I must not seem to capitulate too easily. "Have I any choice?"

"Of course you have a choice. We are anarchists. We compel no one against their will," he said proudly. "But you *will* stay, because this is who you are."

The trust between us ran deeper than reason—perhaps this was what made me speak so plainly. "Is it really, Anton? Would I throw a bomb into a crowded room full of men and women who had done me no wrong—is *that* who I am?"

"This is revenant-talk," Anton growled. "For generations the monsters have murdered and oppressed us. No one has the right to expect us to follow *their* rules."

"The anarchists I met in London would have been surprised to hear themselves described as revenants," I said tartly. I dragged my comb through my hair and began to pin it up again, taking care to include the lock-picks and the wooden stake.

What a pity that neither my umbrella nor my revolver could be concealed likewise!

"Such people think that mere idle words will help us," Anton countered, scowling. "If that was true we would have been free long ago. Are you ready? Come."

"Where?"

"I have something to show you." He took up the candelabra and flung open the door, making the light flare. "You will understand, then."

I followed him into the passage, but before we had taken more than a few steps towards the main part of the castle, there came the harsh metallic sound of a key turning in a lock, and the shriek of long-disused hinges. Anton turned, raising the candelabra as the door set in stone ground open to admit Veronika, the Baroness Sarkozy herself.

She had changed from her sumptuous black velvet into another dress in black bombazine, plain but elegantly cut. As always, she carried her lacquered walking-stick. Two men followed on her heels, one of them carrying a crate of empty bottles like a milkman's, and the other what seemed to be a long flexible tube.

Veronika's eyebrow rose when she saw us. "Anton! Just who I wanted to see. Where are you going?"

"I am taking Vera upstairs."

"No. We have no time for distractions, and she is needed elsewhere."

"What do you mean?" Anton's voice was angry, but I could smell another emotion on him: fear. I found that I was quaking in my own boots. "You promised I would have the chance—"

"My plans have changed." Veronika signalled to her henchmen, who set down their burdens and advanced upon us.

Anton put himself in front of me, his voice deepening to a growl. "Your plans may have changed, but mine have not."

"Don't be dramatic, Lupei," Veronika said, but the tip of her nose paled with anger. "I have a revolution to arrange, and as it happens, Miss Sharp has become an essential ingredient."

"For what?"

"For the experiment. You don't mean to jeopardise this, do you, Lupei?"

He sent me an unhappy look. "No."

"Then stand aside."

Reluctantly, Anton did as he was told. The two henchmen seized me by each arm and marched me to the door from which they had just emerged. Beyond, the round space and winding stairs told me we stood in the old tower. It was quite dark in the tower, and silent, save for a sound so faint and distant that I thought I might be imagining it: the thud of a slow-beating heart.

Anton followed, holding the candelabra high. Veronika shut the door, and I heard the latch on the other side fall into place with a horribly final sound. Echoes ran up and down the stairs, and again I heard the slow-beating heart.

"Where are you taking me?" I asked, carried away on a

sudden tide of fear.

"What is this place?" Anton added, but neither Veronika nor her men answered.

Veronika had spoken of an experiment—what kind of experiment? I might have tried to resist, but I had a feeling that I was about to discover at least one of the secrets of this hidden castle, and so I followed—down into the darkness, into the heartbeat in the depths of Castle Sarkozy. I thought I smelled blood, and mice, and worse things; and then, just as I caught sight of a spark of light below, I caught the faint sharp scent of cedar, like a mothball that has rolled into a corner and been forgotten.

"Vasily!" I exclaimed. "What have you done with him?"

"You will see," Veronika said grimly. Then we descended into a small dark room so silent that I knew we must be underground. A lamp stood there beside a three-legged stool on which a guard sat, occupying himself with a pack of cards. Set in the living stone of the mountain before him was an iron gate that gave onto utter darkness.

It was a dungeon.

I set my feet, exerting all my strength. "Veronika, for the love of God, tell me what this means!"

"I thought you would be pleased to see your friend."

I remembered Vasily as I had last seen him: tethered into bed, pale and ghastly, feral as a wildcat and calling for blood. My lips felt numb. "He is not my friend!"

"Then why," Veronika said inexorably, "did you rush to his defence on the train?"

"I thought *you* were my friend," I whispered.

"Is that why you followed me to Budapest?" Her voice was mocking as she reached into my hair and drew out the wooden hairpin—my one defence—before nodding to the guard. "Open it up. Our guest of honour must not be allowed to go hungry."

"Veronika!" Anton roared, starting forward. "Have you gone mad? What do you think you are doing?"

Veronika gestured to the guard, who unslung the rifle from his shoulders, worked the bolt, and brought it up to point full at my breast. Anton halted, immobile, his face a mask of futile rage.

"The creature must be fed," she told him. "Do you propose we give it one of our own *compagnons?*"

"Let it starve," he said thickly.

"Then we have no revolution."

He looked at me again, and I saw with a thrill of horror that he was really tempted to sacrifice me.

"Did you think she came here for *you,* Lupei?" the Baroness added in a hard voice. "The Vera you once knew is gone. Fool! She is only using you to thwart *me*—to recover her blood-sucking aristo friend, and turn all of us over to the police for execution and worse!"

Anton turned to me. "Is it true?"

Reader, I could not deny it! Terror had unmade me. All I felt was that I owed this man my loyalty, and was even now planning to betray him.

He must have read my answer in my eyes, for he covered his face with his hands and turned away. As my captors forced me towards the cell door, I planted my feet, fighting in earnest.

"Shoot me," I cried. "Better that than *him.*"

A flicker of amusement kindled in the eyes of the man with the gun. Then the rifle roared—a terrible sound in that small place. I screamed as the bullet struck the stones before my feet. Chips of stone stung my skin—I smelled blood—my blood—God help me!

Anton roared.

Suddenly his fists were clenched in the other man's shirt, half lifting him from his feet. "Dog!" he cried in a language I knew but could not speak. "What do you think you are doing?"

"The people's vengeance," Veronika said coldly. "Watch yourself, Lupei."

With a gasp Anton released him, and the rifle fixed on me again.

"Here is the key," Veronika added. "Open the gate, but do not cross the salt."

Anton took the key. In the lamplight he was pale and sweating, and he did not move at once. His eyes fixed on me, and for a moment he seemed unable to speak.

I dared not speak either, but I sent him a look of mute entreaty.

He moistened his lips. "Does *he* know?" I could only imagine he meant the vampire, although what he meant the vampire to know I could not understand.

"I was with him all afternoon," Veronika said contemptuously.

Anton whispered a curse—or perhaps a prayer; and then he unlocked the iron gate and dragged the door open, not looking me in the eye. Impelled by the barrel of the rifle, I backed into the cell, feeling my heel drag through a line of salt on the threshold.

The salt ward, to keep a vampire in. I fell to my knees, ready to beg. "Please!"

The gate slammed in my face and locked. Anton's composure broke, and without a backward glance, he fled up the stairs. Veronika flashed a triumphant smile upon me, beckoned to her men, and followed.

Their footsteps died away. I heard a slow heartbeat in the dark behind me. Suddenly, it picked up speed, quick enough for a dance.

Suddenly, it was close behind me.

I turned with a shriek of terror. Vasily was there—right there—near enough to kiss. He was gaunt and bloodstained, raw skin showing through the rags of his shirt and burn-marks scarring his lips. Every shred of charm and civility was stripped away. In his eyes I saw only murder and starvation.

For an instant only. His eyes were fixed upon the naked sweep of my neck, and he fell upon me with bared teeth.

Chapter XIX.

Salt is its own kind of magic. The tribute of the sea, it gives flavour and preserves meat. Poured generously across a lintel, it acts as a barrier to vampires.

Seized by the handful and thrown into the creature's eyes, it results in a great deal of pain and an abrupt disruption of dining arrangements.

Vasily recoiled with a high, agonised scream. Clawing at his face, he scrambled away until his back hit the far wall of the tiny cell. I fell against the bars of the door, gasping at my narrow escape.

Behind me came the sound of hands clapping slowly.

I turned from the keening vampire to find that the guard was laughing at me. "Very good! Very clever, girl." Then he took a broom and swept the salt away from the lintel, until it formed a new barrier some distance from the bars, beyond my reach. In desperation I seized the broom as it passed—but it was made, not of wood from which I might fashion a stake, but from cheap tin, which would be useless against a vampire.

I let go angrily, and the guard laughed at me again.

Once he was done with his sweeping, the guard rattled the broom against the bars. "Not so fierce now, are we, blood-sucker? Get up and have your dinner! The People's Vengeance needs you alive and healthy!"

"You are not the People's Vengeance," I told the guard with a curl of my lip. "You are only a bully."

"And you're about to be vampire bait," the guard jeered, "so you should worry about yourself." Picking up his rifle and his lantern, he bowed ironically in my direction. "Your grace, madame,"—and he went away, up the stairs, taking the light with him and leaving me in the darkness, alone with the monster.

I sat pressed against the bars of the gate, listening to my hectic heartbeat and Vasily's slow, labouring one—my swift shallow breaths, and his tormented sobs. It was silent in here, and utterly dark, but I could smell a little cold air moving about like a zephyr. I thought there might be a window somewhere high up, that might admit a little light when morning came—*if* morning came.

I waited an interminable time—shivering in the cool liquid folds of the dress like blood—but not even my eyes could distinguish any hint of shadow or light in the utter darkness enfolding us. I found my thoughts straying once again to Short. Someday, no doubt, he would ask himself what had become of me, and perhaps he would feel injured a little that I had never sent to assure him of my wellbeing. If only he knew how devoutly I wished to see him!

Too soon, the vampire's cries of pain faded away. I shuddered, aware that I was alone here and helpless. When Vasily's pain receded, his hunger would return, and I now had no way to protect myself, no way even to see him coming. How I wished for my umbrella!

I clasped my knees to my chest and sat still for as long as I dared, willing him to forget I was there. But as his breath evened out, I heard a long, drawn-out sniff. A shard of stone kicked up by the bullet had stung my arm—a mere scratch, but the blood was slick and hot on my skin, rank in my own nostrils. I dared not think how powerfully it must call to the monster opposite me.

Any perverse pleasure I had once found in the thought of becoming this creature's prey was long vanished. Fantasy had dissolved in the face of brutal reality, leaving naught but blind terror.—Dreamer though I may be, I was never a fool; not where Vasily was concerned.

I heard him shift in the dark, and the words burst out of me: "Vasily! It's me, Liz Sharp!"

The movement ceased, giving way to intent, listening silence.

"Remember me," I whispered, like a prayer. "Remember the train. I tried to save you."

For an endless moment I held my breath. There came another long sniff, and a voice that creaked as though it had not been used in some time.

"Miss Sharp?"

"From the train. Do you remember?"

A sobbing breath. "My eyes."

"Yes, I'm sorry about that. I didn't want you to bite me."

There was a longer silence. "I am...not myself."

I could not afford to trust him. Cunning as he was, he might simply be afraid of what other weapons I might yet be concealing, though in truth I had none, not even my wooden hairpin.

All this time I had wondered what he would do to me if he really wished to eat, and now I knew.

I must try to show him it was worth his while to let me live.

"They want your blood for some experiment," I warned him, thinking of the empty glass bottles I had seen in the passage above. "They must already have used the lot they siphoned off on the train, but until you feed, they can take no more. Veronika has three hundred men out there spoiling for revolution. If you drain me, you'll only help them."

He took a slow, rattling breath. "No. Not true."

"What?"

"You were werewolf-bitten." Vasily spoke with great deliberation, as though his mind was fuzzy, and he had to concentrate very hard to get the words out. "Your blood is different. Stronger."

"What?"

"Give me your blood." His whisper was hoarse, urgent. He dragged himself towards me, and I pressed back against the bars. "Give me your blood, and both of us can escape."

"No—please!"

His hands closed trembling on my shoulders, the long nails digging into my skin. His breath was cold and smelled of pine and carrion. "I will not kill you. I will take you away from here."

"No! There is another way." I peeled his hands off my shoulders and scuttled sideways, nearly knocking over a water-jar that stood there. "We'll work together. You bend the bars on this door. I'll sweep the salt aside."

"The bars," he said vaguely. "I can't. I've tried. Without blood, I am weak."

"Then I'll pick the lock! See—I still have my hairpins. You can't have my blood."

"Why?"

"Because you don't need it," I sobbed, "and I won't give it."

That was all the explanation I could give. Perhaps, if I had not been I…but someone had taken my blood once against my will, and from that moment I would never choose to give it freely, certainly not to this monster. You will laugh at me, you will ask why I could not bend my resolution even to save my life. The truth is that never in my life had my resolve been more fierce than it was at this moment. It is not only the choices we make that define us, but the choices we find ourselves incapable of making: and I was incapable, in that moment, of consenting to his bite. The fact that it was to save my own life made it still more a question of force, not less.

I said, "Ask of me anything but this."

There was a silence. I sensed him slumping against the wall beside me, close enough to send cold revulsion scrambling across my skin. His voice faded to a mumble, and I realised just how fragile this moment of lucidity might be. "Without blood I cannot get us past the Vengeance."

"It doesn't matter. Two people can't go missing like this. Someone will come looking for us. Hush. Rest. I'll make a plan."

He sighed. When he spoke again after a moment, there were dreams in his voice. "Don't leave me, Miss Sharp."

"I won't." I sat stiff and unhappy for a moment. Why must he be so close? Did he mean to inure me to his touch—to make me easier prey, when the time came to drink my blood?

The thought was terrifying, but then it occurred to me—like a voice whispering in the one calm, quiet corner of my mind—that in this cramped place I was hardly going to achieve anything by trying to keep him at arm's length. And then—not only might I become inured to his touch, but he to mine.

I needed him clear-headed, not driven to madness by the

scent of fresh blood and the beat of a frightened heart. I needed him to think of me as something more than prey. If I was to escape this place with my life, I needed him to think of me as a friend.

I took a deep, calming breath and touched his head where it was bowed against his knees. He flinched, seizing my wrist with a snarl. My pulse thundered against his grasp. I could feel it, he could feel it, and I heard a sound rather like a trill of excitement from his chest.

"Vasily," I said very gently. Only terror could have kept my voice so calm. "Don't drain me, please."

That brought him to himself again. He released my hand and inched away. "Don't touch me," he said thickly.

"Why not?"

"Only my dainties touch me."

I did not know why those words should sink a dull pain into my heart. Likely it was the thought of never knowing human touch that was innocent or generous—without fear, without predation. It was also my own despair. Was there *no* way I could conduct myself, that would not cast me as his prey? Let him sink back into the mindless hunger that gripped him when first I entered this room, and I would certainly die.

"Surely your mother touched you," I said.

"She died when I was young." A pause. "I think my father ate her."

"A nurse, then."

"My…nurse." He was silent a moment. "I would lay my head in her lap, and she would stroke my hair until I slept."

I closed my eyes and sent a desperate prayer to my Maker. Then I crawled across the stones and touched his shoulder. "Come here, then. Lie down."

At first when I put my arms around him, he shivered. "You don't know what you are doing."

"Hush," I said. "Lay down your head."

Just then, I think his mind was too weak to resist. He murmured another protest, but did as I said, and laid his head in my lap. Gently I touched his head: the sweep of matted hair, the hollow curve of his cheek. I remembered the first time I had seen Vasily, sleek and self-satisfied beneath the lights of a London ballroom. I had thought of him then as a panther, soft-footed, none the less savage for his perfect self-command.

And now I had the wild beast himself in my lap. Was I mad? Did I really know what I was doing?

I took another slow breath—traced the scars I had seen defacing his mouth. "Who did this?" I whispered.

"I was thirsty," he mumbled. "They put saltwater in my jug."

Oh, the bullies, thought I. Was justice worth anything when those who sought it behaved no better than beasts themselves ?—Repressing a shudder, I stroked his hair again. "Everything will be all right, you'll see. Someone will come for us. Sleep."

To my amazement, he did. As the hours passed, cold and the vampire's weight stole the feeling from my body, leaving half of me numb and the other half aching. I felt the tendrils of the draught play across my face, and prayed that when morning came there would be enough sunlight to see by.

I had already lived far longer than I expected when the night began, and I had a notion that Vasily's appetite might be more easily managed in the daylight. Once the sun rose, once there was light, I might try my hairpins on the lock.—But then what? Walls, and a courtyard, and three hundred men. Vasily was right: we could hardly battle our way through that—and even if we escaped by stealth, there would still be the mountains to face.

Despite my brave words, I must face the truth: no rescue was coming. Short had asked me to telegraph if I was in trouble, but from the moment I had met Anton in Budapest I had been watched too closely to send news. As for May, she did not care if I lived or died.

I had not seen her face once since she sent me away. In Strasbourg, I had watched from the hotel window as she went walking with her mother. On my last day in that city I had gone to pay my respects before my departure, and although the Duchess tried to convince her to see me, May had refused. Nothing abashed, the Duchess begged me to keep her apprised of my address in Budapest. She was sure May would relent; she was sure I would be asked to return.

I knew better than to hope. May was too loyal to break a friendship easily, and too proud to quickly relent. No rescue was coming. Sooner or later, Vasily's madness would return. I could only hold him off so long.

There was one other possibility of escape, one weak point in my prison—but that was a desperate hope, and had failed me each time I had hoped to employ it. I could not put my trust in *that.*

Chapter XX.

Towards morning I must have slept. Upon awakening I found that I had slid sideways along the wall and was lying crushed into the damp, filthy corner. By the dim light struggling in at the window high above—really more of a narrow vent than a window—I saw that Vasily no longer lay with his head in my lap. Instead he kneeled above me.

"Look at me, you dark-black eyes," he crooned. His voice slid into something between a chant and a song in his native tongue; and that I didn't understand at all.

"Vasily? What are—what are you—"

"I see mourning for my soul in you, Ioanna…Look in my eyes."

I was already looking. The shadow of madness was back in his blood-red eyes. He touched me then, running a finger down the curve of my neck. Our surroundings softened and changed. I lay upon a divan in a garden grotto. A pool of water splashed in a tiled bowl and in the distance, birds were singing. Only the thin grey light remained the same, and the cold in my bones. Vasily bent over me. "The sun is coming up," he rambled. "Let me kiss you before it rises."

He leaned closer.

Why not let him kiss me? His teeth gleamed between his

lips, long and sharp. I wondered what it would be like to kiss that terrible mouth. I imagined the razor-sharp teeth cutting my lips—the kiss turning bloody. Such risk—such thrill—

I shut my eyes with a gasp. It was wrong. It was not my own heart speaking thus—it was not sleep that held me in its grasp. It was something else, the compulsion of his terrible eyes.

Not today.

My skin was hot, not with desire but shame. Fine indeed was the line between daydream and nightmare! But his spell was broken now—if indeed it could ever have tempted my better judgement. At the shiver of his breath along my skin, I opened my eyes. Vasily's shirt was in tatters and the raw wound across his heart had not healed in the three days since Anton had peeled the flesh away. I had no salt left, but I had this. With clawed fingers, I raked my nails across the raw wound.

He recoiled with a cry, and I pulled myself to numb, aching feet.

"Vasily, Vasily! Remember, it's me!"

As the blood rushed back into my limbs with exquisite pain, I clutched the bars of the gate, gasping through the agony. But at least the blood was still inside my body; and Vasily stared at me through his own pain, and knew me.

"What did I do?"

I swallowed convulsively. Anger sparked to my tongue. "Oh, I think you know."

"I..." He attempted no apology. "The sun will rise, and you'll be safe."

"For how long?"

"Until it goes down. Talk to me. Don't let me forget who

you are."

"All right." I knelt so that my eyes were at a level with his, though I was not fool enough to look at him directly. "You called me Ioanna before."

He blenched. "Oh… Not that. Anything else."

"Then what was that place you showed me?"

"It was…a place on my estate in Moldavia…"

"You used to meet her there?"

"On the summer afternoons."

"Who was she? Was she related to Anton?"

He looked at me with a flicker of resentment. "I told you, no."

I was still too angry with him to make accommodations. "Well, I can't think of anything else to ask."

Vasily looked down at his hands—seemed to come to a decision. "She was his cousin. She was born the summer before me, and she was—she was beautiful." His voice went hard. "I killed her."

The way he said those words—they were remorseless, calculating. As though he meant to do it; as though he had lulled the girl into a false sense of security before carrying out his bloody plan.

As though he meant to warn me that he would do the same to me.

But then his voice softened. "I killed the only woman I've ever loved."

I did not know if I could trust him—I had no choice but to trust him. I must know why Anton was so implacably angry. So I said, "Tell me."

He looked away. "All that summer, we met in the grotto in the afternoon, between the end of my lessons and the start of her milking. I swore I loved her. I *did* love her. A boy of seventeen gives his heart entirely and in those days I was not a—monster. I said I would make her my wife, but Ioanna laughed at me. 'Foolish boy,' she said, 'your parents will never let you marry the milkmaid.' I knew she was right, but in those days I did not know much about the condition. Neither of us did. So Ioanna told me the story of Vasilisa the Humble. Vasilisa wove cloth so fine that the tsar himself wished to marry her. But Vasilisa was only a peasant girl; the tsar's boyars would not agree to the marriage unless she became noble like themselves. So Vasilisa opened her veins and her blood drained. And then the tsar opened his veins, and Vasilisa drank. And when his blood ran through her veins, the tsar's noble blood ennobled Vasilisa, and so the boyars agreed that their love was true and that Vasilisa was noble enough to marry the tsar."

He stopped and shivered. Into the light that illuminated our prison came a tinge of pale gold. Vasily's teeth seemed less long and sharp than they had been, and his eyes less red.

I wanted to hear the rest of the story. "This made her into a vampire?"

"For the girl in the story, it did," Vasily said bitterly. "But not my love—not Ioanna. She was so sure it would work, and I—I did not know. I drained her blood, and it made me what I am today. But Ioanna, it made her dead, dead as a stone. I dripped my blood between her pale lips, and wept for her to awaken, but she did not."

"And Anton blames you," I said numbly. Much as I distrusted Vasily on principle, it never occurred to me to doubt him in this. His story had the ring of truth—it echoed in his eyes, his scent, the beat of his pulse.

He gave one of those foreign little shrugs. "He had loved his cousin very dearly. And he knew more about my condition than I did. He did not believe I could have been so stupid; he believed I must have deceived her. Of course, later I found out that if that sort of thing works at all, it is for the daughters of great lords, never for serfs."

I blinked, suddenly recalling what Mary Adelaide had told me in Paris—that there was a way for a morganatic princess to make the change. *Most unpleasant,* she had said, and I could well believe it. "I don't quite understand why it has to be that way at all. If it takes only a taste of human blood for one of your kind to make the change, then—"

"Oh, it takes more than *that,*" Vasily interrupted. "It takes lifeblood."

The thoughts in my head congealed to jelly. "What?"

"Power like ours is not given freely, my dear."

"What, werewolves too?"

"From the sirens of Denmark to the dragons of China—and yes, the werewolves of England. What else did you think?"

But that meant the Queen—and the Prince of Wales—and *George* had all become murderers. I clapped a hand to my mouth. I was not entirely foolish, of course. I assumed that most royalties who made the change did so by taking a life, but I had thought—I had *hoped*—that there was a better way; a way to become a monster without being truly monstrous.

Of course there was not. How much else of what I knew was wrong?

"Now you know why Lupei hates me," Vasily said, touching his raw chest. There was still not much light in the cell, but I could see the utter seriousness in his eyes, which had now lost the tint of blood entirely. "And that is also why you should give me your blood—soon, tonight, before the madness returns and I kill you. Spare me the burden of carrying *your* name as penance forevermore."

I considered the wisdom of pointing out that the only person who could spare him that burden was himself, and decided against it. "That won't be necessary," I said.

Now that Vasily seemed restored—for a while, at least—to sanity, I reached into my hair and withdrew my remaining hairpins. Going to the door, I thrust my arms between the bars to get at the lock. This turned out to be a padlock on a chain, but when I pulled it around so that the lock faced me, my heart sank.

It was a Bramah.

They had trained us in lock-picking at Saint Botolph's. The hairpins I wore had come from Saint Botolph's too, specially made to get me past doors the anarchists didn't want opened. I had spent hours at the hospital practicing on Chubbs, Bramahs, and Hobbses. After those, there were not many locks that baffled me—certainly not the Bramah.

Not given enough time. Last time I tried, it had taken me two weeks of steady tinkering to open one. Each lock was unique, rendering shortcuts futile. And now—I did not have two weeks.

"Something the matter?" Vasily asked behind me. I startled, nearly dropping the padlock.

"No, no," I said quickly, "only I was trying to remember what I know of this sort of lock."

Taking my picks, I slipped them into the keyhole and set to work. Vasily leaned against the wall beside me, watching my every movement. To divert his attention, I said: "How did you end up a prisoner, anyway? Don't tell me you allowed

Anton to march into your compartment on the train that day and put laudanum in your tooth-glass."

Vasily uttered a mirthless laugh. His eyes were half-closed, but beneath the lazy, drooping eyelids he watched me with icy shrewdness. "It was the Baroness. She said a little bird told her I wished to speak with her."

I touched the tip of my tongue to my lips. "I owed you no secrecy, as well you knew. I never consented to be your servant."

"Oh," Vasily said with satisfaction, "believe me, I would never have whispered to the little bird had I not intended the little bird to whisper to the Baroness. What I didn't expect was to be welcomed to the meeting with a cup of laudanum-laced coffee, nor to waken hours later strapped to my berth with Anton Lupei sneering at me through the undergrowth. It seems," he added meditatively, "that I underestimated the spectacular Verónika. But, *bozhe moi!* it was worth it."

I had meant to ask why he had been so anxious to speak to the baroness, but that last comment caught me by surprise.

"Worth it? *This?*"

"This will be the saving of my Empire." A look of reverence crossed his face—the devotion of a fanatic. "For my Tsar and for Holy Russia, I would suffer the same again and more."

"Time enough to arrange that when we manage to escape."

He gave me faint, predatory smile that made all my skin crawl. "Oh, *I* mean to escape."

At that moment, footsteps echoed on the stair and I looked up to see Anton with a lamp in one hand and a jug in the other.

I let go of the lock and stood back, concealing the picks in my hand. Anton stared as though he had seen a ghost.

"Vera—." He stopped himself—swallowed, and set his face

like flint. "What's wrong with the monster? Don't tell me you managed to kill him."

I didn't answer. Anton came to the bars and looked through, receiving a hungry glare from Vasily. His lip curled, and he turned to me. "Did the two of you make some sort of bargain?"

"Bargain, pah!" Vasily spat. "Whatever you're doing with my blood, I want no part in it. I'd rather starve."

"It's already too late." Anton smiled grimly. "Doctor Livius runs his first experiment tonight. He expects it to be a great success—and if so, there will be no difficulty in finding other vampires."

"We are Romanovs," Vasily said with pride. "None of us will betray our emperor!"

Natural curiosity, as well as my self-assigned mission, prompted me to ask: "And what experiment is that?"

"If you are still alive when we have triumphed, I will tell you." He didn't look at me, and I felt an instinctive pang. Evidently he felt that I had betrayed his trust; and I supposed I had. But, the dickens!—what else could I have done?

I tried another approach. "Since I have lasted this long, may I see Veronika?"

"She has gone away to Budapest. It makes no difference, though. This is the only way you can serve the People's Vengeance now." Anton pointed. "Bring me that jug and I'll fill it."

I did so, and found him looking down at the lock with a frown. "You ought to know that lock is unpickable."

I didn't want Vasily to hear this. "No lock is unpickable."

Anton shook his head. "Even if you have the skill, you will be dead long before you open it."

"Why, do you mean to starve me?"

He sent me a wary look. "I will bring you some food."

"I also want to wash. I am filthy."

"Use the jug. It's full."

"In front of the vampire?" I gripped the bars. "I may no longer be the Vera you loved, but you might show me some kindness for her sake. I have been here all night. Let me out, only for an hour or two, so that I can eat and wash."

"You think I am stupid? You want to escape."

"I don't," I said, quite honestly. Far better to win Anton over. I dropped my voice. "I want what I've always wanted—only to speak to you. If what you say about the experiment is true, then Veronika lied when she said I was necessary for the success of her revolution. Please—for Vera's sake."

He swallowed hard and looked from the lock, to Vasily, to me. All his bluster had been just that—bluster. In truth, he hated to see me end up as food for Vasily—that much was clear. And with Veronika out of the castle, perhaps—perhaps—

"No." He turned away.

In another moment he would be gone. "Wait!" I cried, clutching at a new idea. He stopped, but did not turn to face me. I whispered:

"Is it true? what Vasily told me about Ioanna?"

He turned, ghastly pale in the light of the lamp he carried. *"What did he tell you about Ioanna?"*

I rattled the bars. "Let me out. Let us speak of it in private."

Conflict—longing—simmering wrath chased themselves across his blunt features. Then, without a word, he snatched the lamp and went away.

When the door above us closed, clawlike hands grabbed the bars to each side of me, rattling the gate. With a shriek, I turned to look up into Vasily's eyes. Was the madness on him again?—but no: his eyes were narrow, clear, and dark with anger.

"You want him to let you leave? You want to leave *me?*"

To think I had begun to pity him! "I have no intention of leaving you to fuel their revolution."

"Abandon me here," he snarled, as though he had not heard me, "and when I find you I will tear your head from your shoulders and use your blood to bathe in."

"You were better company when you were out of your mind." I pushed at his chest. "Step aside. I need to work on this lock."

"The lock is useless." His hand fastened on my throat. "Swear to me you won't abandon me, or I'll strangle you now and drain the blood from your dead body tonight." A pale, shiny, toothy sort of smile. "I can't think why I didn't do it before the sun rose just now."

Every nerve was on the verge of panic, but I must remain calm. "I promise I'm trying to save both of us. Perhaps it's true that the lock is useless. That means right now—until May sends someone to find us—the weak point in this prison is Anton Lupei."

He scowled.

"He's going to bend," I said with more confidence than I felt. "He'll let me out, and I'll gain his confidence, and then I'll use it to free you. I swear it. All right?" Remembering my resolve from last night, I reached up to brush back the lock of hair that fell over his eyes. He backed away, affronted.

"What are you doing?"

"You told me that's what your nurse used to do when you were a child."

"I never told you that." His voice was full of flat certainty.

"You did—last night."

His eyes narrowed. Then, suddenly, he burst into startled laughter. "Well, I'm not a child any more, Miss Sharp."

There was a silence as we both recalled just how far removed we were from whatever sunny youthful days we once had known. Vasily looked about the stone cell with a sigh, and then dropped back into a crouch against the stone wall and looked up at me with a thin, hard smile.

"Talk to me, Miss Sharp. Make me forget where I am."

I was still the jester, then. A role for which I was uniquely well-suited, after all. I retrieved the padlock and gave myself up to badinage and lock-picking for the next goodness knows how long.

When the light was beginning to fade, and my fingers were cramped with the effort of the tiny motions needed to coax the lock, and my voice had become hoarse and anxious as sunset approached and with it danger—then Anton returned, stepped over the barrier of salt, and unlocked the cell door.

Chapter XXI.

"Answer me one question," Anton demanded. There was something curiously vulnerable in his weather-beaten countenance. "In Budapest, you told me you knew you had loved me once. Was *that* a lie?"

Hastily, I concealed my lock-picks within the folds of my skirt. "Would you believe me if I said it was not?"

"Yes, I would."

Again, that curious vulnerability.

"Then yes," I said, "that part was true. And as for the rest, it's as I said on the train—I don't want to see you become a killer, that's all."

He gave me a searching look before standing back and beckoning me to follow him from the cell.

Even with the door open, the salt must have presented an insuperable barrier to the vampire, for Vasily made no attempt to rush the opening. As I stepped over the threshold, I looked into his eyes, pleading with him to understand the message I sent with my glance: *I will not abandon you.*

Then Anton locked the gate again. As the lock turned, suddenly I found myself sweating and trembling, crushing the red satin dress between my fingers.

"Come," Anton said, jerking his head towards the stairs. I

followed almost blindly, for there seemed to be a shadow over my vision. I climbed a little way before the shaking became too much for me and I found myself kneeling on the steps only trying to breathe—letting the terror I had repressed these past twenty-four hours roll over me in sickening waves.

The lantern-light fluttered, and Anton dropped into a crouch beside me. "Vera? What's wrong?"

"Don't," I rasped, "don't touch me—I'm sorry, I don't..."

There was an awful silence. "What did he do to you?" Anton asked, his voice a low forbidding growl.

"He?—Nothing," I gasped. "It was *you* who did this to me; you and Veronika."

He drew in a sharp breath. But he didn't have the nerve to pretend he didn't know what I meant. "I should never have brought you here. This is my fault. I should have known you were not ready."

My fit of the horrors faded a little, and I glanced up to see him looming over me, lit up like a ghost with the lamp he carried. There was something not altogether comforting about the look in his dark eyes, but one question had tormented me all day, and I must ask it of *someone.*

"Is it true," I whispered, "that they must take a life in order to make the change?"

"Of course. Didn't you know?"

I shook my head.

"So he told you *that* much of the truth, at least," Anton growled. "Did he tell you how he tricked my cousin with words of love, then murdered her?"

"Something like that." I drew a deep, sobbing breath. "Don't send me back to that place."

I would return for Vasily, but I would not offer myself up

to him.

Anton straightened, not meeting my eyes. "That decision is out of my hands now."

"You're an anarchist. You don't answer to Veronika or anyone."

"Veronika and I may not always see eye to eye, but we want the same things. The Vengeance is greater than any of us. You must see that, now. The monsters are killers by nature... and I cannot sacrifice the revolution, even for you. You must understand that."

I found, to my surprise, that I did understand it. I found myself no longer sure of right and wrong. Veronika had said that justice was worth anything, and now that I knew just how many lives were at stake...

Had Mary Adelaide knowingly lied to me, in Paris, when she said a taste of human blood would create a monster?

And George must know—why had George never mentioned this fact? Whom had he killed? Did he regret the sacrifice? Did he tell himself it was justified?

Was Short in on the secret?—No, I could not bear it if *he* had known, and concealed it from me.

"Come," Anton added, offering his hand. "There is more for you to see."

As Anton guided me up the stairs, I was able to pick through the questions flocking my mind. "I take it Veronika is still away. When will she return?"

"Tonight, for the experiment."

The experiment for which I had been sacrificed to a monster! "And what experiment might that be?"

"You shall see it." We came to the landing, and the door that led into the house. Anton nodded to my scars. "It means justice—for these. It means showing the monsters they cannot continue to kill."

My throat was dry, but deep down, I could not help feeling a disloyal spark of hope. "What do you mean? How?"

His eyes blazed with purpose. "Wait and see."

He unlocked the door to let me through. This time, when I entered the small room I had used as a dressing-room the night before, I found a fresh gown laid out for me, together with fresh under-things, and—joy of joys—*hot* water in the jug.

I lifted the white dress and noticed, rather impressed, that this was also of a perfect size for me, though it might have been five years out of date. "Where *did* you get all these dresses?"

He stiffened, and some of the triumphal glow faded from his eyes. "That was yours, once."

"Mine?" So many questions flocked to my lips. I dropped the white dress, a little frightened I might grime it with my filthy hands. My dress. It was made from an inexpensive cotton, but with real skill and artistry, and when I looked more closely I saw how carefully it must have been washed and starched, for some of the lace around the shoulders had become a little worn. That told me a little of who I had been, once—neither very rich nor very poor, careful of my things, with a taste for simple prettiness in my dress.

None of the other questions mattered, really, like how a dress of mine happened to be here at all. My voice shook a little. "What, all of this, mine?"

"Not all. I raided Veronika's boudoir for the rest of it. Property is theft!" He winked.

"That's nonsensical," I said, "since the concept of theft presupposes a right to property in the first place."

To my surprise, he shook his head proudly. "There's the Vera I knew."

The door closed behind him, leaving me feeling rather startled by this glimpse into my past.

The white dress fitted me more easily than did the red satin, and I was able to dress myself and even brush and rearrange my hair before a knock came at the door again. When I opened it, I caught my breath.

Anton, too, had changed. He now wore grey trousers, a fresh shirt and waistcoat and—marvellously—a stiff collar and tie. He'd even brushed his hair. The effect, fine as it was, was somewhat spoiled by the rumpled appearance of the garments, and the fact that they had evidently been tailored for someone smaller across the shoulders than Anton.

"You look lovely," he said, when he saw me.

"So do you," I said waspishly, "almost bourgeois." I felt adrift in the wreckage of what I had thought I knew of the world, and I did not want Anton to think I would throw in my lot with him so easily. Nor could I forgive him for standing by while I was thrown into Vasily's cell.

He offered his arm. "You don't remember the promise I made..."

I laid my fingertips lightly on his offered arm. "No, but you might tell me about it."

"I promised you once that when the revolution came, we would dress in fine clothing and dine together like rich people." He led me into the central part of the house, through a magnificent marble-tiled vestibule at the head of the great stairs, and thence into the dining-room beyond.

It was a magnificent room, the one part of the house still furnished like a palace. Wooden parquetry covered the floor, and wooden strapwork and pendants decorated the ceiling. A marble-fronted fireplace boasted a blazing fire that warmed the immense apartment, decorated by massive landscape paintings, while opposite the fireplace, three immense windows looked out upon a twilit sky. Down the centre of the room ran an immense table. Two places were laid across from each other near the head—polished silverware, sparkling crystal, snowy napkins, a cobwebbed wine-bottle.

"Tonight I keep my promise," Anton told me. "Tonight we will eat like kings."

There was an odd sort of ring to his voice, and it struck me that he carried himself like a man who knows he is destined to conquer the world; it was not the kind of posture one would expect from a common labourer. A premonitory chill ran through my veins.

"And the revolution?" I asked, keeping my voice light. Something very strange was happening here in Castle Sarkozy, but I could not push too hard if I wished to know what it was.

Anton went to the table and picked up the wine-bottle. "Step over to the window."

I heard the swish and gurgle of wine and smelled the aroma of a finely aged Shiraz as I crossed the room. Great sweeping curtains in green velvet bordered each of the three windows. There was something beyond one of them—something immense, blocking the light that filtered through the last of the windows. Suddenly, my heart was in my throat. I drew back the filmy veil that masked the window—and there it was.

Massive, buoyant, rising by gentle increments from the courtyard below, where workers cheered and whistled and strained at the ropes that tethered their immense vessel to *terra firma.* As the great cigar-shaped bladder rose past the window, the skiff slung beneath it came in view. It was shaped rather like a flat-bottomed boat, and it was immense—why, there must be at least two decks inside that thing.

I threw myself against the window in delight. I had longed to see one of these at close quarters. "An airship?"

"It was our own Doctor Livius who invented the airship," Anton said, approaching me. He handed me one of the glasses, and clinked the rim of his own against mine. "His patent was stolen by the patron who funded him, and he hasn't received a penny in return for his work. So, we arranged for him to enjoy *some* of the proceeds, at least."

"You *stole* an airship?"

"It would be more accurate to say that we restored the product of the good doctor's labours to his own control." For a moment, there wasn't the slightest ghost of a smile on his lips. Then they twitched. "In fact, we stole three. This is only a test flight."

I nearly choked on my wine. "Three airships? The dickens, that's...extraordinary."

He nodded. Perhaps he heard the undercurrent of panic in my voice as I tried to imagine what three hundred desperate men might do with three airships of this sort. "I don't agree with everything Veronika has done. But...this could break the stranglehold the monsters have on this world. Isn't that worth a little revolution?"

Break the monsters' power—stop the traffic in human blood, do away with the revenants, end the royal murders forever. It might be worth a great deal. "I want to see it," I said huskily. "I do. But not through violent means."

"We have tried peaceful means," said Anton. "We said: we

are suffering. Give us freedom, give us hope. They did not listen the first time, nor the time after that. What makes you think they might listen next time?"

Following the day's revelations, I saw his point. "The social contract," I began.

Anton shook his head. "The contract has already been broken, and not by us. The war has already begun, but we were not the aggressors. Now we must look to our own defence."

The door opened to admit a divine aroma and I turned away from Anton with a sense of relief, for his words went to my heart and I was afraid that in another moment I might find myself agreeing to goodness knew what carnage. The pair of servants that entered with the hot dishes of food were decidedly scruffy-looking, and the young girl poked her tongue out at me. Instantly, I poked my own back. After that she smiled cheerfully, and unloaded her plates onto the table without upsetting them into my seat or lacing them with arsenic. Her male companion was more surly. Slamming his dishes onto the table, he muttered, "Grub's up," and withdrew.

As Anton drew out my seat, I bit my lip to hold back the laughter. "What I wouldn't give to see *them* at Balmoral."

We sat. I could scarcely bring myself to unfold my napkin or wait for Anton to serve me from the covered dishes: the scent of the food reminded me that I had eaten nothing for the last day, and very little the day before that. For a while all I could think of was the dinner.

"So, this is an anarchist feast?" I said, when the meal was finished and I could think again. "No footman to wave each new dish under our noses! It's a wonder we did not starve."

"In the new world, everyone will dine like this."

"The ragout was very good."

"That's Maria's work." I supposed he was speaking of the girl with the tongue. "She used to work as a cook in Prague, but her husband beat her, and after she left him she was unable to get a respectable position. She is much happier here." He took a mouthful of wine, swished it around his mouth rather inelegantly, and gulped it down. Meal finished, he pushed his plate away and leaned forward. "You belong with us, Vera. This revolution—you have earned your place at its head every bit as much as the rest of us." He looked at my scars. "More than most of us."

It would be so easy to say yes. I *wanted* what he promised—peace, dignity, a new world where we were free to look the monsters in the eye and call them what they were.

"You don't agree with our methods?" he went on. "Then why not wait for the revolution to end? The *compagnons* might not like it, but we would not be anarchists if we did not allow everyone the freedom of their own convictions. Wait here in Castle Sarkozy. A month, a year, and everything will be over. You can't stop the revolution, but you don't have to fight it, either."

So this was the offer he meant to make when he descended into that prison, my own private hell. I thought of that little suffocating room, of the constant high-pitched scream of terror that had gone on and on and on in my mind every minute that I had been there. I did not want to go back.

But I had made a promise to Vasily—and perhaps it was only guilt, but I still felt responsible for May. I had a duty to her; a duty I had overlooked for my own gain once already. No matter what excuses my heart made for Anton, no matter how unmoored I felt in the wake of Vasily's revelation, I must not forget that I had seen Anton's war in the Café Terminus, and I wanted no part in it.

"And then?" I whispered, trying to conceal my doubts. "When the revolution is over?"

"And then I'll come back for you." Quiet confidence rang in his voice, as though in his eyes, the victory was already won.

I choked back the questions that rose behind my teeth—*what are the airships for? How can you be so certain? What aren't you telling me?*

"I'll come back for you," he went on. "You promised to marry me once. I won't hold you to that; I ask only that you give me a chance. I'll teach you to love me again. We can have the life we always dreamed of, the life they stole from you."

He lifted his hand—then hesitated, as though afraid to touch me.

"No," I murmured, "do."

He touched my cheek again. His hand was roughened from hard work, not a gentleman's hand at all, but it was warm, and gentle, and loving. His roughened fingers traced my roughened scars, and I closed my eyes to keep the tears from spilling over. Since I had left Saint Botolph's, two princes had seen my scars as an invitation to drink my blood. To everyone else I had been a leper, an outcast, a barely-restrained monster. Even Short had struggled to see me as anything but damaged goods.

Anton saw none of that. He saw the wrong that had been done me, and he wanted to set the world upright again. As his hand slid along the rough striations on my cheek, I put up my own to catch it—to hold it there, warm and gentle. For a moment I felt memory hovering on the brink of unveiling, as unbearable as a forgotten word on the tip of the tongue.

I had loved this man, and he had loved me. My heart knew

it, though my head did not.

"Whoever did this to me," I whispered, "will you bring him to me?"

I half hoped the answer would be yes. If it had been, who can say what I might have chosen then?

Anton shook his head. "I know who murdered my cousin Ioanna. I have never known who took the woman I loved. Sometimes I wish there was a God—or at least a God who cared about such things."

I released his hand and it slipped away, leaving cold defeat behind. "What *do* you know, then?"

"It happened in Stuttgart," he began.

"Stuttgart," I repeated mechanically. I had always been told it happened in London. But—Stuttgart! "It might have been anyone." One of the Württemberg family—or any of a dozen German princes passing through, as travellers or as guests.

There was a delicate irony in the fact that May herself was of Württemberg stock. Was that known, at Saint Botolph's? Did they think it safer to put me into the service of a Württemberg, to bind my heart to my duty lest I think of confronting a member of the family for vengeance?

Anton went on: "You were travelling with an aunt, returning from London to meet your father in Nuremberg. It was late when you arrived. You went to your lodging-house, and your aunt knocked on the door, but there was no answer at first. She went around the house to find a back-door, and just as her knock was answered, she heard your scream from the road. When she returned, there was nothing in the street but the print of a wolf's foot in the mud. …And then I saw you two years later in Paris."

But then—I was not at fault. *I* had not sought out my

attacker. *I* had not sold my blood.

I had never believed what they said of me—but now I did not merely guess, I *knew* I was no reprobate, no dainty. It was as though a burden rolled from my shoulders, and I could hold my head high for the first time in two years.

Scarcely had I considered this than a new implication occurred to me: someone at Saint Botolph's—Miss Scrimpson, or at least some of the board members, or whoever had spirited me from Stuttgart to London—had also known this. Knowing me to be innocent, they had spent the last two years telling me I was at fault.

Infamous as this was, it paled before yet a third implication: that Saint Botolph's did not merely send its girls to work for royalties across Europe. It received their victims, too.—Saint Botolph's was not a purely English operation. It was a clearing-house for all the monster-bitten in Europe—a conspiracy of international magnitude.

"We all thought you were dead," Anton added, as these fire-bursts unfolded in my mind. "If I had known, nothing could have prevented my coming for you."

His words pulled me back to the present. Ah! the sorrow in his voice! And yet—once I had been something quite other than I was. I did not yet know enough to join him in his grief. Was I once as wild and bitter as he? Did I once speak airily of murder and revolution, as did he?

There was only one way to find out; and now, at last, I thought him ready to tell me. I leaned nearer.

"My father," I whispered. "Tell me his name. Please."

He put his hand over mine with a peculiar little smile, glancing at the grandfather clock in the corner. "Wait."

It was nearly seven o'clock. I waited, consumed by a

strange fancy: the clock would strike, and something would happen—a good fairy would come through the door; a pumpkin would turn into a coach; a nutcracker would turn into a prince. The clock did strike. Anton's grip tightened on my hand, and he rose from the table.

"It's time," he announced.

He led me from the room and up one flight of stairs, then another. I realised we were going to the attic—that place which had drawn my attention the night before, with its flickering windows and strange protuberances. Having reached the top of the stairs, we found a small high door that stood ajar beneath the high slant of the roof. From within came a medley of smells—blood and chemicals and grease—and again, the flickering of cold blue light, and the fizzing of electric sparks.

Anton opened the door for me to enter. With some trepidation, I stepped over the threshold.

At once, a figure confronted me. It was dark here, just inside the door, but a little light filtered in from the gaslight in the landing behind me. That light fell on a familiar face—my own.

I caught my breath as the creature advanced towards me. The black hair dressed in a low knot at the nape of her neck—the large grey eyes and the mouth somewhat too wide for beauty—even the dress in sprigged muslin was very like the white I wore.

Two differences struck me at once: she glided too smoothly for human gait, and her cheek was clear and unscarred. I stepped back with an involuntary cry of alarm. I was face-to-face with my *doppelgänger,* and foolish ghost stories sprang into my mind unbidden, whispering that those who met themselves were never long for this world.

I hesitated, but Anton did not. Uttering an exclamation of alarm, he snatched me back and slammed the door. The next instant an explosion rocked the castle. The attic quivered under our feet, and flakes of plaster rained from the ceiling around us.

Anton swore. "The devil! I *told* him to be done by seven o'clock!"

"Who?" I cried, thus recalled to the errand on which we had mounted these stairs. "Who?"—but Anton did not answer at once. I flung the door open and burst inside.

A cloud of thick smoke hung in the air, mixed with the sweet cloying whiff of dynamite. Some of the tiles had been knocked from the roof, admitting rays of moonlight. My *doppelgänger* was scattered across the floor of the attic in shreds of muslin and shards of debris. Jagged bits of shrapnel were embedded in the walls. Somewhere in the smoke, someone was coughing.

I bent down, brushed aside a shred of bloodless flesh, and picked up a cog. My double was not a creature of nightmares—it was nothing more nor less than a very clever automaton.

The coughing gave way to cries of triumph. "Success! Is that you, Anton? Success, I say! It will work!—I'm sure of it!"

A shape loomed out of the smoke, and then a man appeared—a gentleman of medium height, respectably and soberly dressed apart from the smoke and grease-stains smudging his clothes. His hair and beard were both grey and very long, and round dark glasses shielded his eyes.—When he saw me, he stilled at once, and the blood fled his cheeks.

"Vera!" he whispered.

Anton's hands settled on my shoulders. "This is Doctor

Livius, who is perhaps the greatest inventor living today; but he often used to tell me that of all his creations, you were the one that made him most proud. This, Vera Livius, is your father."

Chapter XXII.

"Vera!" my father said. His dark glasses must have obscured his view of me, for he snatched them from his head and extracted a pair of spectacles from his waistcoat pocket. "Vera! Is it really you?"—I stood there like a stunned mullet, gaping with something of that fishlike expression. He crammed his spectacles onto his nose and swallowed convulsively.

"It *is* you," he said. Before I could move, he seized me in a whiskery embrace.

I had often wished that familiar smells, familiar sensations might restore to me some of my lost memories. So far I had been kissed by a former lover, told my true name, and been given a dress that was once my own. All had given me a sense of familiarity; but that feeling was stronger now than it ever had been. I smelled grease and pipe-smoke, coffee and oxy-acetylene flame—and I *knew,* without a doubt, that this was my father.

Tears sprang to my eyes.

"Don't leave me again, my Vera. Don't ever leave me again," he sobbed.

"Papa," I whispered. My mind was full of questions, my heart full of doubts; but my arms tightened around his neck and for a moment I forgot everything else in the world. Home, family, love, acceptance—I had crossed Europe in search of them and here at last, in the attic of Castle Sarkozy, I had found them.

Oh, say I might now rest! Say I might stay here where I had begun, sink back into that old life and never leave! This was my place, these were my people. I was restored to them now, and justice was done.

My papa pulled back with his eyes wet with tears. His hand traced my scars, and his mouth twisted with grief. "Look what they did to you."

"What does that matter, now that I'm home?"

"It matters that no one else should have to suffer the same," Anton growled. He had been tramping through the attic, opening windows to let out the smoke. Now that the fog had dissipated, I saw that I stood in a cluttered laboratory. Each surface was cluttered with Bunsen burners, syringes, beakers, blueprints, flasks, crucibles, goggles, screwdrivers, cogs, gloves, packets of worrisome-looking powders and jars labelled *Poison—Not to be Taken.* One flask held what was undoubtedly blood—Vasily's blood, said a part of my mind I was trying to ignore. The room was criss-crossed by what I guessed were newfangled electrical cords, connected to a large machine in the corner that I suspected might have been the generator. Near it, a half-built steel automaton like the one that lay in pieces around me leaned awkwardly against a window beside a large glass tank full of some glowing green liquid in which another stark, skeletal shape appeared to be growing flesh. But without a doubt the centrepiece of the laboratory was a heavy stainless-steel table, which stood beneath a section of the roof from which the tiles had been removed, allowing it open access to the stars. A tall antenna—one of the strange installations I had noticed yesterday evening—protruded from one corner of the table, and sturdy leathern straps (the dickens! were they the same Anton had stolen from George's compartment aboard the train?) hung from each corner.

I stared about me in astonishment. "Is all this yours, Papa?"

A sad smile. "You would have recognised it, once. The bionic tank was your idea, of course...Anton said you had lost your memories."

"I *helped* you with this?"

"I hoped you'd take over my work when I was gone."

I caught my breath. I had always known myself to have an affinity for mechanics. I could never have guessed I had once been a scientist myself. And now everything I had once known was gone. They had stolen not only my home and loved ones, but my work and my knowledge.

Moving towards the great green tank, I traced my fingers across it as a woman might trace the headstone of a lost child whose face she had never seen. My heart was dull and heavy as lead. "It's gone," I said aloud. "They took all this away from me and all they left me with was *be good, be quiet, God save the Queen.*"

"It will come back to you," Anton said

"I still have some of your old journals about," said Doctor Livius—Papa. He hurried to the table, shifted an old cracked teacup off a stack of papers, and extracted a weather-beaten leather-bound book. He put it into my hands. I found I was trembling as I turned the cover.

My own handwriting looked back at me from the pages. Sketches of joints and skeletons. Dotted lines to show the motion of a walking man. Detailed notes of a visit, in London, to one of the wealthy prosthete heiresses whom the English nobility kept importing from America to give the family fortunes a shot in the arm. Or more accurately, not to the heiress herself, but to her maintenance mechanic. Apparently it was he who had given me the formula for growing flesh on bionic skeleta.

"It's the same technology they use in America," I gasped, reading the notes. "I thought it was possible to grow fully operational automata from scratch: not just limbs and attachments."

"And it *was* possible," Papa said, the gaslight glinting enthusiastically from his spectacles. "It's taken me two years to perfect the process—you would have done it so much sooner."

"I told you! It's all coming back," Anton declared. "You might take a month or two to brush up on what you've forgotten. By the time the revolution ends, you'll be your old self again."

But it wasn't coming back to me. Almost nothing in the journal made sense—none of the equations, none of the abbreviations, none of the formulae.

Yet I was still young and my mind was keen. The doctor—Papa could teach me. I might unearth my old books, my old journals, my old clothes, and carry on where I had left off.

My life was waiting for me. All I had to do was step back in. What was my duty to May, after all, compared to the duty I owed my own father? She had cast me out, but he had taught and raised me. What was my duty to keep my word to Vasily compared to keeping my word to Anton? The one had tried to drain my blood, while the other had secured the promise of my hand in marriage. What was my duty to the monsters compared to my duty to their victims? Veronika was right:

a revolution was bound to come sooner or later. Surely this was my place, then: not to protect May by remaining by her side, but to protect all Europe as a voice of moderation among the revolutionaries.

I have never claimed to be a heroine, and in that moment the temptation was strong. On the one side I was offered love, respect, home, and family—everything I had ever wanted. On the other—but there was no other side for me at that moment. My father held my hand as though he never meant to let me go, and nothing else in the world mattered.

This must be what Anton had meant when he said I would understand, if he could only show me upstairs. And I did understand. I opened my mouth to say it, but at that moment a distant commotion reached our ears. Anton glanced through one of the little dormer windows to the darkness-shrouded courtyard below.

"Veronika has returned," he said.

A sense of my danger returned to me. "Veronika!" I cried. "Papa, did you know she tried to feed me to a vampire?"

He started. "She what?"

"Didn't she tell you? I've been here since last night, locked up with the Grand Duke on Veronika's orders."

He paled, took off his spectacles, and polished them frantically. "No, no, she can't have known who you are."

"Anton," I appealed, but a distant growl of thunder sounded overhead, and Doctor Livius glanced up at the lowering clouds visible through the opening in the roof.

"The experiment!" he cried, seizing a bell-pull, "it's now or never!"

Any thought of Veronika seemed to vanish from their minds. Anton began to unbutton his waistcoat. "I am ready."

My father caught him by the shoulder. "You don't have to do it, my boy! The risk is too great—for Vera's sake—"

"I tell you I can control it," Anton said fiercely, throwing a glance in my direction. "Don't fear for me. With Vera here, I can master any beast."

"Quickly, then!"

"Papa?" Already my resolve was wavering. "What beast?"

He dropped a kiss on my forehead. "Don't let Veronika frighten you, my dear! She couldn't have known—Everything will be explained—You shall see. Stand back. If we have success, the results will be truly magnificent!"

I backed away as the door opened and a couple of men in shirtsleeves entered. "Ah, my assistants," Papa welcomed them. "Have you your cattle prod, Dmitry? And Heinrich—I see you have brought the silver, garlic, saltwater, laudanum—good. Stand here. The Livius Serum is ready for testing. My dear, you should be proud of Anton; he is a brave man."

At those words Anton hesitated. Stripped to the waist, he'd dropped his shirt and waistcoat to the floor beneath that ominous steel table. Now he seemed to think better of it. Bending to retrieve one of his cufflinks from the little heap of clothing, he raised it to his lips, then took two swift steps and pressed it into my hands.

"I'll be wanting this back, my Vera," he said, putting a roughly caressing hand to my cheek. "I promise."

"Whatever this is, you don't need it to impress me!" Yet despite my alarm, wild horses could not have dragged me away from the laboratory. I was too eager to learn how my father planned to defeat the monsters.

Anton smiled and climbed onto the table. Dmitry and Heinrich strapped him down by the wrists and ankles. Outside the attic, the storm rose to a crescendo. The rain-laden wind forced itself in through the great opening in the roof, sending notes and blueprints flying. Lightning flashed—thunder growled.

Doctor Livius raised a flask containing a thick red liquid. "The Livius Serum," he whispered reverently. "Vera, we've been awaiting this day for so long!"

"What is it made of?"

He plunged a syringe through the wax seal at the head of the flask and drew off a carefully-measured quantity of the liquid—let us say two or three tablespoons-full. "The werewolf blood Veronika brought back from Paris. Vampire blood from our own cellars. Refine them, extract the essence, combine, and then give them a little kick—"

He slipped the needle into a vein in Anton's elbow. "Heinrich!"

The burly German hurried to a wheel and began to turn it. Shaking, banging, the antenna rose, telescoping up into the storm that raged overhead. Anton grunted when the needle went in, but after that he made no sound, no movement. I crossed the attic to better see his face without getting underfoot. My heart beat half with suppressed curiosity and excitement, half with terror. I thought I knew what Doctor Livius was trying to do—but would it work?

The antenna was at its full extent now, rattling and shaking as though the wind meant to tear it from its moorings. Doctor Livius motioned his two helpers to stand back, to pick up their weapons.

"Wait for it," he cried. His hair and beard whipped around his face in the storm-wind.

Lightning struck the antenna.

The whole attic lit up with cold blue flame, accompanied by a shattering crack of sound. I felt as though I had been kicked in the heart. The same instant, a bank of cabinets struck me in the back. Sparks erupted from the cables looping from the pitched roof.

Anton's whole body lit up with light, so bright I could see every bone.

So much I saw—so much I heard—before my wolf-bitten senses failed me, overwhelmed beneath the burden of so much light and sound. Even my nostrils were clogged with the stench of ozone and heated metal. The first faculty that returned to me was touch, as I found myself stretched out on the floor at the base of the cabinets.

I pulled myself to my knees. Anton's bones were still printed with fire on my vision each time I blinked, but slowly a little sight returned to me: upon the steel table a dark shape was moving, heaving, battling his restraints. Faint and far away was an endless howl of pain—Anton! I tried to call out, but no one heard. I closed my eyes and put my hands over my ears to gain some relief.

When at last I regained my feet, my ears still rang, but the thing on the table had fallen still and silent. Doctor Livius and his two assistants had unearthed themselves from shattered equipment and smoking cables, and now stood over the thing that had once been Anton. One of them was reeling the antenna in again. The doctor's voice was distorted and fuzzy: "He lives."

My eyes were yet too dazzled to see what had become of Anton. I stumbled forward one step, then another. "Test the silver first," I heard my father say from very far away. "See if it burns—"

I didn't see Dmitry carry out the instructions, but the creature on the table reared up with a shriek like a lost soul. A misshapen head broke into one of the weak globes of light emerging from the gaslights and a scream forced its way between my lips. Where Anton had lain was something half beast, half man. Grotesque and misshapen, it might have been a man caught midway in the change to wolf: the fur on its arms was patchy but its head was more like a goblin's than anything else—its skin grey, its teeth long and sharp, and yellow hatred shining from its eyes.

"Anton!" I cried. "What have you *done* to him?"

"Now: saltwater," my father said tersely. Heinrich dropped one clear drop onto the creature's naked chest. I smelled burning hair and flesh. The creature went fighting mad, screaming and clawing and fighting its restraints.

Doctor Livius snatched his spectacles from his face. "Success! It carries the attributes of both wolf and vampire—the Livius hybrid lives! My dear girl, behold our revolution!"

"*This* is your revolution?" I cried, aghast. I had suspected something like this; but the reality was far worse than I could have imagined.

"Too long the creatures have hoarded their power in their own hands," Doctor Livius cried over the snarls and snaps of the terrible creature. "Now everyone will be monsters!—Let the workers of Europe only inject the Livius Serum into their veins, and administer the correct voltage, and the revolution will begin. Now we have only to observe how long—"

It was not a very loud sound compared to the shouting and howling going on the attic—only a soft, leathery sort of *snap*—but I heard it, and so did everyone else.

A look of terror crossed my father's face.

Anton—the *thing* that had been Anton—reached out a free hand, seized Heinrich by the throat, and hurled him bodily through the window opposite. An anguished scream rang out as the man plunged from the castle's topmost height. It went on much longer than any of us cared to think—and abruptly stopped.

I shrieked in horror. The Anton-beast reared up from the table, clawing at the restraints on his left arm.

"Anton," cried Doctor Livius, "remember yourself—remember Vera!"

The creature only snarled.

"Subdue him, Dmitry! Quickly!" The terrified Dmitry raised his cattle-prod.—"Not that, you fool! The laudanum!" my father cried.

I leaped towards the table. Before the sparking electrical nodes could come in contact with the enraged creature, I seized the prod and snapped it in two.

"Don't," I cried, "stop, you'll only make him worse."

But already there was nothing worse that could happen.

Anton's claws were razor-sharp. A swipe of his hand cut his left arm free. Then he threw himself from the table, upending it over himself. As he wrestled with the ankle restraints, I seized my father. "Papa! Quick, we must go!"

He blinked at me. "He isn't himself—he must be restrained—and my observations—!"

With a pealing roar, the steel table flew across the attic, sweeping Dmitry before it. The terrible vampire-wolf reared to its feet, sniffing for prey—for us!

The attic was still full of the scent of lightning, and that is what must have saved us. The creature gathered its powerful limbs, springing for the opening in the roof. Claws scrambled across the tiles, then the front of the building. "He's getting away," I gasped, dashing for the broken window. In the courtyard below, screams sounded as the Anton-beast scrambled down the face of the house. A crowd of people had gathered in a ring around the pale smudge of clothing that had once been Heinrich. As Anton sprang from above, they scattered in panic. All I could see was the seething, running, falling crowd—all I could hear were screams and growls.

I turned on my father. "Papa! What have you unleashed upon the world?"

He dug a notebook out of the ruins of his desk, and was scribbling desperately upon the pages. "Just a moment, Vera! Let's see, the serum should wear off in twenty-four hours, give or take—Quick, by how much do you suppose he was stronger than the average vampire? the average werewolf?"

I could smell blood. Beneath the heavy steel table, Dmitry twitched once and was still. "He *killed* them, Papa!"

He blinked at me. "Sacrifices have to be made, Vera."

"That's monster talk!"

He sounded bewildered. "Your mother always used to say—"

"My mother?"

He didn't seem to know what to say to that; only cleared his throat and looked harried. "Anton told me you wanted justice. For your scars—for everything. Don't you?"

"Yes, but not at *this* cost! If our rulers are monsters, the answer is not to create more of the same! *Please,* Papa. Things have to change, but not like this."

He hesitated, a look of doubt crossing his face. I seized his hand. "I don't want to stay here, Papa. I don't want to be a part of this. Come away with me. We'll make a new start and invent things that help people, not hurt them."

For an instant I thought he might agree—but then the attic door burst open. In the glare of the gaslight on the landing stood Veronika in another of her black-velvet gowns, breathing hard. The streaks of grey in her hair were askew, and she had broken apart her lacquered walking-stick to unsheathe the blades.

"Kurt! Kurt!" she cried. "Are you injured?"

Doctor Livius lifted a calming hand. "Only—a little shaken, Veronika."

Her eyes fluttered shut. She drew in a deep breath, and her lips moved soundlessly. Then she put away her swords. "Three men are dead, and your experiment has escaped the castle. I feared..."

Doctor Livius looked a little nervous. "As I suspected, the beast took over. I *did* warn him!"

"We knew the risks. The question is, will it be a match for the royal monsters?"

"It was stronger than I could have imagined."

"Then our success is assured. My love, I've never been more proud. And now, I have brought you the gift for which you asked. The next stage of the revolution..."

The words died on her lips as she saw me. Her white throat worked. For a moment she, too, seemed to have seen a ghost.

Seeing that it was no use to hide, I attempted to brazen the thing out. "Good evening, Veronika. Are you surprised to see me?"

She did not reply at once. Then another pair of henchmen appeared at the door—they must have followed her up the stairs at a slower pace. They showed a certain amount of apprehension as they stared at the wildly flapping papers, the overturned benches, the broken windows, and the rain pouring in through the gap in the roof.

To these newcomers, Veronika said crisply: "One of you, get a tarpaulin over the roof. O'Grady, choose three of your men and take this girl back down to the vampire's cell, where she belongs. And ah! My gift."

More men trouped into the room—Veronika had brought her full entourage with her. Two of them held an upright, defiant figure between them—a figure wasp-waisted in rumpled white, with the pale gold hair and the heavy-lidded blue eyes of a little china doll. At the sight of her, I let out an exclamation of horror.

It was my mistress. The anarchists had captured Princess May.

Chapter XXIII.

May's look of sickened betrayal went through me like an arrow. I had no time to appeal to her, for O'Grady seized me by the arm. "Knock it off, Jim," said I in desperation. "There's an explanation for this. Tell them, Papa…!"

My voice trailed off as I turned to Doctor Livius. My father glanced from me to Veronika, evidently caught in an agony of indecision. Doubt struck me. For one moment I had imagined he would leave this terrible place and come away with me. Would he be overcome by the force of Veronika's personality? What did she mean by taking his hand and calling him her love? How dared the woman put her hands on my father?

What did she mean, that May was a gift?

"Take her away, O'Grady." Veronika repeated her command in a voice like ice. "The revolution depends on our getting the Livius Serum into the hands of as many *compagnons* as possible. Now we are assured of success, the vampire must be fed so that we can harvest more blood."

"Veronika! No! You don't understand." Doctor Livius put an arm around her shoulders and reached out his hand to me. A tentative smile broke over his face. "This is Vera, my love—*this is our daughter.*"

O'Grady swore under his breath and let go of me. May

looked appalled. Veronika's face was deathly white.

"It can't be," I whispered.

But how could he be lying? His daughter—*their* daughter—Veronika Sarkozy's daughter. The daughter of whom she had told me that first night in *Le Chat Noir*, from whom she had been so cruelly parted.

The daughter she must have known—even then—was identical with myself. My heart gave one throb of fear as I realised just how terrible was the danger in which I stood.

"It's true," my father told her. "This is the child we have sought so long."

Slowly she pushed away from his embracing arm. "Yes, I know," she said in a very cold voice. "I have known it for days."

In that moment I knew what it is to learn that the woman who gave you life means to have you killed—that the woman who carried you in the safety of the womb can no longer bear to look upon your face. Perhaps you think she was an unnatural mother; but in that moment all I could think was that I must be a monstrously unnatural daughter.

The doctor was aghast. "And you would throw her to *that* creature below us?"

Veronika's eyes narrowed. "I do not know what lies she has told you, but she is no anarchist. She serves our enemies. I questioned her on the train."

Doubt crept into my father's eyes. "Vera? You don't really want us to flee the revolution, do you?"

"Oh! so she has already been trying to subvert you, has she? I'm glad I came in when I did. Take her away."

"No," my father protested. "You wanted to stay, Vera! I could see it in your eyes. You wanted to remember what you had forgotten. You wanted to make automata with me again.

You—you promised you'd never leave me!"

His words tore at my heart. "And I *don't* want to leave you," I cried in a voice choked with tears.

"No, Sharp!" May cried out. "Please, Sharp—don't join them—please!"

I glanced at her in time to see her captors rudely shake her, warning her to be silent. Even now she did not show a great deal of outward terror, but her lips were parted, and I could smell her fear and desperation.—Days ago she had refused to speak to me or see me. She had cast me out in anger, yet now she wanted my help. I did not know how to refuse her. I did not know how to refuse what my father asked. I did not know what to do.

In the distance, a faint far-off howl rose into the night air, piercing through the storm. Anton, in beastly shape, roaming the mountains in a blind rage. The cry made me shiver. Then Veronika spoke in words like chips of ice. "Well, child? It seems I must give you another chance. Will you assist your father in his work, or will you go below to feed the monster?"

I shuddered again at the thought of returning to Vasily. This was a way out, surely. Agreeing to help my father, I might yet retain some form of freedom. I might sabotage his work—I might find an opportunity to set Vasily and May at liberty—I might survive the coming cataclysm, the airships and the monsters, in safety.

"Of course, you should have to prove your allegiance to the People's Vengeance," Veronika added. "I think we shall have you assist in draining Princess May of her blood. Yes, that would be convincing. I should then withdraw every objection to your joining us."

"Sharp," May appealed in a whisper.

There was a way out. Surely there had to be a way out. "If you mean to use her blood for your serum, it's impossible. May is morganatic—there's nothing remotely monstrous about her."

"We know," Veronika said.

"Ah, yes," my father put in. "You see, there's a possibility that morganatic blood, when delivered directly to the—"

"Kurt," she said warningly. My father fell silent, and Veronika fixed me with a remorseless gaze. "Make your choice, my dear."

I cannot tell you with how much of my being I wished to agree—but I could not say the words, not even to save myself from the hell that awaited me below. I trembled at the thought of being returned to Vasily, but in the end I had already betrayed May once and could never do it a second time.

"I won't do it. I can't."

"Veronika," Doctor Livius appealed.

"It's no use, Kurt," she said briskly. "We lost our daughter years ago; we have done our mourning already. This is no longer the child we loved."

He glanced at me, anguished. "Don't have her killed. Please."

"She knows about the serum. She knows we plan to send it to anarchists across Europe. Perhaps she also knows that we mean to load the airships with bombs, and use them to obliterate the emperors of Germany, England, and Russia." A tight, ruthless smile. "Or if she didn't, she knows it now. Take her back to the vampire's cell. Oh, and—O'Grady, you might as well take Miss Teck downstairs as well, and lock her in one of the servants' rooms. I don't think Kurt is ready to resume his experiments just yet; this place looks like a bomb hit it."

Accordingly, May and I were seized and marched downstairs again. Doctor Livius did not try to protest. I did not try to resist. There were six of them, and they had seen very well that threatening May was a simple way to control me.

As they hustled us downstairs, it occurred to me that this might probably be my last opportunity to speak. "Ma'am, I'm so sorry," I told her, as we tramped down the narrow stair. "You can't imagine how sorry I am."

She didn't answer at once. Since I followed her, I was speaking to the back of her head.

"Only say you forgive me for lying," I said miserably.

At that she spoke, in a tired colourless voice: "There's nothing to forgive, Sharp. Mamma was right. It was her duty to tell me, not yours."

A pang ran through my heart. The Duchess of Teck, as difficult as she could be as a mother, could at least admit when she was wrong.

But it wasn't the lying that had outraged May, so much as the truth she wished to escape, concerning her family. "If it's any consolation to you," I said, "it seems that both our families are pretty monstrous."

We had spoken in English. Now—"Enough of your chit-chat," O'Grady growled in an Irish brogue. By this time, we had come to the narrow passage leading through the servant's quarters. Our escort paused to force May through one of those doors, locking it behind her. Then my captors closed ranks around me, and the cold muzzle of a revolver settled in the small of my back.

"None of your fancy tricks, now," O'Grady warned me as we moved towards the tower door.

The night was come—the waning moon had risen—the

vampire would be delirious, and hungry. Terror wormed its way into my mind. Tonight, tomorrow night—at some point I must die, helpless, in the dark. Not even Anton could help me now.

Down to the bowels of the tower, and the scent that ever after would haunt my dreams, of cedar and terror and damp. The roll of thunder, the crack of lightning were muffled by the immense weight of stone that pressed down upon us. My strength failed me, for I no longer cared to walk to my doom on my own two feet; but the men on either side of me seized me by each arm and dragged me. The lock clicked. The chain rattled. The men drew out fragile glass bulbs of saltwater, ready to throw if the vampire attacked. The door opened, and I was shoved within. I landed with a whimper on hands and knees, and the door slammed behind me.

I caught one glimpse of Vasily's eyes and teeth shining in the lantern light, before the light went away, and I was once more alone in the dark with the monster.

A silence followed. I found that I was weeping in great, heaving sobs. The tears ran down my face and neck. A hand reached out of the dark with curving sharp nails on the ends of the fingers. I felt it, cold and loathsome, caressing the pulse at my throat.

"I hunger." The voice slid out of the dark like a nightmare. I closed my eyes. Perhaps it would be easier this way, and over quickly. *"Give me to drink."*

I shivered as his cold arms went about me, drawing me into the suffocating stench of cold carrion. His nose traced my cheek. A cold tongue flickered out and tasted my skin—tasted my tears.

A flash of heat—I felt it on my skin; heard the sizzle of

burning flesh. He pulled back with a cry of pain, shocked into lucidity. "Ah! salt!"

I reached up with a shaking hand, found his hair and brushed it back from his forehead. "Vasily. Vasily. It's me, it's…it's Liz Sharp. Remember me. Oh, for pity's sake, remember me."

"Sharp?" he said dizzily, letting go of me, and catching my wrist. "Stop it, I know who you are. What's wrong? Why are you crying?"

"I…I know their plan," I said, forcing myself to breathe more steadily. I could not allow this dreadful secret to accompany me to my grave. "They have three airships. They mean to load them with bombs and send them to London, and Berlin, and Saint Petersburg."

Vasily gave a sharp hiss. I stopped, afraid his mind had been submerged once more in madness, but he quickly spoke again. "Go on—don't be afraid."

"They're using your blood," I added, "and they got some werewolf from somewhere—that's what Veronika was doing in Paris—and they've made a serum which turns people—ordinary people, anyone in the streets—into monsters, and they mean to make more and send it to anarchists all over Europe. Vasily, it's going to be a bloodbath. I—I know I might not survive this; this is why I'm telling you. Do you understand what I'm saying?"

It might be night, but he was himself now: sober as a judge, cold as a stone, focused and furious. "I understand. How do you mean to get us out of here?"

"I…"

His voice was desperate. "They're going to incinerate your Queen, my Emperor, and the German fruitcake. Tell me you have a plan, Sharp."

"I... They have May."

"And?"

"A princess can't just disappear," I said desperately. "Half the policemen in Europe are crawling over Budapest right now. Depend upon it, by this time tomorrow they'll all be here."

"At which point," Vasily said, "the baroness will send a man down here with a bullet for you and a stake for me, and our information will go with us to our grave."

I shuffled backwards, away from him. "It won't be a problem. They might shoot me, but they'll never manage to stake you. You're stronger than that. You'll kill them and warn the police."

"Sharp." Oh, the dickens—he was following me inexorably across the cell. "You're telling bedtime stories, Sharp." My back hit the wall and I pulled myself to my feet.

"You can't have my blood. No."

Vasily was near enough that I could smell the drought on his breath. His hands were on the stone to either side of me. Desperate, I clawed at his raw chest. He grunted with pain, but caught my wrists.

"I can get you out of here."

I twisted my hands in his grasp—to no avail. "No. Let them shoot me. I don't care."

"You'd rather be shot than give me your blood? Even a little of it?"

"Yes," I wailed. Until now I had not been desperate enough to wrestle the monster. Now I reached out with my trapped fingers and latched them into the shreds of his shirt. In the same moment I threw my weight sideways, dragging him after me to the floor. With the momentum of my roll I got on top of him, hooked my fingers into the reinforced collar of his

shirt at each side of the neck, and ground my knuckles into his carotids.

It was no use. No sooner had I applied the choke than Vasily released my wrists and slipped his arms between mine, forcing them apart and down. I found myself pinned in an iron embrace.

"I'm sorry, Sharp. They must be stopped…I'm so sorry."

His mouth met my skin. "Please, no," I whispered as his teeth sank in.

In the end, he was perfectly sane when he did it.

Chapter XXIV.

I don't clearly remember what happened next. All I have are dim flashes—vague impressions.

I remember lying on the floor of the cell thinking how tired I was, and how much worse it would be getting anyone to take me seriously now that I had vampire punctures to match my werewolf scars.

I remember the shriek and snap of tortured metal as Vasily plucked the gate from its hinges.

I remember kneeling on the stones sweeping open the ring of salt with my hands because I was afraid of what he would do to me if I refused.

I remember being carried in his arms through the castle; I remember the screams of terror as the anarchists fled at our approach; I remember the scent of burning hair and flesh as they sprayed him with saltwater—followed by the scent of blood as he swept them aside with one clawed hand. Then for a very long time there was only wind, rain, lightning, and thunder, as the whole of nature seemed to revolt against the unholy deeds of mankind.

Above all I remember the cold, bare white room, with its open window lit up by the failing moon as it sailed through straggling clouds. I remember long white curtains blowing on a wet gale, and the distant rumble of dying thunder.

The stark white walls—the devotional pictures hanging just a little askew—the cold impersonality of it all was familiar to me. He had brought me back to Saint Botolph's. I was a prisoner again. They would take my memories, and I would forget all I had learned—

"No, no," I whimpered, struggling as he laid me in the narrow bed—to no avail, for I was weak as a kitten. Vasily seemed hairier than I remembered, with patches of fur growing along his arms; and there was something wrong with his ears—they were long and pointed like a wolf's. Later, I would realise that this must have been an effect of my wolf-bitten blood, but at the time, it only added to my confusion and terror.

Running footsteps sounded in the passage and a starched nurse appeared in the doorway, no doubt hurrying to close the window that had blown open. Vasily straightened and snarled at her. She recoiled with a shriek, putting a hand to her mouth. A shadow leaped for the open window, and Vasily was gone.

Vasily was gone. I was alone. But I ought not to be alone—I ought to be by the side of my mistress.

"May," I whimpered, as the darkness swallowed me. "May!"

I remember one other image: white-wimpled faces peering down from around my bed. A man stood over me with his naked arm held out, a clear tube conveying blood from his arm to a raised bulb.

I tried to speak, to beg them not to take my memories a second time, but it was no use. I sank back into darkness as quickly as I had emerged from it.

When I opened my eyes again, it was broad daylight.

Outside was a fresh, golden sort of day; the window had been raised a few inches, and I could hear horses and carts rumbling to and fro in the street below. Looking up, I saw an image of the Virgin in dark polished wood on the wall to my right. No medieval supplicant ever looked upon Our Lady with more of hope in her heart. Saint Botolph's was not a Roman Catholic institution—I was not at Saint Botolph's.

"Where am I?" I asked feebly.

I did not expect an immediate answer, but a nurse hurried to my bedside. She was carrying a basket of rumpled bed-linens, for she must have been stripping another of the three beds in this room. "You are awake," she said kindly in a language I understood but could not recall ever having learned—Hungarian, as I later discovered.

"Where am I?" I spoke in German.

"You are in the Women's Hospital."

"Where?"

"The Vincés Sisters—"

"What town?"

"Eger, in Hungary." She watched me with shadowed eyes, and I wondered whether she had heard the story of my appearance in this room at night, carried through the billowing curtains by a monster which then fled, leaving my crumpled, drained body behind.

"Eger," I muttered. Now I remembered it: the town in the shadow of the mountains, nearest to Castle Sarkozy, where Anton and I had transferred from the train to a horse-drawn brake. It was a sleepy, pretty town, full of red brick and red tile and walls of cream-coloured plaster. But it was too large to be safe for one such as myself. "Don't let them take me away. Don't let them take my mind—"

"Calm yourself," she said kindly, putting a hand on my shoulder. "You have had a transfusion of blood, and in a short time you will be well again."

"If anyone comes for me..."

"There is a policeman waiting to see you when you are ready, but..."

"No," I gasped, rising from my bed with a surge of returning strength as every instinct told my body to fight. I had originally been attacked in Stuttgart, not London. *Someone* had taken me to Saint Botolph's after my first attack, and I did not think it could have been a private individual. Was the same about to happen again?

Barefoot, I staggered into the passage-way beyond, whence a stair led down into a vestibule soaked with golden sunlight. I reeled towards the stairwell, pushing my way past a nurse who gave a shriek of alarm and then tried to intercept me. I was still in my white dress from the previous night, now stained with blood and grime, and I must have looked like a ghost.

"Miss Sharp!"

A dark figure loomed between me and freedom. Tall and angular, yes, with sadly drooping eyes, tight bloodless lips, and a sweeping greatcoat—but he appeared to me like an angel of help.

"Short!" I sobbed. Unable to arrest my steps, I fell into his arms and pressed my cheek to his buttons to assure myself he was real. "Don't let them take me!"

"Good Lord, Miss Sharp!" He patted my back. "Don't be afraid, my dear. No one is going to take you."

The nurse from my room arrived, sounding a little out of breath. "Ah, Inspector. I see you've found her."

As Short thanked her, I realised my mistake. "Oh, *you're* the policeman?" I asked of the buttons.

"You don't mind?"

I let out a shaky chuckle and extracted myself from his embrace—not that he seemed eager to relinquish his hold, for he slipped an arm around my waist to support me. "For you, I'll make an exception. However did you find me?"

He glanced around the hospital, which had now reverted to tranquillity. "Is there somewhere we can talk?"

I led him back to the room in which I had awoken. By the time we reached it, I was shivering with cold—a reaction which may have had something to do with the terrifying memories that now returned to the forefront of my mind. Sinking onto the bed, I touched the bandage that swathed my neck, finding the sore place where Vasily had bitten me.

Short's voice—*such* a nice, calm, unworried voice it was—broke into my reverie. "Thankfully, when I escorted Prince George to Coburg, there were already a handful of other Special Branch men there, making ready for the wedding. His grace was kind enough to reassign one of them for himself, so I came post-haste to Budapest."

"You must have moved pretty quickly," I murmured. Later, when I had the chance to calculate travel times, I realised how very anxious he must have been to travel more than six hundred miles in two days. Post-haste, indeed!

"I feared for you." Kneeling before me, he pulled a blanket around my shoulders. His hands lingered on my arms as he searched my face. Worry lines were etched in his brow, and it occurred to me that if he seemed cheerful and calm, it was because he must wish to spare me his own distress.

I wasn't ready to speak to him about it—not yet—so I said

the first idiotic thing that came to mind. "Why, didn't you think me capable?"

He blinked and released me. "No—no. That's not what I meant."

"And after Budapest? You tracked me to Eger?"

"No, I went to the Hungarian police and received a list of Vera Sarkozy's properties. Her castle here in the mountains seemed the most likely spot. When I arrived here an hour ago and found confirmation that I was in the right place, I came to this hospital at once. I didn't expect to find *you* among the survivors."

A chill fist fastened about my heart. "Confirmation? Survivors? What do you mean?"

In answer, he silently handed me an edition of the morning paper. Although it was in Hungarian, I found I could read the words as easily as if they had been English—well, that riddle was solved; I knew Hungarian because my mother—

I forced myself to focus on the words. *Horror at Egerbakta,* a small headline read. It contained a paragraph to the effect that a small village about midway between the town and the castle had been attacked the previous night by a dreadful apparition (the papers were not permitted to say *monster*)—but whether it had been werewolf, vampire, or something else, no one knew. A dozen people had lost their lives, and the injured had been brought to hospital in Eger.

My hands were shaking. Had Vasily—? No, for having been fed, Vasily was quite sane, and I did not think this was something that would appeal to his coldly calculating mind. No, this was the work of a monster untrained in the governance of its sanguinary appetites.

"Anton," I whispered. My heart weighed on my breast like a

stone. I had begun this quest seeking justice, and now where was I? Vasily gone; May left behind at Castle Sarkozy to be drained of her blood as soon as my father's laboratory was in working order again; my mother about to unleash a bloody revolution. I closed my eyes and saw in my mind's eye the bloodshed at Egerbakta village: throats torn out, skin peeled away, houses smashed. "Anton," I repeated. He had tried so hard to become a killer, to have his revenge on the vampire who'd slain his cousin. He had been so confident of his ability to control the beast my father had created. Now he had become the very thing he despised, a monster that murdered without knowledge or remorse—and it wasn't people like Vasily who were dying. It was those poor people in Egerbakta.

Someone was saying my name. I opened my eyes to see Short kneeling before me, gently chafing my hands to bring warmth back to my cold fingers. "Miss Sharp," he said. He looked at the bandage around my neck, but didn't ask about it directly—for which I was grateful. "I'm sorry to ask this of you, but I urge you to tell me what you know."

"The last time I told someone this, he drained my blood."

Short swallowed hard, as though something in my words had pained him. "You are safe with me."

After that I was able to speak. "I found my family, Short. I found them...and now I have to stop them."

I told him the tale of the last few days in as few words as possible. At first Short listened in silence, only once or twice drawing a sharp breath. But when, falteringly, I explained how Vasily had taken my blood, he leaped to his feet.

"What! against your will?"

I don't know what else I had expected—but not this. Not after everything we had been taught at Saint Botolph's. "You don't think... I mean, perhaps he was right? With so much at stake..."

Short had paled to the lips. "Against your *will?*" He leaned down swiftly—for a moment I thought he would touch my cheek—and looked in my eyes. "There is no excuse for that, Liz. Never. Good God! I could kill him myself."

He said the words softly and clearly. I think my heart stuttered to a halt. Here was a side of Short I had never seen before!

Then he turned away and the moment was gone, so swiftly I might almost imagine it had never happened at all. All the same, I felt deliciously light and warm, as though all the nightmares were floating away from me. It meant a great deal to know that not even Short would countenance what Vasily had done.

And he had called me by my Christian name!

"If this is how the Romanovs treat their friends, I do not wonder at the bitterness of their anarchists. I think you are right, Miss Sharp. Even if we manage to foil the anarchists today, a revolution will come one day, if royalties do not learn to do better."

"Such things could never happen in England."

"No, thank heav—. You're laughing at me." He thrust his hands into his pockets and looked at the ceiling with a sigh. "It's true, Miss Sharp. To think what pride I once took in serving the only empire in the world not ruled by monsters! I have been wondering, lately, how much of what I once believed is true. If I was wrong in this, what else might I not have been wrong in?"

It did me good to know that he was able to ask the question at all. A ray of hope in a world that felt rather hopeless at present; but how far did his doubts really go? "Vasily told me that they cannot become monsters unless they make a kill," I said, in a small voice.

Short's mouth lengthened in distress. "I have always supposed as much. Did not you?"

I shook my head. "I thought…surely *George* would never do such a thing!"

"I think his grace has been taught to subject his conscience to his duty, and to the prestige of his family."

"Careful," I said, "they'll be arresting *you* as an anarchist next."

His lips twitched in a smile, and the corners of his eyes perked up a little too. "We can both agree that whatever the solution is to the world's wrongs, it ought not to involve this sort of violence. Let me telegraph to Budapest, and once we have some reinforcements, we can make a plan of attack."

Reinforcements—he meant police. I found that although I could not condone what the People's Vengeance intended to do, neither could I stomach the thought of handing them over to equally monstrous authorities. It struck me that questions of order and chaos, regardless of what I had always been taught at Saint Botolph's, were quite irrelevant to any notion of right and wrong; and I would always prefer to be right than to be orderly. But I could not quite bring myself to put it so plainly to Short.

"That will take too long. They have May up there at the castle, don't you understand? They mean to harvest her blood—I don't know if they mean to kill her or not, but I can't leave her to suffer alone. I must go back at once."

"You aren't strong enough."

"On the contrary, I think I am. They have given me a

transfusion—and I'm both wolf-bitten *and* vampire-bitten now. Look." I pulled at the bandage around my neck. The loops of white cloth fell into my lap, and I brushed my fingers over twin punctures that were already knitting together. "I feel stronger. I'm healing faster. You can't stop me, and neither can they."

"And Anton Lupei?" Short levelled a sceptical gaze. "You said Doctor Livius wasn't entirely sure how long the effects of the serum would last."

He didn't tell me what to do—only left those words hanging in the air. Anton was still a monster. How many must he have killed? How many more would he kill before the effects of the serum wore off?

I looked through the window. Already it must be past noon. "If we go to Egerbakta, I may be able to pick up his scent."

Short nodded grimly. "And then we'll have evidence with which to prove what Veronika is planning. I'll find us some horses. Do you have other clothes?"

I glanced down at my tattered white dress, a sad reminder of my tattered dreams. "I don't have a riding-habit folded up in my pocket, if that's what you mean."

"I suppose not," he said with the ghost of a smile. "Come along, then; we've no time to lose."

Chapter XXV.

It took a little longer to prepare for our journey than either of us had bargained for. While Short was inspecting the public stables, I found a rag-and-bone shop at which to buy myself a new suit of clothes, which included—oh, bliss—a pair of bloomers to wear beneath my blouse and waistcoat. I was careful to select a blouse with a high collar to conceal the fresh bite marks on my neck; and after a moment's consideration, I added a muslin scarf to the ensemble.

Werewolf scars might be considered accidental. But vampire scars in addition would confirm me as the worst sort of reprobate, and I found I had enough pride remaining to wish to cover them up.

So attired, I went to a post office, where I sent a telegram to the Duke and Duchess of Teck, addressing it to the hotel in Strasbourg. From there, presumably, it would be forwarded about Europe in search of them—the party had been headed to St. Moritz next, although I did not suppose the Tecks would have remained in that resort following the disappearance of May. I was not quite sure what to write, so I simply said *May traced to Hungary. More news soon. Sharp.*

This done, we set out on our journey. We did not approach Egerbakta until late that afternoon, when the last light of that lovely golden day slanted low through the trees. Now, as we made our way through a fringe of trees towards the main street of the small village—a long double row of houses—I reached for one of the bottles hanging at my saddlebow, and handed it to Short.

"What's this?" he asked.

"Saltwater," I explained. "They didn't have a great deal of laudanum at the pharmacy, so I asked them to make up some saline solution as well. It won't kill Anton—he has far too much wolf in him for that—but it ought to make him stop and think."

Short watched me meditatively. For a moment I wondered if he was looking at my new blouse and scarf, perhaps divining their purpose—seeing through to the sore spot beneath. Instead he said, "We *do* plan to kill him, though, don't we?"

Both of us carried a pair of sharpened wooden stakes, each about four feet long, slung across our backs. These I had soaked in wolfsbane, which I *had* been able to find at the pharmacist's. We were equipped to kill Anton, of course; that was only sensible. He could not be permitted to live at the cost of innocent lives. But I hoped—I prayed that choice would not need to be made.

Rather than answer Short's question, I pointed ahead, reining my horse in. "Oh, look." I was glad, in truth, for the distraction.

The village was still a short way ahead of us, but I could see the main street now, and a familiar horse-brake tethered outside the public-house. The cart was empty, but there could only be one reason for its presence.

"The anarchists are out looking for Anton, too," I told Short. "That hunting brake belongs to the castle."

Short stood in his stirrups to survey the countryside. "I see them."

He pointed ahead and to our left, where pastures swept down towards a belt of trees that hinted at a river running down from the mountains. There I saw the flat proletariat caps favoured by the People's Vengeance bobbing along in the pasture perhaps a quarter of a mile away as they made their way from the village towards the river. I thought I counted four or five of them, but they were hidden by a rise in the ground, and for all I knew there might have been more.

Here was a pretty kettle of fish! We could not follow Anton's trail without falling afoul of the Vengeance; but we could not allow him to fall into their hands either, for upon Anton depended my best hope of rescuing May.

"Perhaps we don't need to do this," Short said in a low voice. "Those people will deal with the beast themselves."

"Wait." I lifted my face, sniffing the air. Then a stronger gust brought the scent to me, and I knew I was not deceiving myself. "I smell blood. Quick, take that gate. We can get ahead of them."

Short looked dubious, but opened the gate to the pasture beyond. Cajoling my mount to a canter, I followed the faint, sickly stench of death towards the river. Not much further, and the horses scented it too, baulking at the smell of blood and torn flesh.

"By Jove," said Short in dismay, as we surmounted a rise, and saw the ground sweeping down to the river before us.

A flock of sheep had been feeding here when their death came upon them. Now they lay dotting the slope in little fly-speckled heaps—perhaps two dozen of them. Other puddles of blood, and the wheel-ruts of carts spoke to an even greater slaughter. No doubt the owner had been hauling carcases home all day to salvage what he could in the way of meat.

"This wasn't done for hunger," Short said in a subdued voice. "This was done for the joy of destruction."

I threw Short my reins and dismounted, unslinging my stake. The scent of blood and meat and guts was too strong in the actual killing-field, so I made a wide circuit of the corpses, bending low to sniff at the grass.

"Just like old times," I called to Short.

He sent me a tight smile and went back to watching the slope above us, no doubt waiting for the anarchists to appear. "Miss Sharp, the sooner we move on from this particular chapter, the better I shall like it."

I stopped downslope of the dead animals. Dropping to hands and knees, I buried my face in the grass. If this had been a city—or if last night's biting had not left me with yet more finely-honed senses—there would be no hope of picking up a scent after so many hours. But in the fresh, untrampled grass, I smelt it like a lingering memory: dynamite, ozone, carrion, wolf.

A distant shout.—"Miss Sharp!" in a warning tone from Short.

"I've found it," I called, jumping to my feet. The anarchists had come in view at last, and the foremost of them began to run.

"This way," I called.

The trail led us down to the river. Here I did not even have to stop and smell, for there in the soft mud at the water's edge, terrible clawed footprints (still more human than dog) left their mark in the clay, pointing south. "He went downriver," I told Short.

"You should mount," he said with a glance behind, where the Vengeance were hastening toward us.

"Can't risk losing the trail."

One of our pursuers paused, the brass barrel of a gun glinting in his hand as he raised it skyward and pulled the trigger. A white-hot flare shot into the sky. A signal—but to whom?

"I don't like that," Short muttered. "For pity's sake, Miss Sharp, I don't want you falling into their hands again."

"Anyone would think you were my mother." Then I remembered what a poor comparison this was, given the disposition of my own mother. Sighing, I beckoned Short and set off at a run. He kept pace with me at a trot, often glancing behind him as we went. Little by little, we gained on the Vengeance until they were no longer visible through the trees behind us, and Short looked more at ease.

We were still on Anton's trail: once or twice I glimpsed more footprints in the soft ground beside the stream. The beast had run abreast of the river for some way, never stopping. At last we passed through a belt of forest as the river widened into a small lake.

Short and the horses joined me on the flat white shore. By now the sun was truly getting near the horizon, and I could not help wondering if Anton, too, would be stronger and more frenzied by night. The Vengeance had sent up another flare half a minute ago, and as for the footprints, they had disappeared.

Seeing the look on my face, Short unslung the stake from his shoulders. "Something wrong?"

"I've lost the scent.—Hullo, no, here it is again, and stronger than ever. It smells as though he's been here within the past hour." In one direction the trail ran north into the wood; in the other, it curved south skirting the eastern shore of the lake. I chose to go north, leading Short through bushes and over rocks until we came to a massively-girthed tree split at the foot to provide a dry and sheltered den. The dry leaves and ferns collected there were trodden down and flattened as though a large beast had bedded here for some hours; and the scent shouted of Anton.

"That looks like—"

"Yes, he slept here until recently." I placed a hand on the leaves. Although the den was cold, the scent was nearly strong enough to taste. Overwhelmed, I backed away to draw breath. In the west, the sun rode the mountains, ready to set. "He must have woken as the sun was going down. I wonder how hungry he'll be."

"He wasn't hungry in Egerbakta," Short pointed out, his mouth thinning. "That didn't stop him killing who knows how many people and beasts."

"Then we had best move." I got up and turned to follow the scent back to the lake.

That was when I realised we were not alone.

My father—Doctor Livius—stood behind us, panting from exertion. He was not dressed for the outdoors, but his shoes and trousers were splashed with mud, and there were twigs stuck in his white hair.

He seemed to be alone—but he, too, held a brass Very pistol in one hand, and I thought I knew to whom the Vengeance had been signalling.

"Vera—alive!"

"Yes, and extremely fortunate to be so," I said cuttingly. "This is my friend, Inspector Short. Short, my father, Doctor Livius."

Short looked awkward, but nodded politely anyway and lifted his bowler hat. My father looked distressed. "Then Veronika was right. You're consorting with policemen."

"Consorting sounds so scandalous. Fraternising would be nearer the mark. I take it you're also looking for Anton."

"He's gone south," my father said, taking off his spectacles in a harried sort of way. "I...I think he's going to Eger."

Horror struck the words from my lips. "As a beast?"

Anton had wreaked enough destruction upon the village. I didn't want to imagine what would happen if he found his way into the town.

"The serum ought to wear off any time now," said the doctor. "It was only supposed to last twenty-four hours or so, and then he will be himself again."

"Why are you telling us this?" Short put in.

My father seemed to shrink in on himself. "Someone must stop him. Veronika has given strict orders we aren't to go into Eger. Too much is at stake."

"Your revolution is at stake, you mean?" I found myself too angry to mince words. "Your plans to create thousands of creatures as dreadful as this one?"

He didn't look at me.

"Veronika has gone mad," I protested. "You mustn't create more of the serum, Papa. It isn't too late; you can stop this happening."

He groaned. "I can't. She wants more, but I've already made a great deal of it—hundreds of doses."

Before either of us could reply to that, my ears caught the faint sound of footsteps in the wood. I grasped my wolfsbane stake, but the next instant a flare erupted from the trees and hung over us, painting the scene in harsh light. While we lingered in conversation, dusk had fallen and the anarchists had come upon us.

"What about May?" I hissed, turning upon him. "Is she alive?"

"Yes—but you must go. I'll misdirect them. Quickly!"

As I went to mount, Short caught my arm. "We should take him for questioning," he murmured.

What—hand over my own father to the very authorities who winked at murder when it was committed by their masters? That was out of the question, but now was no time to argue.

"Anton first, then May." I seized my horse's reins and swung into the saddle. "To Eger!"

Together we followed the lake-shore a short way east, before the trail—strong enough now to scent from the saddle—left the water and struck east across the rolling, twilight-grey fields. Topping a hill, we found that the trail did in fact lead straight back toward the glowing lights of the town.

We followed, urging our mounts to a reckless canter.

Darkness falls quickly at that time of year. By the time we reached the outskirts of Eger, the night had fallen but the moon had not yet risen. It was so dark that for the last quarter-mile even my eyes struggled to make out a safe path for the horses, but at last we made it into the narrow winding streets of the old town. Although Eger was so picturesque in the daytime, with the walls painted cheerful yellow beneath their red tiled roofs, we now found ourselves feeling our way in darkness from one streetlamp to another. Still more troubling was the fact that we were now unable to follow Anton's scent: walls, houses, fences—none were a barrier to him. Within a few minutes of our entering the cobbled streets, I ran the scent to a blank wall surrounding someone's garden. The way was barred.

"We might split up," I suggested. "You take the horses back to the stables, and I'll follow over the wall."

"Isn't he stronger than you are?"

Thanks to Vasily's bite, I could feel myself stronger than before—but I was no match for Anton's double monstrosity. "I expect I am sufficiently pure in heart to overcome him alone."

Short looked quizzical. "Pure in heart? Really? That makes a difference?"

"I was—it was a reference—Tennyson. *My strength is as the strength of ten because my heart is pure.*"

"Ah." Short cleared his throat. "All this is very new to me. Anyway, I'm not leaving you. Not after what happened last time. No matter your strength, you need someone to watch your—"

I stiffened as a scream cut through the night. "Did you hear that?"

"It came from that tower on the hill." Short pointed towards a low hill at the north end of the town.

"Let's go." I quickened my horse to a trot. We had not gone far before I picked up the scent I sought. This time it ran straight up the road and ended at the foot of the square white tower itself. Nearer, I saw that this was surmounted by a small onion dome and attached to a little white church.

Here Anton's scent was fresh and pungent, making the horses dance nervously. Looking up, I saw a dark shape scuttle in at one of the high windows, just like a spider glimpsed from the corner of your eye on a warm evening.

Short reined in beside me and slipped from his saddle. I drew him close to whisper. "He's in the bell tower. Hush! If we speak too loud he'll hear us."

"So ring the bells to cover our approach," Short murmured.

That was a clever idea; so clever, I felt a faint twinge of annoyance that I hadn't thought of it myself. "With his sensitive hearing, they will be unbearably loud. If I do that he's likely to burst out the window again."

"Then we'd better split up, after all. I'll ring the bells, and you wait out here to follow him." Short tried the handle of the door—locked. Without a word, I pushed him out of the way and had the old-fashioned lock picked in a trice. Easing the door open while Short watched the tower, I sniffed at the dim interior. Despite the darkness, my eyes picked out the long thin shadows of the bell-ropes in the corner of the square vestibule formed by the tower's base.

"All right," I whispered, standing back. "Inside, left corner."

I backed several paces from the tower, the better to keep my eyes on the windows. Short must have found the ropes, for the bells began to ring—loud and booming in a harmonious, if not melodious clamour. Wincing, I clapped my hands to my ears. For a long, terrible moment, nothing happened.

Then came a whiff of wolf, and the horses went mad. I dropped my hands from my ears just in time to hear Short cry out and be silenced.

I had misjudged. My heart stood still for a long, terrible moment as the truth struck me: Anton had chosen to descend the tower within. I threw open the door. Short was a crumpled heap in the corner, and Anton—

Anton was already gone.

Sniffing, I determined he had fled through the vestibule into the main body of the church. Clutching my wolfsbane stake, I followed.

He was not difficult to find.

By now the moon had risen, sending a thin beam of light through the high windows of the church. An immense gilt-edged iconostasis separated the sanctuary from the altar beyond—a wall displaying dozens of painted panels divided by frames of gold-leaf and braid. A low door in the massive screen gave onto the altar beyond, so that through it one could glimpse the golden candlesticks, lit up by the moon.

Anton stood before this door with his head bowed, breathing heavily as though something in his surroundings had frightened him. As I tiptoed nearer, I smelled blood, and saw wet drops on the pavement underfoot.—His own? Short's?—At that second thought, my heart stuttered again.

My foot scuffled against the stones. Anton growled suddenly and lashed out. A small gilt table, with the open Bible it bore, flew across the sanctuary and crashed into the wall. Then he turned to face me.

A growl rumbled deep in the monster's throat. In this ornate jewel-box of a church Anton looked like a demon risen from hell, his eyes flaming yellow as he crouched to spring.

I ought to face the truth: no matter what my heart told me, Anton Lupei was a killer. As long as I had known him he had been single-minded in his pursuit of death. I had followed him across Europe in hopes of changing his mind, all to no avail. Now he had succeeded in turning himself into a monster, but that was only what he had been inside all along.

I ought to know he was beyond salvation—as Vasily had been beyond salvation. I ought to lift my stake and strike true, because violence was the only language some creatures understood.

I ought to, but I didn't. You see, I knew what had made him who he was.

"Anton," I said softly, reaching into the pocket of my bloomers for the tiny thing I kept there. "I know you can hear me. Don't you remember me? Don't you remember Vera Livius?"

He paced forward a step, his sharp teeth locked into a snarl that might have been fitting on the face of a wolf but seemed immeasurably more frightening on him.

I moved forward, reaching out to show him the cufflink he had given me as a promise of his safe return. "Don't you remember this?"

He flinched and growled. I hesitated, my heart beating. At last, he let out a tiny whine and sank to all fours at my feet, putting his chin to the pavement. Quickly I knelt before him, setting my wolfsbane stake aside.

You may ask why I trusted him. I didn't trust him. I knew he was a mad beast.

I knew the last beast to attack me had been firmly in possession of all his wits.

"Anton," I murmured. I touched his deformed face—cradled his cheek in my hand, the great curving teeth only inches from my skin.

He growled deep in his throat, those smoking yellow eyes fixed on mine, but he didn't turn and bite.

I whispered: "Let me teach you to love again."

Some of the yellow light went out of his eyes. "Vera…"

"It's me."

Suddenly, he was shaking under my touch. "Help—help me."

"I will." Gently, I reached into my pocket, this time for a small glass vial. Anton pulled back, interpreting the raised hand as a threat, but I shushed him. "It's time to rest now.

Open your mouth."

He did as I asked. My hand shook a little as I reached towards those bared teeth and dropped one, two, three precious drops within.

There came a scuffle from the vestibule, and Short's panicked voice. "Miss Sharp!"

He burst into the church behind me. I turned, lifting a warning hand. "Short, no!"

Anton's eyes flared with madness as the beast took hold.

I never saw the blow coming. With a sweep of his arm, Anton threw me bodily across the church. I hit the wall and fell to my knees, gasping, as Anton unleashed a terrible howl. Stunned, I could only watch as Short braced himself to receive the monster on the point of his stake.

I tried to cry out, but there was something wrong with my lungs—they cramped, robbing me of breath and speech.

Anton drew his claws against the pavement like a bull pawing the ground. Sparks flew from the stones, but there was no charge. Instead, his head began to droop. Short moved forwards a step, stake ready. Anton jerked back to vigilance with a growl, but as he tried to move he staggered— toppled to the pavement—lay still.

After a moment's hesitation, Short moved forward, raising his weapon.

I found my voice at last. "No, don't hurt him!" I staggered to my feet and went down on my knees at Anton's side. I found his pulse: it was steady, but his eyes were closed and when I pushed back an eyelid, no yellow gleam escaped them.

"What happened?—Miss Sharp, are you hurt?"

"I'm perfectly all right," I said, sitting back on my heels. A little glass bottle rolled on the floor nearby; I recaptured it. "I gave him laudanum—poppy-juice."

Short didn't lower his stake. "Being part wolf, he'll be more resistant to the drug than a real vampire would. We can't risk him waking."

I felt suddenly very tired. "Go on, then. Stake a helpless creature, if you must."

"Helpless?" Short was incredulous. "We should hand him over to the police, at least."

I climbed to my feet, sighing that I must fight a new battle. "That's out of the question. If we're to get inside Castle Sarkozy to rescue May, we'll need Anton's help."

"You can't seriously think—"

"Nothing easier," I said muzzily. "Until the Livius Serum wears off, he has the combined vulnerabilities of both the monsters that made him."

"So, what, we wait for him to awake in his right mind? I do not recall his being any more tractable in that state, Miss Sharp!"

"Give me one more chance with him, Short." I thought of how Anton had released me from my prison; I thought of his insistence that he could tame the beast, and how only moments ago he had whispered my name. "I was *so* close to reaching him just now. Let me try once more—please."

His long mouth screwed up unhappily, but I could tell he had already yielded. "Can't you give me a better reason than *close?*"

"I'll give you a big kiss."

Let the reader note that I only said the words out of pure exhausted caprice.—George had always responded with *such* gratifying discombobulation to my pretended flirtations! Short, however, did not respond at all in the same way.

His eyes widened in surprise. Then he choked on his own surprised laughter and said, "By Jove! *will* you? Then I have no further objection to make."

"Wait a moment," I said, distinctly rattled by this development.

But Short, crouching by Anton's side, already seemed to have forgotten the offer. "Someone will be here in a moment to investigate the bells. If you can find the strength, will you help me to move him?"

Chapter XXVI.

Before coming to see me at the hospital, Short had taken a room in a tenement not far from the church where we had captured Anton. With Short's greatcoat flung over the anarchist's half-naked, half-furred body, we were able to pass him off as a friend who had partaken too freely of the city's hospitality. When he was slung over my shoulder, Anton's great bulk more or less obscured my own feminine curves, but for all that I got some funny looks from passers-by as I pulled him off Short's horse and carried him up the steps.

"This feels wrong," Short muttered, as he unlocked the door to his room and let me in.

"It's all right," I said, intentionally misunderstanding him, and still a little rattled after that exchange in the church. "I trust your intentions are honourable."

He actually blushed. "I mean letting you carry him all by yourself." A pause, as I slung Anton gratefully off my back and onto the bedside rug. "I say," Short added uncomfortably, "would you rather I got you your own room?"

That made *me* uncomfortable. "I was joking, Short. What reputation do I have to lose?"

"I thought you might prefer the privacy—"

A troubling thought struck me. "If *you* would prefer it, then by all means—"

"Miss Sharp." He put his hands on my shoulders, staring at our feet so that all I could see of him was a slight flush across the forehead. "I—I don't know what to do for you. That's all. If you want to be alone tonight, I'll get you a room. If you don't want to be alone, I would be honoured to host you here. Either way, I am yours to command."

Without warning, I felt as though I was trying to swallow a marble—one of the big ones—and I was glad he wasn't looking at me. "Please don't send me away," I said in a voice much shakier than it had any right to be. "I don't want to be alone tonight. I don't know if I'll ever want to be alone at night again, but I'll cross that bridge when I come to it tomorrow."

He patted my shoulder in a brotherly sort of way. "All right. I need to return the horses to the stable. Can you manage by yourself for a while?"

"Of course."

"I won't be long." He left, and I collapsed onto the bed. As exhausted as I was, I felt I ought to be up and doing something. Inexorably, my worried thoughts returned to May, who had now been in the hands of the anarchists for twenty-four hours. My father said she was still alive, but she might be hurt—or afraid—or anything. Perhaps I ought not to wait any longer. Perhaps they would surrender May in exchange to Anton. I should run downstairs now and tell Short I would return the horses to the stables, then hire a fresh mount and set off for Castle Sarkozy at once. Yes; that was a better plan. I jumped up and was running down the stairs when a falling sensation came over me. I started awake to find myself lying across the bed in Short's room.

It was no use; I was going to fall asleep in another minute. I could be of no service to my mistress in this state. Getting up, I shovelled coal into the stove, then found a packet of salt on the shelf above. This I poured in a circle around Anton, then dropped a little more laudanum between his teeth for good measure. He was warm and heavy, completely subdued by the drug. Perhaps I ought to have left a note for Short, telling him to wake me if he wanted to take a turn to sleep; but that did not occur to me. Stripping down to shift and knickers, I crawled onto the bed, wrapped the blankets about me, and fell into a deep sleep.

Apart from the nightmares, nothing disturbed me all night.

I woke in the cold before dawn. The room smelled close and stuffy, and my feet were like blocks of ice. Grey light had just begun to pierce through the thin curtains of the window. When I pulled the blanket closer, I found that Short had added his overcoat to my coverings. He himself sat against the wall near the stove with his legs stretched out, his arms folded, and a stake balanced across his knees. He was also very decidedly asleep.

I peered over the edge of the bed. The Anton-beast still lay on the rug, curled up on his side and breathing slowly. Short, to my astonishment, must have put a cushion under his head. As little by little the light grew stronger, I wondered what we would do if Anton did not soon return to human form. I wondered whether he would ever return to human form at all! Would he need to be put down—killed like a mad dog? Every thought revolted. The same impulse that had prompted me to subdue rather than destroy him in the church last night was still deep in my bones—but was it that irrational sense of trust I felt for him, or something truer?

After all, I had hope for May—and yes, even for George, who

had certainly killed at least once. One did not think twice of extending grace to a prince—so why not to an anarchist?

As for May... Once again, the thought of her danger pierced me through like a knife. It had been right to deal with Anton first, but I could not help feeling I had once again wronged my friend. Today, come what may, I would go back to Castle Sarkozy, and I didn't mean to leave until she was safe.

The thought, however, was a daunting one. All yesterday I had told myself that going back would not be so bad, now that Vasily was gone. But then—*she* was there. My heart quaked at the thought of falling back into the hands of Baroness Sarkozy—I could not call her my mother. Veronika wanted me dead. I thought of our conversation on the train, when she had tried to recruit me to her cause and failed. At the time I had thought her grieved, but I had been wrong. In fact, she must have been wildly angry and embittered, although no doubt she had congratulated herself for keeping her calm in the face of my wilful obduracy.

Since Vasily's attack, I was beginning to think that calm was overpriced.

As the light grew stronger, Anton twitched in his sleep. Then, quickly and quietly, his body diminished. Tufts of grey hair drifted from his body, melting like snow, and what I could see of his head changed shape. As he groaned softly and began to shiver, I sat up.

"Anton," I whispered.

He stilled.

"Anton, it's me."

Slowly he turned over—human once more. "Vera?" He looked confused—lost—miserable. "Please tell me I've been having nightmares."

"You might have been," I said. He *looked* himself again, but so did all werewolves and vampires, when the sun had risen. "There's a circle of salt around you. See if you can cross it."

It was a simple test: if the barrier still held, he was still a monster. But, when Anton glanced down at the white crystals, his face crumpled. Instead of attempting to cross the salt, he bent over and put his hands to his face.

"Anton," I whispered again.

His voice shook. "It was true—all of it was true—the blood—the screams—all of it—and I couldn't stop it!"

I touched his shoulder. "You did get the better of yourself in the end. Only for a moment; but it saved your life."

He dragged the back of his hands across eyes red with tears. "Oh, hell. Did I hurt you?"

I felt a moment's gratitude that whatever bruises I had incurred last night must have faded by now, although I could still feel Vasily's bite, sore and stiff when I turned my head. I wished devoutly that I had not removed my high-necked blouse to sleep. "I'm made of stern stuff, Anton. Do you realise Veronika is sending all the rest of that dreadful serum to other anarchists around Europe?"

"No—she mustn't! I couldn't stop myself. I was possessed by rage. It was terrifying—it spared no one, man or woman or child. Hundreds—no, thousands of people will die. It won't be a revolution; it will be the apocalypse." His expression was haunted. "I thought I could control it. I never imagined…"

"I know," I told him softly.

Glancing up at me, he saw something that brought fresh horror into his eyes. "Vera!" He got swiftly to his knees, scattering the salt. I flinched, but he seized my blanket, drawing it aside to show the twin punctures on my neck, and the fading bruise around them.

In his eyes blazed a remembered wrath. "Vasily Nikolaevitch," he breathed.

"Yes," I whispered. My heart quickened. I wasn't afraid of him, not physically; the fact that he had crossed the salt showed that all the beastliness was out of his system. But I sensed he stood at a tipping-point, and the right words might set him on a path from which he might never return. "Veronika sent me back to him, you know."

He frowned up at me, uncomprehending. "But Doctor Livius, surely—"

"Doctor Livius is in love with her," I said gently. "It turns out that as he is my father, so Veronika Sarkozy is my mother."

Anton swore. "And she did *this* to you?"

"We *are* speaking of the woman who means to unleash hundreds more monsters upon Europe."

He shook his head in disbelief. I continued:

"Veronika told me once that justice is worth anything. *I* say the difference between justice and vengeance is the rules that we have." I held out my hand to him. "Veronika needs to be stopped. At once. Will you help me do that?"

As Anton considered my outstretched hand, his mouth twisted in uncertainty. He might no longer believe in Veronika's revolution, but opposing her must feel like a betrayal of all he held dear.

"I need you, Anton," I pleaded. "I can't do this alone."

With that he took a sharp, almost pained breath, and put his hand in mine. "All right. You have me, Vera. You followed me into anarchism once. The least I can do is follow you in this."

I offered him a tentative smile, and a moment later, he returned it.

Somewhere in the building nearby, a door closed with a bang. Short jolted awake with a grunt of alarm. The sight of Anton so close to me gave him a second fright, and he scrambled to his feet brandishing his stake.

"Oh, move along, Short," I said, "there's nothing to see here."

Anton swallowed hard and gave an awkward wave. "I...I am myself again."

"That's not precisely a comfort," Short muttered, but he lowered his weapon all the same. "I apologise for dropping off, Miss Sharp. It won't happen again"—and he glared at Anton.

"All's well that ends well," I declared. "Now, Short: Anton and I are off to storm the castle. Do you want to come?"

Chapter XXVII.

Short took some convincing. In his view, the only sensible plan was to wire Budapest for reinforcements, and pass the time until they arrived in watching the road from the mountains to ensure that Veronika could not distribute her existing supplies of the Livius Serum. Neither Anton nor I were happy with the thought of calling in the police, be they undead or mostly alive. Moreover, Anton pointed out that although Eger was the train station nearest to Castle Sarkozy, it was far from being the only road by which Veronika could move her supplies across the mountains in any direction she chose—and that wasn't counting the airships. Given Vasily's and my escape, and Anton's own failure to return, she was certain to do just that, and soon.

All that, and I insisted I would not let another day pass without mounting an attempt to rescue May. Short's final objection was to our bringing Anton with us at all: "I don't wish to cause undue offence, but to be very plain, Mr Lupei, what guarantee do we have that you are not baiting traps for Miss Sharp?"

At those words, Anton had glowered murderously and knotted his fists again. "You are most welcome to remain behind if you don't trust Anton," I said levelly, before he could respond, "but *I* trust him, and I intend to take him with me."

With that Short had to be content. Soon after our council of war finished over an early lunch, he slipped off under pretence of hiring more horses. Anton watched him go with some misgivings. "He is going to telegraph Budapest for more damned corpses."

"Oh, you mean policemen. Well, I'm sure he is," I said equably, drawing on my jacket. "We shall have no peace until he does. You'll just have to warn your friends to disperse before they can be surrounded and taken in, that's all."

Anton grumbled something about making deals with the devil, but—I had to admire his pluck—he refused to back out now that he had committed to the expedition. I told him what a stout fellow I thought him, and then took myself out of the house and went directly to the post office, from which Short emerged just as I was about to enter.

"Fancy seeing you here," I said, opening my eyes very wide.

He flushed. "Look, Miss Sharp, I would have told you I was wiring for reinforcements, but I knew you wanted to be honest with Lupei, and—"

"Don't worry; I've already explained it all to Anton." That rattled him, and as he went off to find the horses, I pushed into the post office wondering if Short was perhaps capable of greater guile than I had hitherto suspected. Having inquired at the desk, I found that Mary Adelaide had not yet replied to my telegram of yesterday, so I sent off another: *Still pursuing inquiries re: May. More news tomorrow. Sharp.*

Despite my worry over May, on one thing both Short and Anton had agreed: our plan was more likely to succeed if we approached Castle Sarkozy under cover of darkness. Accordingly, we did not begin our journey until mid-afternoon. By the time we climbed into the mountains and tethered our horses to the trees in the valley beneath the fortress's shadow, twilight had fallen.

Anton groaned as he dismounted.

"Sore?" I asked. My own legs felt like jelly, for a few half-hour riding lessons with the Tecks' coachman that winter had not sufficed to inure me to the saddle, and I was already aching after yesterday.

Anton shot a disgusted look at his horse. "Symbol of bourgeois arrogance. Next time I will walk."

Short, meanwhile, had crept forwards and peered up towards the castle. "Miss Sharp," he called softly, "what do you make of this?"

I followed him and saw at once what he meant: two of the airships floated beside the castle, tethered by long mooring-ropes. A third was on the ground in the courtyard, the curve of its massive balloon barely visible as a smooth line beyond the ramparts.

Anton muttered a curse. "They are loading the airships already! All three of them! Something has changed."

"Something—but what?" Short asked.

I caught a glimpse of movement on the road winding down from the castle, and the hurried beat of horse's hoofs. It was our old friend the shooting-brake. Four shadows sat within it, and as it jounced across the stony road I caught the jingle of glass.

I knew at once what it all meant. "The revolution," I whispered. "There are the airships, with the bombs meant for Berlin, London, and St Petersburg—and here is the Livius Serum, setting out on its journey. Veronika has fired the starting-gun!"

Under his breath, Short muttered a word I'd never heard him use before.

Anton stared. "Did he just say *Crikey?*"

"Pay attention, Anton. This is serious."

"He's the one not taking this seriously."

"Shush," Short and I chorused together. There was a moment's silence before I added, "I think you know what I'm about to say."

Short sighed. "Yes, and for once, I think I agree with you."

"We'll do something together one of these days," I reassured him, "defuse a bomb or something. Anton can be in it too, of course; we're unlikely to find any bombs if he isn't about."

"Are you two going to stop talking in riddles and explain what the plan is?" Anton growled. "Or will you give me a gun and let me shoot their horses?"

"No, no, no," I murmured. "That would alert them up at the castle, and we mustn't risk that."

As the cart reached the valley and took the road towards Eger, we hastily discussed our new plans. We must split up. Short would deal with the serum in the cart. Meanwhile, Anton and I must carry on with the plan—to get into the castle, rescue May and disable the airships.

"I wonder if we haven't bitten off more than we can chew," Short said gloomily, as he checked that his revolver was loaded.

"I agree," Anton said, surprising both of us. "This is madness. All of us should go after the serum. Then we can find the princess if we must. The airships can go about their business and explode the emperors. Then everyone will be happy."

"Don't be a fool, man," Short put in. "The only thing that will happen if you kill the emperors is that new ones will ascend the thrones and send thousands of men to die in a great useless war."

"I don't know about that," said I. "What I *do* know is that I could have been rescuing May yesterday, but instead I chose to go in search of you, Anton. So that's what I mean to do now, with *or* without your help."

Seeing that the cart carrying the serum had rattled off into the forest on its way to Eger, I jumped to my feet and started up the road towards Castle Sarkozy. By now I was desperate enough to face the fortress alone. I was relieved, however, when Anton quickly caught up to me. "Ah, Vera," he said, "you are still in so many ways the woman I loved."

"You'll have to tell me all about it someday," I said, tying my scarf over my head in an effort to hide my scars. I threw him a glance out the corner of my eye. "Are you sure you're ready to help stop these airships, Anton?"

"I promised to follow you." He was silent a moment. "And also, when the revolution comes," he added, "it should come without the involvement of the baroness."

I let that pass without comment, and then frowned as a thought occurred to me. "I never said goodbye to Short."

"Yes, he noticed," Anton said maliciously.

I contented myself by quickly petitioning Heaven for his safety. Then the walls of the castle loomed over us, and our adventure had truly begun.

As we approached the gatehouse, Anton slung an arm across my shoulders, and his gait changed to a cocky swagger. "Boys!" he shouted. "Open up—it's me, Lupei!"

The small postern set into the larger gate opened. "Lupei's back! A pretty chase you led us over this damned mountain, *mon compagnon!"*

I followed Anton through the small gate. I could not help feeling a little trapped, like a wild thing with nowhere to run, but May needed me and I did not mean to disappoint her. Beyond, the courtyard was full of people working hard on the airship—carrying supplies aboard, checking the rigging, or crawling across the great balloon to find and deal with any last-minute leaks. At Anton's entrance, many of them flocked towards us with cries of welcome. "It's the big monster himself! Who've you got with you, Lupei?"

"A pretty *compagnonne* who wants to join us," Anton said, hugging the scarred side of my face a little closer to his chest as the welcoming-party flocked around us. "I thought she might do as an attendant for that useless princess they've got locked up in the Hall!"

Still shyly smiling, I trod on his foot. May was not useless to *me.*

"You can have her and welcome!" a girl shouted from the crowd. "I'm sick of waiting on her hand and foot!"

That made me feel almost dizzy with relief. So May had survived another day!

"But what's this, eh?" Anton added quickly, pulling me further into the courtyard, further into the crowd. "Don't tell me the revolution begins tonight?"

"There's been a change of plans." That was O'Grady's dour voice. I tucked my chin, hoping that the dim light and the shadow of my headscarf would serve to hide me.

"And a change of targets," someone else put in. "We're hitting Paris now, instead of Saint Petersburg."

A momentary silence. A chill went through my bones. Short would doubtless have telegraphed the police of Saint Petersburg to warn them. They would be on the lookout—but

Paris would not. Paris would burn.

"Wait a minute," said Anton, "what's the point of hitting Paris? I thought we were going after the emperors. Surely if you were going elsewhere, it should be Vienna."

I kept my smile on, but jabbed him warningly in the ribs. It was no help if Anton merely redirected the airships! He made no sign, but jabbed me merrily back.

"Paris has the revenants!" someone called. A chorus of cheers agreed. "Down with the corpses!"

"I'm just curious, that's all," Anton said with a shrug when the chant ended. "Did Baroness Sarkozy take a vote on this decision, or did she hand it down from on high like everything else?"

Silence—deafening silence. I began to understand the seeds of doubt that Anton meant to sow. The anarchist creed relied upon equality, and if Veronika was giving orders without even a show of consultation, she was no anarchist.

"Take that girl to the house, Lupei, and stop rabble-rousing," O'Grady growled. "Back to work, the rest of you! These ships are supposed to leave by dark, and you don't even have the first one loaded!"

"Oh, so rabble-rousing is forbidden, now? Seems like there are a lot of rules around here all of a sudden."

"Are you trying to make trouble, Lupei?"

"Just exercising my privileges, O'Grady."

Quickly the crowd dispersed, and Anton guided me towards the narrow stair up to the hall. "I beg your pardon," I murmured. "That was good."

"Leave them to me," he said, opening the great front door, and glancing inside to be sure the coast was clear. "You remember where they are keeping your friend?"

"Yes. Be sure I don't catch you flying one of those things to Vienna."

He grinned. "Ah, tempting. But no. I'd never leave you stranded in the house of this harpy. I owe you more than that."

It struck me that he was serious—which, in turn, struck a chill into my heart. He had put his life into my hands. He was quite serious that he meant to stand by me, which made me, in a way, responsible for his safety.

His grin had softened a little. He was looking at me almost appealingly. "I begin to understand why I might have loved you, once," I said in a voice much too soft and uncertain.

"I thought you might," he said.

Had not my heart always recognised him? In that moment I wondered whether I loved him still—whether, in time, it might be possible to imagine a future for such a love. Then I did imagine it, and found to my surprise that the prospect of a future with Anton left me peculiarly indifferent. It was not *he* who occupied my thoughts.

"Godspeed," I said before he could read the emotions in my eyes. Without a look back, I crossed the empty hall and ascended the stairs. Upstairs, I overheard the faint sound of voices from the direction of the great dining-room in which Anton and I had sat two nights ago. In the opposite direction lay the servants' quarters. Venturing into the dark passageway, I visited the room to which Anton had first taken me. Oh, joy!—my umbrella and valise awaited me, untouched. I snatched up the former, and rifled through the latter, finding that it still held my revolver and the old sock in which I kept a handful of ammunition.

Armed and feeling once more myself, I returned to the

hallway, withdrawing the lock-picks from my hair. Well I remembered which of these narrow rooms held my friend. The lock was old, and I made quick work of it. Pushing the door open, I whispered, "Ma'am? It's me—Liz Sharp."

"Sharp!" May stood at the other end of the room, looking as though she had leaped from her bed upon hearing me at the door. Her hair, usually so crisply dressed, was disarranged, and her grey travelling-dress was rumpled. As for her eyes, they were like two enormous stains of ink in a pale, stiff face. "Sharp!" she repeated, and although she neither fell on my neck nor burst into tears, the quiver I heard in her voice meant just as much. "You came for me!"

"Could you have doubted it, ma'am?"

"And I treated you so terribly!" She moved forward, shaking a little—perhaps from cold, perhaps from nerves. "But how did you get free? Are you really the child of those dreadful people?"

"So it seems." I did not feel like answering her first question—not yet, at any rate. "Still, it isn't all bad. I suppose you will have to pay me a higher salary now that we know I'm the daughter of a baroness."

May pressed her lips together. Her eyes flashed with fierce resolve. "It would be an *honour,* Sharp."

Now I would have to explain that it was only a joke, but that could wait until later. "Are you well, ma'am? You look terribly pale."

She shuddered. "They took some of my blood. I don't know why. It isn't as though—oh, Sharp! Mamma says I cannot become a monster, but are you *certain*—"

"There is a way, but it's most unpleasant, and I don't recommend it." I glanced into the passage. "Dear ma'am,

I'm afraid the next half-hour may be both dangerous and uncomfortable for you, but if you're game for it, I think we may be of some real use in stopping a revolution."

"Anything."

"Good egg." Now came the ticklish part: getting May safely out of the castle, and then returning to help Anton sabotage the airships. He had given me directions to a small postern gate leading out onto the hillside from the castle's kitchen garden, which was located at the foot of the service stair at the other end of this building. "Come along and be very quiet; the fat will be in the fire if we're seen."

I took May's arm, for she did not seem quite steady on her feet, and we tiptoed as quickly as we might through the servant's wing and then into the more lavish apartments beyond. To reach the service stair we must pass the imposing doors to the grand dining-room, which at that moment stood ajar. It was as we approached these that I heard the one voice in all the world I least expected.

"To your success, Baroness."

The words overlaid a chime of crystal. I nearly tripped over my own feet. That voice—it was the Russian Grand Duke, Vasily Nikolaevitch Romanov!

Signalling May to remain still, I peered through the open door. Veronika and Vasily stood side by side at one of the great windows, looking down upon the courtyard. Only his profile was visible from my vantage-point, but I saw that the burns and bruises that had covered his face in the dungeon were healed—thanks to my blood—and that he was once again clothed in an exquisitely-tailored coat of black velvet.

"It is all very well to drink toasts," my mother said icily. "When you return to Saint Petersburg, you should give my compliments to your emperor, and remind him that if he fails to uphold his end of the bargain, the People's Vengeance is quite capable of sending a fourth airship to call on him."

"So long as our arrangement continues to be mutually beneficial, there's no reason to alter it," Vasily said with a shrug. "The Tsar has promised to provide you with all the blood you need for your serum, and will allow your revolution to proceed, so long as Russia is left out of it. We need not bother ourselves with Europe; once Britain crumbles, we shall have more than enough scope for our ambitions in India and China."

"Naturally, we shall be calling upon the emperor to address the state of his peasantry," Veronika snapped. "The People's Vengeance cannot be seen to neglect our Russian brothers."

"Naturally," Vasily said with a chuckle. "What a statesman you might have been, Baroness!"

"Shall be, Duke. It is not only the barriers of class that I mean to sweep away, but also those of sex."

I glanced at May to find that she too had heard everything being said within the room. Her lips moved soundlessly: *How dare they?*

I found myself holding back tight-lipped outrage of my own. What a nerve Vasily must have, to drain my blood without my consent, and having effected his own escape, to sell out the rest of Europe for the benefit of his own empire! I should have known! Doubtless *this* was the meaning of the secret business upon which Vasily had come to the continent. Rumour of the revolution must have reached Saint Petersburg, and the Russian Emperor had chosen to exploit it to weaken his imperial rivals.

As much as they turned up their noses at those below them,

the royalties of Europe were quite ready to rend each other for the sake of a few acres of empire in some out-of-the-way tract of the Himalayas, or the Kalahari, or some such place.

A commotion drifted through the open windows of the dining-room, causing Veronika to stiffen. "What's that?"

"One of your airships appears to be on fire," Vasily said in lazy amusement.

Then Anton had already acted. Our eavesdropping must come to a swift end. I caught May's hand for a dash to safety—but not quickly enough. The dining-room door banged full open, and we stood face-to-face with Veronika.

The baroness paled as she saw me. In the first unguarded moments of surprise you can tell a great deal about a person; and in that moment, the emotion I saw on my mother's face—beneath all the shock, all the outrage—was remorse.

"Mother," I cried, unable to resist this one last chance at reconciliation. "Please—a word!"

She turned away from me. "Kurt!" she cried. "Take care of this, will you?"

For the first time I saw the third occupant of the room. Doctor Livius sat at the foot of the great table, staring at the loosely clasped hands in his lap. When he looked up, he seemed tired—exhausted.

Veronika didn't wait to see if her orders were obeyed. Instead she brushed past me and hurried down the hall.

"Veronika," I cried, lunging after her, "will you make a mockery of all your principles?"

Before I could follow her more than a step or two, a cold hand fastened on my wrist. The smell of cedar drifted into my nostrils, bringing dreadful memories to mind. Vasily drew me inexorably into the dining-room and said, "Do come and join us, Miss Livius—Princess May. There is still a little champagne in the bottle."

I didn't try to resist, for at his touch a terrible faintness had come over me. "I don't care what you do to me, so long as you allow my mistress to leave."

"I'm not leaving without you, Sharp," May said shakily from behind us. She felt her way to a chair at a wary distance from Doctor Livius, and fell into it. From there, she fixed her huge haunted eyes upon Vasily. "How *could* you, your grace? Russia is supposed to be England's *friend.*"

Vasily sniffed. "Clearly, you can't have read what England says about us in the papers."

My father was slumped at the table, watching me with eyes nearly as dark and despairing as May's. "Papa," I appealed to him. "You saw what the Anton-beast did in the village of Egerbakta! Help me put a stop to this!"

He remained silent, looking down at his hands again. Anger rose in my bosom, bright and all-consuming. "No matter what remorse you may feel, you have still become the very thing you vowed to destroy. As for you, Vasily!" I turned on him—on his hooded eyes and lazy, catlike grin. For an instant the words were wiped from my mind. My wounds throbbed as I recalled his hands on my wrists, his teeth in my skin. I swallowed and found the words. "You drank my blood without my consent. I can well believe you would throw all the poor people of Europe to the wolves for your own aggrandisement."

"Oh, *Sharp!*" May's soft cry was little more than a whisper wrung out of her by surprise. Of course, she had not known what price I had paid for my freedom.—But just as Short's indignation had given me strength, so did May's distress.

"Not for myself," Vasily said fiercely, ignoring May's cry.

"For Russia. For my tsar. For my people."

I hadn't expected to deal with monsters tonight, and I had no salt, no stake. Through the great open window, it sounded as though a riot was in process, but I dared not look away from him even for a moment.

"No," I said, "you did it for yourself, Vasily Nikolaevitch. One day, I pray God, you really do experience the sensation of doing something for others. I think you will find it unaccountably painful."

His brows drew down like a forbidding bar across his eyes. "If I had done this for myself, do you think I would be sipping champagne with that woman? I would already have torn out her throat. I did it for Russia. For Russia I suffered days in that vile hole—"

"And half drained me for Russia, too, of course." I might even have forgiven him, had he meant it for the good of all Europe. "Self-interest is no less abominable when it is national rather than individual in effect."

"If it makes you feel any better, I took no joy in what I did to you."

"No," I said almost savagely, "you did it out of pure calculation, quite cool and dispassionate. Thank you for saying so; that negates insult and wipes away all injury. I find myself quite reconciled."

Vasily's mouth tightened—but he released me, and at last I could approach the window.

I looked below, and the blood turned to ice in my veins. Veronika stood in the glare of the lamp at the head of the narrow steps that ran down into the courtyard. Beyond her, one of the airships at anchor above the courtyard blazed like a torch, shedding a weird, hellish light upon the scene. In the courtyard itself, O'Grady and a couple of the other anarchists had seized Anton and now dragged him struggling to the foot of the steps, throwing him down on his knees before Veronika.

"Here is the saboteur!" O'Grady cried.

Anton tried to cry out, but was silenced by roars from the crowd. The mood down there had turned ugly. Veronika raised her hands for silence. "Anton Lupei is an enemy of the revolution," she said crisply. "People's Vengeance, carry out your sentence."

"Death!" O'Grady cried, and to my dismay, the word was repeated—"Death! Death!"—by many voices.

A stone flew, striking Anton in the shoulder. Veronika grasped her lacquered walking-stick, and its blades flashed as she pulled them free. Within moments Anton would be dead. The revolution would proceed, and there was only one thing I could do to stop it.

Vasily stood by my side, rapt in the scene that unfolded below. Even having been bitten by him I was no match for his strength, but at Saint Botolph's they had taught us to be quick, to be daring, to use the body's own weaknesses against itself. Vasily was no less susceptible than anyone else to a surprise attack. Before he had taken my blood, I had got the upper hand of him—only for a moment, to be sure, but a moment was all I needed now.

I offered up a silent prayer and moved. A quick step—a shove—a grab and a curse from Vasily, parried by the umbrella in my left hand—a ladylike yelp from May—and the Grand Duke toppled from the window, shrieked like a demon, and smashed upon the stones of the courtyard.

An instant later his champagne-bulb shattered beside him.

The crowd recoiled. Someone screamed, and then for a

moment silence reigned and every eye was fixed upon the window—upon me. I leaped to the window-sill and stood there silhouetted against the glowing light within. With a grand gesture, I pointed to the fallen vampire. "People's Vengeance, you have been betrayed! Behold—the monster with whom Baroness Sarkozy has allied herself!"

I assure the reader I had no intention of killing the duke, for then my ploy would have been worse than useless. Any mere mortal should have been dead upon impact, and it was my intent to show them a monster. Indeed, mere moments passed before Vasily's crumpled body stirred, then dragged itself to its feet. The crowd backed away with cries of horror as the vampire's battered body reknit itself, until all the sign of his fall that remained was the sticky wet patches upon coat and collar.

A terrified silence fell upon the courtyard.

Then Anton surged to his feet, pointing at Veronika. "You traitorous harpy! What you plan isn't a revolution—it's a holocaust! Your serum turned me into one of them!"

"Silence him!" Veronika ordered. O'Grady turned to backhand Anton, but before his hand could fly, a well-aimed stone toppled Veronika's lieutenant from the stairs.

"I vote we hear Lupei!" someone yelled.

"That's right!" cried another. "We don't take orders from anyone, certainly not a baroness!"

Anton turned to face them. "Listen to me, my *compagnons!* You know how loyal I am to the revolution! Yet what I have to say fills me with shame. Under the influence of the Livius Serum, I slaughtered every living creature I came across, without prejudice, without pity..." His voice broke. "I cannot excuse it. It was not the monsters who suffered at my hands, but those whom I had pledged myself to aid. There is not an unfortunate alive who is one penny the better off for what I have done. This is what Veronika's revolution means—the same destruction, magnified a hundredfold! And now she is in league with the monsters themselves?"

He pointed towards Vasily. "Shame!" someone yelled from the crowd. "Burn him! Burn the vampire!"

Vasily, who had been leaning against the hall's foundations as he recovered, now drew himself up to his full height. *"Canaille,"* he spat. Then—he moved.

The crowd hurled stones at him, but as with the saltwater two nights before, he shrugged them off. One of the airships was still moored to the battlements to my left. Moving with dreadful, beastlike speed, Vasily scrambled up the rocky wall of the house, then leaped for the battlements. Upon reaching the walkway atop the castle wall, he hurled first one, then another guard to the courtyard below, then began to swarm up the airship's aft mooring-rope.

I gathered that Veronika was shrieking orders to the crowd, but the uproar was too great and drowned her voice. In no time Vasily pulled himself aboard the airship skiff and slashed the mooring ropes. Two more guards fell screaming from above. Then the ship drifted away into the night and was gone.

The crowd raged, and Anton, who had waited events stoically, lifted his arms and gained silence.

"Forget him, *compagnons!* This is a war we must fight—with violence if necessary—but one cannot solve injustice with more injustice. What good does it do us to topple the monsters, only to create more in their place? Throw down your burdens, my friends! You have made a great many bombs:

there is no need to send them away! Ignite them here, and burn this cursed nest to the ground!"

They were frantic with rage at having lost Vasily, at having been lied to, at the news which Anton had brought. They shouted their approval, but when Anton turned to face Veronika again, she was gone.

She had slipped away—but where? I leaned from the window, searching the crowd as it swayed and milled in confusion.

Then the third and final airship began to move, the one cinched near the ground to my right. Realising whence their prey had vanished, the crowd made a dash for the vessel—to no avail. Veronika must have done something to the ballast, for within moments it rose beyond their reach.

"You fools," she cried, leaning out from the skiff. "You have thrown away your best chance of freedom! Very well! I am not angry—I shall end this myself!"

It was the last of the airships—and unlike the two others, it was already loaded with bombs. I glimpsed the insignia on its balloon as it rose past the dining-room window: the black imperial eagle of the German Reich.

I knew then what it meant.

Berlin, the fuse of Europe, would go up in flames. After that it didn't matter if London and Saint Petersburg stood. There would most certainly be a war.

"Papa," I cried, turning from the window. "The bombs—tell me where..."

The words died from my lips as I scanned the dining-room. Doctor Livius was gone. Only May stood behind me, looking pale and sick.

Outside, the airship skiff rose swiftly past the window. My

heart smote me as I saw the suppressed terror burning like fever in May's eyes. "Ma'am," I said gently, "I wish I could stay with you, but I can't. If you can find your way to Anton, perhaps he will protect you."

I stepped up onto the windowsill, hooking the curved handle of my umbrella into the waistband of my bloomers. May said, "Stop."

Something in her voice kept me there, even though I knew I could never obey her if she ordered me to stay.

"The bomb bay," May said evenly, "is in the lowest level of the ship, just forward of the engine rooms. The main ship's ladder leads straight down to it."

I stared at her in blank astonishment.

She smiled wanly. "I caught a glimpse of the blueprint that first day, in the lab. God-speed, Sharp."

There was no time to waste in thanking her. Already the skiff had passed. One last trailing mooring-line whipped past the window: gritting my teeth, I flung myself after it, into the void.

Chapter XXVIII.

I suppose that very few people have ever found themselves able to record the thoughts and sensations that pass through the mind at the point of death—such as, for instance, having leaped from a high window in pursuit of a small and rapidly-moving target. It would be pleasant to say that my whole life had flashed before my eyes, since this was a point of such great personal curiosity. In fact, it did not. The one thing that *did* flash before me was the terrifying certainty that I had committed myself to a very costly mistake. The human body, I find myself in a position to say with the utmost authority, was never intended to plunge through open air with no tangible means of support.

My terror was blessedly short in duration. The thick mooring-rope smacked into my palms, burned through my fingers—and held me. Thanks to my bloomers, I had no trouble in getting my knees locked around the rope too. Thus momentarily secure, I glanced below.

The mountainside dropped sharply away below me, putting me instantly at a dizzying height from the ground. Castle Sarkozy was a pool of wrath and fire as the Vengeance shook their fists at the sky or hurled themselves upon the last of Veronika's supporters. A bullet whizzed past my cheek close enough to ruffle my hair, although whether the marksman meant to impede the airship or to hurt me, I could not tell.

I looked up. I was dangling about ten feet below the skiff, and in another moment, as soon as Veronika had the ship set on its course, no doubt she or her helpers would be reeling in the mooring-ropes. It took every ounce of courage I had, but I unlatched one hand from the rope, reached a little higher, and hauled myself up.

It was cold in the sky. The wind plucked at my bloomers, and my fingers began to go numb, warning me not to dilly-dally. Foot by foot I pulled myself up until I was nearly level with the skiff gunwales. Then I hooked my umbrella-handle over the rail, and a moment later got one arm up beside it. Some way off I saw Veronika standing in the pool of light in the cabin that housed the ship's wheel, frowning over a compass. No one else was on the deck, but deep within the hull I could hear the engines humming, driving the propellers at the airship's rear. I didn't know much about airship crews, but surely someone was down in the engine-room.

A hatchway in the centre of the deck led below. With one last effort I pulled myself over the gunwale and sprang the short distance to the hatch, umbrella poised for action. A narrow ladder led downwards. I hastened to descend, passing through the middle-deck living quarters without seeing a soul. When I reached its foot, as May had promised, I found myself in the bomb bay.

Like the quarters above, this room was lighted with one of the new electric bulbs, flickering a little in time with the steady rhythmic chug of the engines. An entrance-way aft of the bomb bay led into the engine-room, which must have been massive. There was no door, but I couldn't see anyone there amongst the machinery, either. After a moment, I decided not to begin by incapacitating the engineer—much less bombarding him with questions regarding the ship's inner workings, as bitterly disappointing as this was. I did not have much time, and the task I had to perform was a distinctly ticklish one.

The skiff had a flat bottom, and as I approached the racks of bombs, I saw massive hinges to either side of the floor below the bomb-racks. Cold perspiration broke out on my skin. I was standing upon a pair of great doors, and if they opened—as I had no doubt they were designed to do at the pull of a lever—I would be spinning helpless in mid-air, falling this time with no plan and no escape. There was no help for it, however. I tested the floor with a foot, then stepped up to examine the bombs themselves.

These numbered about three dozen, and were encased in heavy cast-iron cooking-pots. In the smooth motion of the airship they barely rattled. Steadying one in my hands, I tried to open the lid; but to my horror I saw that it was welded shut—as were all the rest of them. A small hole drilled into each lid admitted a fuse, each of which ran to join a great rope waiting only for a single match.

I stepped back and smoothed a hand over my disarranged hair, wishing fervently that my eyes had deceived me. Welded shut! What could I do? I carried a great many useful things in my pockets, but an oxy-acetylene torch was not among them. I might cut the fuses, but that was easily repaired, and in any case it was still quite probable that the bombs would explode upon impact with the ground. I might try slipping the bombs off their racks, but what would I do with them then? I might crash the airship—

I might crash the airship, but the easiest way to do that would be to ignite the fuses, now—to explode the bombs, now.

I would die. Veronika would die. But how many thousands would live?

A paper of matches had been left wedged behind a spar at the side of the hull, ready to light the bundled fuses. I snatched them with a shaking hand—but could I really do this? I did not know how to escape the truth that this woman had once been my mother.

As I entered, I had seen the speaking-tube on the wall by the door—a rubber hose with a brass bell on the end, placed beside a brass lever. The tube must connect with the pilot's cabin, and I turned to pick it up. It was then that I found I was being watched. Doctor Livius stood in the door that led to the engine-room, his scent masked by the powerful smell of grease and smoke from the furnace beyond.

His face was in shadow, and my hand clenched on the paper of matches. I had not bargained on killing him, too. But now it seemed terribly fitting. Everyone else might have turned on Veronika, but he evidently still meant to help her, even knowing her for the madwoman she was. And then, what of the Livius Serum? Even if Short managed to stop the shipment, the secret to its making was still a weapon in the doctor's hands.

"Hello, Papa," I told him. I brought the speaking tube to my mouth. "Hello, Mother."

From the other end of the tube came a sudden clang. It sounded as though Veronika had dropped something. A moment later, footsteps raced across the top deck.

Doctor Livius started forward. "Stay where you are," I cried, striking a match, and holding it near the bundled fuses.

"Vera," he gasped, "put down those matches! You ought not to be here!"

The doorway darkened, and Veronika stepped through, apparently not out of breath in the least.

"I'll put down the matches," said I, "if she puts down the airship. Please. If we can only talk about it—"

"Talk!" Veronika said scornfully. With a twist, her lacquered walking-stick came apart.

"Please," I said again. Something had gone wrong with my eyes. The lights had halos around them, and Veronika's face blurred. "I don't want to do this. I've wished for my mother so long, and I—I remember thinking to myself on the train how happy I would have been to have you."

"And you could have had me. You could have had both of us." There was murder in her eyes, but she did not move, seeming mesmerised by the dancing flame in my hand.

My match was burning low. I took another and lit it at the flame of the first. "You told me, once, that you didn't believe in senseless bloodshed. I have been telling myself that it was not a lie. I have been telling myself that you simply meant that you don't believe in useless violence waged in a battle that can never be won." I took a deep breath. "I thought you were a woman of principle. Was I wrong? Because surely you must see that with only one airship, and with the Livius Serum denounced by your own followers, this has become an empty gesture."

"And whose fault is that?"—Doctor Livius tried to say something, but she silenced him with a gesture. "In any case, you are wrong. Let one empire fall—make just *one* of the monsters bleed—and the whole of Europe will catch fire."

"Losing how many lives in the process? Better if all of us died at once."

"Prettily spoken, child, but you don't fool *me.* If you meant to light that fuse, you would already have done it. Come! Give me the matches. No one need ever know. I will set you on the ground after Berlin falls, and you can claim any reward you like from your royal friends."

I blinked at her. "Do you think I am doing this for a *reward?"*

"Give me the matches," she repeated, stepping forward, and raising her twin swords.

Through my tears I could scarcely see more than the glow from the tiny flame I held cupped in my hand, but that was enough. I moved it a little to my left, and the fuses flared with a scorching wave of heat.

"Goodbye, Mother," I said softly.

Veronika lunged forwards, her blades flashing as she aimed a slashing blow at the fuses. I engaged her with my umbrella, grateful for the fencing-lessons they had given us at Saint-Botolph's. With a parry and a precisely aimed jab towards the busk of her corset, I sent her stumbling out of reach of the sputtering fuses. Still, she was using sharps, and my umbrella was an unwieldy substitute for a real sword. How long before she gained the upper hand?—It was no thought of my own safety that impelled me; I had made up my own mind to die. Only I could not allow her to save the bombs.

"Kurt," Veronika cried as she staggered backward and nearly collided with my father, "fetch water!"

She made to lunge forward again—and tripped over my father's foot. As she measured her length across the hull, his hands fastened on my shoulders.

"Whatever you do," he said urgently, over Veronika's

protests, *"don't let go."*

He thrust into my hands a pack of the sort that attaches with straps to the body. A string ran from the pack to a hook on the inside of the hull.

Veronika struggled to her feet. "Kurt! What are you *doing?"*

He looked at her sadly. "Veronika, she's right. I love you too much to let you do this."

With that, he reached out and pulled the lever beside the speaking-tube.

The hull dropped away from beneath my feet.

I screamed, reached for the hull with my umbrella-handle, and missed. The next instant I was hurtling through clouds. The pack clasped in my left arm twitched as the string connecting it with the airship pulled free. Remembering my father's last words to me, I tried to get my flailing right arm around the pack.

An enormous, rippling white canopy opened above me, attached by a hundred fine silken lines to the pack. The next instant there came a jerk that ripped the whole contraption clean out of my arms.—And that would have been the end of me, had it not been for a bit of exceptionally good luck, for at the very last moment the crook-handle of my umbrella caught upon one of the straps of the pack. I found myself clinging desperately to the ferrule, hovering between earth and sky while the airship continued serenely on its way to the north-west. The moonlight filtered among the clouds; below the countryside was wrinkled and dark, and the lights of a small town shone like jewels set in black marble.

Then the airship exploded.

I shrieked and held more tightly to my umbrella as a great gust of hot wind tossed me through the air. Fearful, I looked up; but to my relief no sparks had caught in the canopy above me—I did not yet know that this was called a parachute. After that I could only watch as fire lit the clouds. The airship tilted towards its engine-room, then slipped gently from the sky.

I clung to my umbrella, and although I am a good Protestant, I said a prayer for their souls.

Chapter XXIX.

From that day to this, I have adamantly refused ever again to set foot in any sort of aerial conveyance—and that is all I care to say about the painful experience of landing an improperly-secured parachute without any sort of formal training. It took me an hour's walk on a strained ankle, across very rough terrain, to reach the small town I had noted during my descent. On my way, I paused to search the wreckage of the airship where it lay burning on a hillside. I found no trace of my parents' bodies, but at some distance from the wreckage—impelled, no doubt, by the explosion—I found my mother's swords. After some hesitation, I decided to keep them. I had little else by which to remember my parents, and it would be nice to have something of theirs other than the nightmares.

By the time I reached the town it was too late to arrange for a conveyance across the mountains, certainly not without ready money. I pass over any further details. Suffice it to say that I arrived in Eger the next day around noon, rather stiff and sore from an early start and a long, jolting journey.

As my cart rolled through the narrow, winding streets of Eger, I wondered what I ought to do next. I had last seen Short going after a gang of desperate anarchists, Anton surrounded by a volatile crowd, and May alone in the dining-room of a castle that was about to be burned to the ground. What had become of them? I had had all of the previous night and the long journey across the mountain to brood upon the question, and by now I was in the depths of despair. I had prevented a senseless act of violence, it was true; but I felt that I had gambled away my friends' lives in a futile attempt to save my family.

And what good had it done? In the end my father had taken my part; but Veronika had refused to relent, and so I had been forced to destroy both of them together. I could not help mourning what I had lost. Perhaps we had never truly *been* a family, and perhaps we would never have seen entirely eye to eye—but surely, if things had been different, we ought to have been able to build *something* together.

It was not my fault, but my very bones ached for the waste of it, and for the heartsick knowledge that I now had no shelter from the unfriendly world. I realised, now, just how much stock I had put in the thought that somewhere in the world I might have a mother and father who loved me.

And now—which of my friends might have perished because I was chasing a phantasm? May, whom I had abandoned at the moment she needed me most? Short, to whom I had omitted even to say goodbye?

It was as I was lost in these thoughts that I heard a faint jingle of glass. A familiar horse-brake approached, driven by a stocky young man wearing a cloth cap pulled low over his eyes. The dickens! it was Anton—with the Livius Serum!

Involuntarily, I called out to him. Anton peered up from under his cap and winked. Then the brake passed us, heading north towards the mountains.

I settled on my seat again with a racing heart. "Just someone I know," I said, as my driver looked at me inquiringly. I felt, quite suddenly, that perhaps everything was going to be all right after all. But I could no longer remain in the cart, waiting passively to be delivered to the town square. At first Anton's scent lingered in the street, mingled with a faint aroma of smoke, but soon it turned off to my left.

"Thanks for bringing me," I said as my driver slowed to allow a carriage to pass, "please do check at the post office before you go home tonight, and I will try to leave some money waiting by way of thanks." With that I slipped into the road and followed Anton's scent, still limping slightly on my sore ankle.

The whiff of smoke led me to the police station. I hurried in to make inquiries, which I attempted to do without drawing anyone's attention to the fact that the brake which had recently been tethered outside the station had quite decidedly vanished.—I trusted the monsters with the Livius Serum no better than I did the anarchists. They told me that yes, an English policeman from Scotland Yard had alerted them last night to some anarchist activity, and a cart and four men had subsequently been seized outside the train station.

Before departing, the Englishman had given an address at Eger's finest hotel. This I hastened to visit at once, and nearly collided with Short on the doorstep.

His whole face lit up in a smile more brilliant than one would have expected from a man who habitually looked so dour. "Miss Sharp! What a sight for sore eyes!" He seized my hand and shook it in both his own. "Her highness told us what you did—I have been down at the post office, wiring all over Europe, trying to find out what became of you!"

"May is alive?"

"May is here. Come up at once, and you shall see her." He ushered me through the vestibule and into the lift. "I take it you have *not* been as far as Berlin?"

"No," I said, with a glance towards the lift attendant, "there was a—shall we say—accident, with the cargo. What about the castle?"

"A similar accident, which involved the remainder of the cargo." The lift opened, and Short followed me into the passage-way beyond. "I was up at Castle Sarkozy again in the early hours of the morning, with the police. We found an astonishingly composed princess sitting on an ash-heap. There's nothing left of the place but broken stone."

"What—all gone? The lab, and—everything?"

"I saw Anton half an hour ago; he gave me to understand that he took some pains with the laboratory."

"Ah yes," I said, "I'm sure he did."—And the sorrow I felt at having lost all my journals, all the things I had once known and might yet have done? That could not be helped; nor could the outstanding question of what my father had been planning to do with May's blood. "Strange that you should have seen Anton this morning; so did I, a few minutes ago."

"Behaving himself, I hope?" Short stopped outside a door.

"In fact, I do believe he was engaged in a spot of larceny. You didn't happen to let drop, in the course of your recent conversation, the whereabouts of the last of the Livius Serum?"

A smile quivered in the corners of his mouth for a moment, before he drew them down and looked very doleful. "That might have come up in the course of discussion. Come to think of it, I *did* mention that it had been handed over to the police. Why do you ask?"

I shook my head. "And you a representative of the Law."

"Just so," said Short, "which is why I found myself in need of our friend's services." He tapped deferentially at the door, and May called, "Come in."

Short led the way inside. "I've brought you a tonic, ma'am."

May sat at a table, finishing what appeared to be a late breakfast. Setting her teacup on its saucer, she said: "Indeed, I was wondering when the two of you would stop whispering in the hallway and come in to see me."

"I won't stay," Short said. "Besides Miss Sharp, I was only stopping to deliver this." Depositing a telegram on the table by May's elbow, he bowed himself out.

May didn't even glance at the message. She glanced up at me, very composed, although there were still signs of her ordeal in the puffiness beneath her eyes. "Tea, Sharp?"

"Thank you, ma'am."

"Do sit." She glanced at my mother's double sword-stick, which I still clutched beneath one elbow. "Am I still to call you Liz Sharp, by the way?"

A fireball bloomed across my vision: the descent of my parents' airship. "I should prefer that, ma'am. There was some effort made to resurrect Vera Livius, but I think I may definitively say that she is dead."

"Poor Vera! And her parents?" May asked, very gently.

I took a long sip of tea and a deep breath. "They, too, are dead."

"Oh, Sharp, I can't tell you how sorry I am."

I didn't answer—there seemed nothing to say. The hurt was too raw, and too fresh. "Whatever you may feel about the secrets your own mother kept from you, at least she's never had you locked up with a hungry vampire. Bear *that* in mind."

"Yes, but dishonesty still hurts." May sighed.

I bit my lip. "I ought to have told you, ma'am, and hang the consequences."

"You *did* tell me, in time," she answered. "And I took out my hurt on you, because I was not willing to accept the truth about Eddy. But I ought to have known better—I *did* know better, although I did not know he was a monster." She gave a small, wry smile. "You see I have had plenty of time to think it over, during my misadventures."

"Better late than never, ma'am."

"Can you bring yourself to forgive me?"

I was a little startled to hear her say that. "Of course! All the same, you will allow me to say that I owed you the truth."

"As my maid, you owed me nothing."

"But as your friend, I did."

"As my friend!" Her voice was a little wistful. "Is that how you think of me, Miss Sharp—as your friend?"

"Yes. I do, ma'am, if it isn't too bold."

She turned a little pink with pleasure. But then, decidedly, she shook her head. "No, I am not your friend. Not so long as you feel you must beg my leave and call me *ma'am.* I *do* beg your pardon. From now on you must call me May, and feel free to speak quite plainly, whenever you wish."

No pretty speech from a man—even from Short, though *that* was unimaginable—could have filled me with quite the same sense of happiness. There is something so disinterested about an offer of friendship!—and from one of May's standing!

"I wonder if you know how much that means to me," I said, with a catch in my voice. It had not occurred to me to think that a friendship contracted upon terms of inequality must be null. Evidently May had been conscious of it, if I had not. It was comforting to think that if I had doubted my friendship because of the lies I had told, at some point May must have come to doubt her own because of her insistence upon royal prerogative.

"Then you'll agree to it?" she said, a little anxiously.

"Of course—at least in private, when it will not attract comment."

"Oh, thank you." She heaved a deep sigh. "I can still hardly believe it, Sharp. Mamma says they are *all* werewolves. Surely not!"

"Near as makes no difference," I said.

"Not Uncle Bertie?"

"Very much Uncle Bertie."

"And Aunt Augusta—of Mecklenberg-Strelitz, I mean?"

"It seems rather likely."

"And..." May gulped. *"Her Majesty?"*

"I saw her transformation with these two eyes."

"Good Lord!" she said faintly. "I don't know what to make of it, Sharp. Heaven must have *some* purpose for it. Those who are appointed to rule have many prerogatives by virtue of their office that the ordinary sort of people do not."

And that was precisely the response I had always feared. Still—now, at least, there was a chance she might listen to me. "Personally, I am more inclined to believe the origins of the monsters to be less *heavenly,* than downright infernal."

May swallowed hard. "Of course," she said faintly, "it is very wrong for them to abuse their power, like that horrible Duke Vasily! I shall never forgive him for what he did to you, Sharp! Never, never!"

She had had rather a difficult week, so I did not press her further. No doubt we would have opportunities to discuss the matter in the future—or so I thought, not guessing just how soon or how urgently the question was about to make its presence known.

In any case, this opportunity had already passed, for another tap came at the door, and this time it was Anton who entered, carrying a bulging messenger-bag over one shoulder.

May stiffened a little. "Ah," she said frostily, "it's you."

He grinned cheerfully at both of us. "I came to see Vera, if she has a moment."

May looked imperious, but I shot her a pleading glance and she melted at once. "Inform me when Mr Lupei is gone, Sharp," she said, picking up her telegram, and withdrawing to her bedroom.

Anton threw himself into an armchair, a picture of insolent lethargy with his legs stretched out and his hands thrust into his pockets.

"It's all right, you can knock it off," I advised him, taking a sip of tea. "She isn't watching you through the keyhole or anything."

"She is angry with me for leaving her sitting on an ash-heap last night. *You can come with us anarchists,* I told her, *or you can wait for the police.* She seemed to think that we ought to wait for them too."

"Poor May! She must have had an anxious time of it, waiting there alone."

"Not half so anxious a time as we would have had, knowing what they do to people like us. But aristos don't understand that. Policemen are like a sort of well-armed butler to the likes of her."

"I wish you knew how far she's come in the last three months. You might begin to realise just how much is possible."

"Bah! It's not your job to save them." He leaned forward. "No, hear me out. Veronika lied to me, and now I don't know if the things I used to believe were true anymore. How does any revolution succeed without turning the new order into new monsters? Look at France—all the revolutions in the world, and they're still marching revenants down the Champs Elysees. ...I don't know what the solution is, but I know I'd rather sort it out with you than without you." He jumped up and held out a hand. "Leave the bloodsuckers, Vera. Come with me."

Instinct told me to take his hand. But that was what it had always been: instinct and memory, not true emotion. My heart might not yet have learned to doubt him, but in the end it was not he who occupied my mind and gave purpose to my future—at least, not any more.

I shook my head. "I never enjoy saying these words, Anton, but you were right. I'm no longer the Vera you once loved."

He looked down at the table with shadows of guilt in his eyes. "Nor am I the man who loved you first."

"I'm Elizabeth Sharp now," I went on. "I don't know yet exactly what that stands for. I do know one thing for certain, though: it means faith in a higher law, and not the ones made by monsters to keep themselves in power. I mean *thou shalt love thy neighbour as thyself.* There's a lot of scope for revolt in that, Anton, but it's not the same law as yours."

He forced a smile, disappointment in his eyes. "So that's what you meant when you offered to make me love again. But that's not the sort of love to keep a man warm at night."

"Is that so terrible, my friend?"

"It's a damn' shame. They've tamed you, Elizabeth Sharp. They've made you safe for their world." He got up, brushing his cap against his trousers. "You should know, anyway, that the Livius Serum is gone. I poured it into the first paddock I came across. Some farmer is going to harvest toothy cabbages this year."

"That should be all right, so long as the lightning doesn't strike them."

He grinned, but there were still shadows in his eyes. "I brought you a gift." He picked up the bag and dropped it on the table heavily enough to make the china rattle. "Go on, open it up. I think I got them all."

"You didn't!" I cried, already guessing what he had brought. Sure enough, when I pulled the flap open, I found books—journals—the result of all Vera Livius' work. "Anton! I could hug you!"

"Don't let me stop you."

We were still embracing when the door to May's room opened and she emerged with a faint pucker between her eyes and a distant, absent-minded note in her voice. If she noticed the impropriety, she gave no sign. "Sharp, do you know what all this is about? It's addressed to you."

I took the telegram from her and pursed my lips in an unladylike whistle, before reading the startling missive aloud:

Cannot imagine what you mean hounding me with telegrams across the continent. May traced to Hungary? What do you mean May traced to Hungary? May perfectly well in Coburg with parents and fiancé Prince George of Wales. All this most upsetting. Heart palpitations each time the post arrives. Franz distracted. Kindly explain. Mary Adelaide of Teck.

"I didn't even know you *could* send telegrams so long," Anton said, dazedly. "How much do you suppose she spent on that?"

May's eyes flashed. "I'll thank you to keep your valuations

to yourself, young man. Hang it all, Sharp, what can she mean, when she must know very well that I was kidnapped in Stuttgart? Me, in Coburg? I've never been to Coburg in my life! And engaged to George? It must be some frightful hoax."

"I don't know," I said thoughtfully. "Your mother's telegrams *are* awfully expressive, as a rule."

Anton had been lounging aggressively against the wallpaper ever since May entered the room. Now he slouched an inch or two lower and said, "Oh, the telegraph is genuine, all right. Veronika was planning this kidnapping for some time."

I stared at him. "You mean—"

"Yes. I take it that when they snatched Her Nibs in Stuttgart, they simply substituted an automaton."

May blinked rapidly three or four times. "I beg your pardon!"

"An automaton," I said, thinking furiously. A memory formed in my mind: a blast—smoke—the laboratory sweet with the scent of dynamite. My father, crying *Success!*

"I am affronted," May said severely.

"The dickens," I cried, "my father had those automata rigged to explode—and now one of them is in Coburg—at the wedding—with George!"

May stared, and one pale hand fluttered to her throat. "You mean," she said in a soft and jerky voice, "they mean to explode—*George?*"

"Don't leave, Anton," I said, getting up and sliding a chair beneath May just as her knees gave way. "Or, no—go and find Short. No—" as a knock sounded at the door—"that would be him now. Come in, Short!"

He entered, reaching up to take off his bowler hat; and then stilled in astonishment as he beheld the tableau: Anton slouching villainously against the wall, May fainting in a chair, and me ransacking the room in search of smelling-salts.

"Miss Sharp," he sighed, "I was away for a *mere* half-hour! What now?"

I located the needful in a box upon the mantle-piece, and sent him my sweetest smile. "I hope you packed a tailcoat, Short. We're off to a wedding!"

S.D.G.

Unhistorical Note

I flatter myself that Miss Sharp's second volume is still more disembarrassed by historical fact even than her first. As always, however, I *have* taken some inspiration from history: namely, from the Continental holiday which May of Teck and her family took following the untimely death of her fiancé, Prince Albert Edward. Starting out on the French Riviera, they took a trip to Paris, where they stopped by the Restaurant Véry in the aftermath of a terrorist attack by the anarchist Ravachol. They then took the Orient Express to Switzerland and passed some quiet time there. Prince George did pursue May as far as France, and remained in correspondence with her afterward, evidently encouraged by his family to pursue her.

Everything else is more or less my own invention. I've taken the liberty of transforming the *Akbar* boys' reformatory, which was the centre of a scandal in the early 1900s, into a sibling institution to Saint Botolph's. The real bombing of the Café Terminus (by the anarchist Émile Henry) actually happened in February 1894, though not (as far as we know) with the object of assassinating a Russian vampire prince. If you want to learn more about the anarchists—about the policemen that hunted them, the regimes that went to tyrannical lengths to repress them, and the dreadful social conditions that drove many of them to acts of radical terror in 1890s Europe—I highly recommend John Merriman's very readable book *The Dynamite Club*; although you may find it somewhat lacking in terms of airships, mad science, and werewolf-vampire hybrids.

As always, profound thanks are due to my wonderful beta readers: Christina Baehr; Schuyler McConkey; Stella Dorthwany; Intisar Khanani; Kate Ravenna (who provided some fascinating information on historically-accurate airships of the period, which information I then proceeded blithely to ignore—sorry, Kate); and W.R. Gingell, without whose trenchant insight and commentary this book would have been finished in a fraction of the time.

Suzannah Rowntree
March, 2021.

About the Author

Suzannah Rowntree lives in a big house in rural Australia with her awesome parents and siblings, drinking fancy tea and writing historical fantasy fiction that blends real-world history with legend, adventure, and a dash of romance.

You can connect with me on:

https://suzannahrowntree.site

Subscribe to my newsletter:

https://www.subscribepage.com/srauthor

Also by Suzannah Rowntree

The Miss Sharp's Monsters Series
The Werewolf of Whitechapel
Anarchist on the Orient Express
A Vampire in Bavaria

The Watchers of Outremer Series
A Wind from the Wilderness
The Lady of Kingdoms
Children of the Desolate
A Day of Darkness

The Pendragon's Heir Trilogy
The Door to Camelot
The Quest for Carbonek
The Heir of Logres

The Fairy Tale Retold Series
The Rakshasa's Bride
The Prince of Fishes
The Bells of Paradise
Death Be Not Proud
Ten Thousand Thorns
The City Beyond the Glass

Lightning Source UK Ltd.
Milton Keynes UK
UKHW010854070223
416609UK00007B/2028